MORE . . .

ALSO BY JOAN HESS

Strangled Prose
The Murder at the Murder at the Mimosa Inn
Dear Miss Demeanor
A Diet to Die For
Roll Over and Play Dead
Death by the Light of the Moon
A Conventional Corpse
Out on a Limb
The Goodbye Body
A Holly, Jolly Murder

**AVAILABLE FROM
ST. MARTIN'S PAPERBACKS**

DEATH BY THE LIGHT OF THE MOON

Joan Hess

St. Martin's Paperbacks

This is a work of fiction. All of the characters, organizations and events portrayed in this novel are either products of the author's imagination or are used fictitiously.

DEATH BY THE LIGHT OF THE MOON

Copyright © 1992 by Joan Hess.
Excerpt from *Damsels in Distress* copyright © 2006 by Joan Hess.

Library of Congress Catalog Card Number: 91-37884

ISBN: 0-312-94905-7
EAN: 9780312-94905-1

Printed in the United States of America

St. Martin's Press hardcover published 1992
St. Martin's Paperbacks edition / September 2003

St. Martin's Paperbacks are published by St. Martin's Press, 175 Fifth Avenue, New York, NY 10010.

10 9 8 7 6 5 4 3 2

To Michael Denneny, for seven years of encouragement, guidance, and friendship

"Driver," Caron said, somehow managing to combine the imperiousness of a dowager with the poutiness of a thwarted toddler, "I demand that you stop this car right now. This whole thing is Too Absurd for words. I refuse to participate in this farce for one more mile."

The taxi driver, a youngish man with doughy white skin and shiny black hair, obligingly pulled over to the side of the gravel road and cut off the engine. He took a stained cigarette from some mysterious hiding place, stuck it between equally stained teeth, and caught my eye in the rearview mirror.

"Whatever the little lady wants," he said with a wink, "is okay with me. On the other hand, we might make better time if I didn't stop every other mile while you two argue."

"A valid point," I said. Warily, I turned to study my daughter. Her expression epitomized the intensity of every fifteen-year-old martyr whose mother continually insists on throwing her to the lions. Although we share red hair and freckles, I consider myself an agreeable sort of person, with perhaps only a tiny inclination to irritability when provoked. Caron's inclination is much steeper.

I took a deep breath, blew it out slowly, and continued. "Listen, dear, we've been over this no less than four times since we left the airport. We are going to see this through, and with a modicum of grace. Three days with your father's family will not—and I repeat, will not ruin the remainder of your life."

"This place is dismal," muttered the martyr. "It's hot and smelly and ugly. The mosquitoes are big enough to be barbequed. The creepy stuff on the trees looks like rotting flesh. That icky water's probably full of poisonous snakes and sludge and primeval slime."

The driver flipped his cigarette out the window and lit another. "Yeah, we got water moccasins in the bayous, along with your coral snakes, alligators, and leeches bigger than my thumb."

"Thank you for the insight into the local ecology," I said, admittedly without a modicum of grace. I noted the rigidity of Caron's shoulders and tried a different tactic. "It's not going to hurt you one bit to spend some time with your grandmother and cousins. You've never even met any of them except for your Uncle Stanford, and that was more than ten years ago at your father's funeral. I know your father would have wanted you to establish a relationship with his family."

"He couldn't stand any of them. You know perfectly well what he used to say about Miss Justicia and all those screwy people. We never once came to visit, and he choked on his eggnog when he felt compelled to send Christmas cards every year. Remember what he used to say about Uncle Stanford and his bratty kids? And about pompous—"

I cut her off before she could elaborate further for the driver's edification. "They're still members of your family.

Miss Justicia was too ill to attend the funeral and that must have been very difficult for her. Now she's been kind enough to invite us to visit her for her eightieth birthday. We accepted, and we are going to have a lovely time. We are not going to sit here and sweat, nor are we going to continue to screech at the taxi driver, who is attempting to carry out his half of the bargain."

"I don't mind," the gentleman under discussion contributed through a cloud of gray smoke.

I gazed at the back of his collar, which had enough oily rings to gird Saturn. "I'm delighted by your flexibility. Now would you be so kind as to drive on without interruption until we arrive at the house?"

As he pulled back onto the road, he looked over his shoulder at Caron. "And there's always your *Diphyllobothrium latus,* of course."

"What's that?" she asked suspiciously.

"Tapeworms, honey. Louisiana's got the biggest tapeworms in the country, maybe the world. Be real careful about going outside in your bare feet, and for heaven's sake, don't eat any fish. Once one of those ol' tapeworms gets inside you, it sticks its hooks in your intestine and sucks away until it's fifteen or twenty feet long."

Caron buried her face in her hands and began to whimper. On the whole, it was not an auspicious beginning for a jolly family reunion. I had to agree with Caron that the idea seemed rather flaky, but I was not about to share my reservations with her. I'd felt so guilty about my lack of contact with Carlton's family that I'd kept up the Christmas card list. But from the day of the funeral until a few weeks ago, I'd never heard from any of them, and it hardly kept me awake at night.

The ink on the invitation had been almost as washed out as my memories of the few photographs Carlton had shown me on a maudlin occasion induced by a vast quantity of cheap red wine. There had been the obligatory family portrait: Miss Justicia, seated in a high-backed wicker throne; a mangy dog at her feet and her two sullen sons on either side; several of the boys and a squatty, pigtailed cousin.

The invitation had been addressed to Caron; I was an afterthought. It had been more of a directive than an invitation, and had I not fished it out of the wastebasket in her room, it would have been rat fodder at the landfill.

"Mother!" gasped Caron, jabbing me on the leg. "Look at that horrible old house. This is too gothic for words. I am not getting out of this cab, not even for one second. You can stay and visit if you want, but I'm going back to the airport to wait for you. Nobody'll bother me. I'm positively not—"

"Yes, you are." I leaned forward to look at the house, which indeed was intimidatingly gothic. It was a large structure with rows of dusty, blind windows, paint-flecked pillars, a wide veranda, and a general air of decades of decay. Massive trees surrounded it, their contorted branches dripping with Spanish moss (in Caron's vernacular, rotting flesh). The vast yard was clotted with sprawling shrubs and patches of spiky yellow weeds.

The driver parked behind a slinky red Jaguar and a more sedate black Mercedes. "Here we are, ladies. Malloy Manor, home of the loons."

I shoved Caron out of the taxi, then followed her, my expression determinedly calm. "Isn't this impressive? This is such a wonderful opportunity for you to explore your roots, Caron. You can learn all about your ancestors."

"Aunt Morticia and Uncle Lurch?"

As I opened my mouth to issue a stern maternal warning, a flash of silver passed between an opening in the azaleas on the side of the house. A raucous cry was followed by a cackling noise that might have been described as laughter—if one was in a charitable mood.

I grabbed Caron's shoulder before she could fling herself back into the sanctuary of the cab. The driver snickered and said, "That, ladies, was Miss Loony Tunes herself."

Seconds later, a gray-haired woman in a plaid housecoat and high-topped jogging shoes skittered into view, froze long enough to give us a deeply disconcerted frown, and then continued in the direction of the cackles, which were still audible but fading.

I glanced back at the driver, who was tugging on his ear and grinning. "Don't know about that one," he said, "but I wouldn't leave any valuables lying around my room."

Caron stared at him, then turned on me. "If you want roots, call Alex Haley."

I could think of no appropriate response. I waited while the driver unloaded our luggage, paid him the amount we'd agreed upon, arranged for him to pick us up Sunday afternoon, and glumly watched him drive away . . . to the airport, where one could catch a series of flights back to Farberville, the site of a charming bookstore, an apartment with a view of the undulating lawn of Farber College, and the amorous attentions of a cop with molasses-colored eyes, a vulpine smile, curly black hair, and talents best left described in steamier novels than this. He had his faults, but at the moment I couldn't think of any of them.

Trying not to sigh too loudly, I picked up my luggage. Caron gathered up hers, and we trudged through the weeds and up the weathered steps to the veranda. I knocked on the door. After a minute, I knocked more forcefully.

Caron brightened. "Well, I guess nobody's home. If you carry my cosmetics bag, I can handle the rest of my stuff. We can walk to the highway, and it shouldn't be too hard to hitch a ride to the airport . . ." Her voice dribbled off as the door inched open in a series of squeaks and protests.

He was not the sort of butler I'd read about in cozy British mysteries. Although he remained in the dimness of the foyer, I could make out stringy shoulder-length hair, some of it in his face and the rest tied back in a ponytail. Beneath an oily curtain of bangs were sunglasses, pock-marked cheeks, and thick, unsmiling lips. He wore a tattered flannel shirt over a dingy T-shirt. His jeans were fashionable, which meant they were threadbare and covered with frayed holes.

"I'm Claire Malloy, and this is my daughter, Caron," I said, ordering myself to hold my ground. And Caron's arm.

He froze for a moment, then brushed past us and went down the stairs. I caught a whiff of acridity, a view of headphones nestled in his hair, and the faint sound of rock music, which I presumed was blaring between his ears.

"Okay," Caron announced. "To the airport, *tout de suite*. Enough is enough, Mother, and this is More Than Enough!"

"Why, look who's here!" boomed a voice from within the foyer. A plump man with peppery hair stepped onto the porch and began to pump my hand enthusiastically. In contrast to the mysterious butler, he wore a crisp white suit and a pink bow tie that matched his shirt. His cheeks were pale and smooth, his mouth stretched in a broad grin, and his blue eyes unmasked by sunglasses.

"Claire and little Caron," he continued, still jerking my hand up and down as if hoping for water to spew out of my mouth. "I am charmed that you could come. How long has it been, my dear sister-in-law? I must say, you're looking prettier every time I have the good fortune to see you."

"Stanford," I said, trying to disengage my hand before he dislocated my shoulder. "I suppose it's been ten years."

He released my hand, but before I could retreat to a

prudent distance, he threw his arms around me and smothered me in a hug. "Since the funeral," he said damply to my earlobe, "and such a tragedy for us all. Such a tragedy. Why, Caron was just a baby when her daddy died in that terrible automobile accident, and you had to be a brave little widow. My heart was torn to pieces, Claire." His tongue slinked into my ear. "You poor lonely thing, you."

I abandoned any pretense of tact and squirmed free. "It's nice to see you again," I said coolly. "Caron and I are looking forward to spending a few days with the family."

Stanford turned on Caron, his eyes sparkling dangerously. She'd edged all the way to the railing, and looked more than willing to tumble off backward if he moved on her. He clasped his hands together. "And haven't you grown into a pretty young lady! Your daddy would be bustin' with pride if he could see you here on the veranda."

Caron wiggled her fingers at him but kept her other hand clamped on the railing. "Hi, Uncle Stanford."

"Isn't she perfectly charming!" he said, easing slyly toward me. He tried to put his arm around my shoulder for another display of kinship, but I ducked at the crucial moment to grab a suitcase.

"She's perfectly charming, and we're exhausted," I said. "Perhaps we could have a few minutes to freshen up before we meet the rest of the family?"

Stanford Malloy, Southern gentleman extraordinaire, assessed the luggage, swooped in on Caron's cosmetics bag, and grandly gestured at the open door. Caron and I picked up the rest and meekly entered Malloy Manor.

The foyer was paneled with oppressively dark squares of mahogany. On my left was a door, and beyond that a hallway as inviting as a passage in a poorly lit subway station. A staircase was directly in front of us; adjoining the bottom step and on my right was a set of double doors, the glass panes blocked by white sheers. A table held a vase of brittle flowers and a scattering of dried petals.

"Miss Justicia thought you'd like to stay in Carlton's old bedroom," Stanford said as he herded us toward the stairs. "There's a little bathroom with it, and a fine view of the back lawn and the bayou. I'll bet Carlton used to tell you tales about how he and I fished for gars in the bayou, gigged bullfrogs, and even scared up moccasins for the hell of it."

"Bullfrogs and moccasins and gars, oh my," intoned a hollow voice behind me.

I rammed Stanford with a suitcase to nudge him into motion. "Who was the boy at the front door?"

He paused on the landing to wipe his forehead with a folded linen handkerchief. "That was my son, Keith. Neither he nor Ellie could come to the funeral, so I don't guess you've ever met them. Twins, though you can't tell by looking at them. Ellie's doing real fine these days; she works for a television station in Atlanta, but before too long she'll be on one of the big networks. She's got an unemployed bum for a boyfriend, but she'll grow out of it and find herself a nice lawyer or doctor to marry."

"And Keith?"

Stanford stuffed his handkerchief in a back pocket and snorted. "He's still trying to find himself, as he's so fond of saying when he calls to try to wheedle money out of me. Last I heard, he'd found himself in a jail in New Jersey for car theft, so I was downright startled when he showed up with Ellie this morning. He's still as surly and obstinate as always. Why, he hasn't said more than two words to any of us—which is fine with me." With a snort to punctuate the sentiment, he stomped up the remaining stairs.

A humming sound caught my attention. I looked back, to see Caron gliding up the stairs. It was unsettling, at best, and it took me a minute to realize she was perched on a seat attached to a track along the wall. As she passed by me, her luggage stacked neatly on her lap, she managed a regal nod. I managed a blink, maybe two.

We went down a dark hallway lined with family portraits. Caron stared at her ancestors with an increasingly black frown, but we arrived in our assigned room without any editorials. Once Stanford had elicited a promise that we would be down shortly, he left us alone.

Caron's nostrils flared as she took in the dingy wallpaper marred with blotches of mildew, the worn carpet, the battered furniture, and the two narrow swaybacked beds. "You must get the name of their decorator, Mother—and have him put out of his misery."

I held back the curtain and gazed out the window. Beyond the tangle of shrubbery was the bayou, an expanse of swampy water and half-submerged skeletal trees. Rather than dark and mysterious, it merely looked unappetizing. Carlton, a fastidious sort who ran notoriously tight seminars (and, would have alphabetized his clothes had I allowed it), had not related stories of his boyhood adventures. Now I could understand his general aversion to any memory of it.

I closed my eyes and imagined myself in my lovely, dusty store, where there were boxes to be unpacked, invoices to be checked, quarterly tax reports to be decorated with whimsical figures, and even a customer or two to be cosseted. Then, in a display of maturity that impressed only me, I told Caron it was time to go downstairs to meet the family.

"No way. You may go downstairs or upstairs or out to the swamp to shoot snakes. I'm staying right here on this pitiful excuse for a bed." The treacherous child flopped across the nearest pitiful excuse and pulled a pillow over her face.

I debated the wisdom of attempting to drag a recalcitrant teenager, who was, among other less charming things, a skilled actress in the gentle art of melodrama, down a flight of stairs and into a parlor to meet her eighty-year-old grand-mother.

"I'll tell everyone you're taking a nap," I said, acknowledging defeat. "You will appear for dinner, and make a sincere effort to be attentive and well bred. Deal?"

Her reply was somewhat muffled by the pillow. "I think I'm getting a pimple on my chin. I'll probably be covered with them before morning—if I live to see the sun rise. Talk about your haunted houses! This has to be the—"

I closed the door and started down the hallway, pausing periodically to study the portraits of the family. The pouty expression at which Caron was so adept seemed to have a genetic basis, I thought as I peered at one particularly tight-lipped woman with eyes so small, they were almost invisible in the fleshy folds of her face. The man in the next painting was dressed in a Confederate uniform several sizes too small for his girth, and looked painfully constipated.

I stuck out my tongue at a bewhiskered man with a walrus mustache. And at that moment, of course, a door opened and a very attractive young woman stepped into the hallway. She had thick auburn hair, a generous mouth emphasized by scarlet lipstick, and the flawless complexion of a model. Two cool blue eyes appraised me.

"Like, hi," she said in an amused drawl. "Trying to butter up Great-Uncle Eustice?"

I pulled in my tongue and stuck out my hand. "I'm Claire Malloy. Are you Ellie?"

She continued to study me for a few seconds, then briefly touched my hand. "You were Uncle Carlton's wife, right? Yeah, I remember Daddy saying you were coming this weekend. Isn't this whole thing ghastly? It's straight out of some dreary old black-and-white movie."

"The house or the family reunion?"

"Is that what she told you?" Ellie chuckled, although

with a malicious tinge. "You really don't know, do you? This might be entertaining, after all, Auntie Claire." She slipped her hand through my arm, escorted me to the top of the stairs and pointed at the elevator seat. "Walk or ride?"

I halted. "Neither. I'm in the mood to chat, Ellie. What is it that I don't know, and why is it likely to be entertaining?"

"How could I possibly know what you don't know? I met you less than three minutes ago, so I'm hardly able to make any sort of in-depth analysis of your deficiencies."

Her glibness was beginning to annoy me, and I allowed my expression to indicate as much. "I have had a difficult day. It took three plane changes to get to the ultimate airport, each plane smaller than the preceding one. My daughter currently is supine and moaning about the likelihood of being throttled by the ghost of Great-Uncle whatever. I'm not in the mood to play games. Will you please explain your remarks?"

Her smile faded. "Sorry. It's so bizarre, so . . ." She searched for a word, and I wasn't surprised when she said, "Gothic, if you know what I mean."

"I don't know what you mean," I said grimly. "Caron received an invitation to visit on the occasion of Miss Justicia's eightieth birthday. What's so gothic about that?"

She sat down on the top step and gestured for me to join her. "She's changing her will. Haven't you ever seen those old movies where the matriarch demands that the family gather to find out who's to be the heir apparent and who's out in the cold—or in this case, out in the stupifying humidity?"

I had, and they were pretty darn gothic. "Miss Justicia is using the birthday ploy to announce she's changing her will? Why didn't she just do it and send everyone a postcard?"

"You obviously haven't met her yet," Ellie said with a shrug. "She loves this kind of thing. Ten years ago, she informed us that every penny was going to a televangelist in Shreveport, and when I was in high school, she decided to give it all to a sperm bank in Baton Rouge. Daddy sputtered like a lawn mower all weekend. It was classic."

"What's the existing situation? Is the bank still at the top of the list?"

"No one's sure, of course, but the prevailing theory is that the estate's divided among the loyal family members who show up whenever she tells them to. Not divided evenly, mind you, because then we wouldn't squabble across the coffin."

"That would include Stanford, your brother, and you, I suppose," I said.

"And Cousin Pauline, who's been an unpaid companion for a million years or so, and Cousin Maxie and dear little Cousin Phoebe. I'm afraid your branch was cut off years ago when Uncle Carlton refused to scurry home with his tail between his legs to listen to her threaten to cut him off."

"Then why were Caron and I invited to this . . . party?"

"Only the shadow knows," she said in an appropriately lugubrious voice. She stood up and dusted off her fanny. "I'm sure we'll find out, Auntie Claire. Come along; it's time for a spot of sherry in the parlor."

I've always disliked sherry, but suddenly I realized that I loathed it.

2

Ellie led me into the room opposite the double doors. It might have been spacious had it not been crowded with sofas and love seats, brocaded chairs, tables cluttered with ceramic bric-a-brac and brass boxes, enough spindly lamps to comprise a small forest, and a vague redolence of furniture wax and camphor. Heavy draperies hung like folds of liver-spotted skin, blocking out most of the late-afternoon sunlight. The cobweb-encrusted chandelier glinted weakly, its low wattage bulbs unable to conquer the gloom. Ellie's hand on my back was the only thing that prevented me from retreating upstairs to pack my bags.

Stanford stood in front of a wicker cart, a bottle of liquor in one hand and a glass in the other. "So I see you two have met," he said as he poured himself a stiff drink and gulped it down without spilling a drop. He had the decency to ask if he might be honored to offer me a wee libation, and I assured him that he certainly could. Once I was settled with scotch and Ellie with bourbon, he frowned at her.

"Where's your brother? I told him we were having drinks before dinner. Not that he necessarily heard me, since he goes around with that foolish thing on his head, and those sunglasses over his eyes so we can't tell if he's awake, asleep, or dead. And that hair's a disgrace. I ought to drag him down to the barbershop and—"

"Cool it, Daddy," Ellie said. "It's a little late in the game to start with the paternal authority routine. You're liable to get yourself all fired up and have a heart attack in the middle of the parlor. That'd play holy hell with Miss Justicia's plans, wouldn't it?"

"I don't want to hear that kind of language from you, young lady," Stanford began, then broke off with an uneasy smile. "Why, here's Miss Justicia now, and Cousin Pauline."

I stood up and turned around. The photograph I'd seen of Carlton's mother had been taken at least thirty years ago. She had shriveled with age and barely managed to fill the shiny wheelchair she drove into the room. White hair dotted her scalp like clumps of cotton. Nestled in a high lace collar, her face was emaciated and harshly wrinkled, but her faded blue eyes were as sharply appraising as Ellie's. Although her hands were misshapen with arthritis, her fingers darted over the control panel of the wheelchair. She braked in front of me.

"So you're the gal Carlton married, are you?"

"I'm Claire," I said. "My daughter, Caron, is napping upstairs, but she's looking forward to meeting you at dinner."

"It was kind of the two of you to come all this way for a pathetic old lady's birthday. It well could be my last, you know." Miss Justicia shifted into first gear and spun around neatly. "Stanford, my dear boy, why are you standing there like a wart on a toad's butt? Fix me a drink."

The woman in the plaid housedress approached me. Her face was long and angular, and her oversized teeth added to the unfortunate equine effect. I doubted she was sixty years old, but her aura of grayness made her seem older. When she smiled, however, the effect was surprisingly appealing, and I found myself smiling in return.

"I'm Pauline Hurstmeyer, Justicia's cousin," she said, so softly that I could barely hear her.

Miss Justicia had the same problem. "Speak up, Pauline. This isn't the front room of a funeral parlor, so you don't have to whisper."

"Of course I don't, Justicia," she said, although without any appreciable increase in volume. "I'm pleased to meet you, Claire. We're so glad you and your daughter have come to Malloy Manor for our little party."

"I'm pleased to meet you," I responded mendaciously, in that I wasn't pleased about anything that had taken place since the airplane had landed several hours ago. She again gave me a warm smile before she sidled away from me and sat down on a love seat near the window.

Stanford placed a glass in his mother's hand. "Here you are, Miss Justicia. A nice glass of sherry."

The old lady sniffed the contents of the glass, then held it to one side and dropped it on the rug. "Oh, my goodness," she said, "how terribly clumsy of me. I've spilled this glass of dog piss. You'll have to fix me another, but this time I'll have a vodka martini, straight up, with two olives."

"Absolutely not," said Pauline. "Justicia, you know what the doctor says—"

"The doctor says, the doctor says," she said mockingly. "If I want to hear his words of wisdom, I'll call him on the telephone. Better yet, I'll drive over to his office and park in the hydrangeas. Stanford, please stop hovering over me like the Goodyear blimp and fix me a martini." She wheeled around and drove back to me. Resting her hand on my knee, she said, "Isn't it wonderful for us to have this chance to get acquainted, Claire? I wanted to attend the wedding, but my doctor wouldn't allow it, and the funeral was out of the question. May I hope Stanford represented the family well?"

"It was a short, simple service, as Carlton would have wanted." I ignored the reference to Stanford's presence, but I shot him a dark look.

Turning red, he said, "I was happy I could be there to stand beside you and Caron." Neither of us added that he'd offered to lie beside me that same night. I was amused to see he still remembered the well-articulated vehemence of my response.

"Stanford told me that you own a bookstore," Miss Justicia continued, her hand bearing down on my knee. "Is it profitable?"

"It's pleasant, but not impressively profitable. I opened it in order to be surrounded by books. I didn't realize they'd all be ledgers filled with red ink."

"And in a train station. So very quaint and clever of you." She gave me a vaguely reproachful smile. "Women of my generation would never have competed in what was considered a male dominion. It would have been quite ill-bred, so we were obliged to occupy ourselves with charitable endeavors and taking proper care of our families. Do tell me, dear, why did you and Carlton have only one child?"

The others may have been willing to be bullied, but I was not. I took a sip of scotch, then said, "It was our decision, Miss Justicia."

"But here you are in the bosom of the family, surrounded by your loved ones, and you can confide in us. Was it on account of money, or did Carlton lose his . . . Oh, what shall I call it? His resolve?"

"Miss Justicia, you are such a hoot," Ellie said languidly.

Stanford bristled. "Ellie, I won't have you speaking like that to your grandmother. Apologize right this minute."

"She doesn't need to apologize to anyone," Miss Justicia

said, cackling. "She's blunt, and I like that. She doesn't pretend to have any great fondness for me. She simply wants my money, as do the rest of you."

"Don't be absurd," Stanford protested weakly. "Ellie is very fond of you, as am I. I know I don't visit too often, but what with the business and all, it's difficult to get away for even a weekend. I can't remember when I last had a vacation."

"I can, Daddy," said Ellie. "Weren't you way down yonder in New Orleans a week ago? That's what your secretary told me when I called."

"That was business." He busied himself with a plastic pick, trying to coax olives out of a jar. "Darn these things," he muttered as several of them popped out and bounced on the floor like marbles.

"Good heavens, Stanford," Miss Justicia said, "where did I go wrong?" She took the glass from him and drained it. A purplish tongue flicked out to catch a drop on her lip. I stared, mesmerized. Ellie's face was lowered, but I could hear her throaty chuckle in the silence. Stanford looked as though he wanted to speak, his lips quivering as he blinked at the old woman. Pauline sadly shook her head.

The doorbell interrupted the unsettling stillness. Stanford flinched, then hurried out of the room and into the foyer. The front door creaked open and the sound of footsteps was accompanied by the mumbling of low voices and the thudding of what I presumed was luggage. A great deal of luggage.

"More vultures," Miss Justicia said. She maneuvered the wheelchair to the wicker cart and picked up a bottle. Vodka splashed on the carpet as she refilled her glass. "Stanford can no more make a decent martini than he can profit from the family business. My grandfather founded it more than seventy years ago, and it was a decent company until my incompetent son took over and ran it into the muck. Don't you agree, Ellie?"

"Daddy doesn't have much of a head for business," she said, facetiously sympathetic. "He says he's undercapitalized, but I suspect his girlfriend in New Orleans has expensive taste. It's really not fair for him to keep her in diamonds while I'm reduced to rhinestones. He cut off my allowance last year when he found out about my fondness for roulette and my teeny-tiny problem with a gentleman in Atlantic City. Can you imagine such a brutal thing?"

"So you're hoping to get all my money?"

"Every last penny of it. I'm going to buy a penthouse in Manhattan, a town house in Paris, and a doghouse for Daddy, should he ever visit." She paused for a moment to study her scarlet fingernails, then gave Miss Justicia an angelic smile. "But I'll have to wait until you're dead, won't I? It's so utterly boring. I don't suppose you'd advance me a few thousand? Lately Big Eddie's been saying all kinds of crude things about my line of credit and my kneecaps."

Miss Justicia began to cackle. The sound grew until it filled the room like a sickly sweet perfume. Tears zigzagged down the creases in her cheeks, and her hands jerked spasmodically in the air. Seconds later, I realized she was struggling for air, her face red and her eyes bulging. She snatched at the cameo holding the collar around her throat as if to rip it off. Pauline and I both rose, but even in the midst of the attack, her glare warned us not to approach.

"Isn't it nice to see we're having fun?" oozed a voice from behind me.

Feeling very much as if I'd been dropped in Oz, I spun around to look at the woman in the doorway. She was short and round, with a monumental bosom, a soft jaw, and too many chins to count. Her hair, twisted into a cone of improbable height, was the color and texture of bleached hay.

She wore a linen dress that spoke of money, and a strand of pearls that screamed of it, as did the assorted rings on her fingers. If she was wearing bells on her toes, I had no doubt they would be made of the finest crystal.

"Maxie, my dear," Miss Justicia managed to gasp, "I should have known you'd be here in a Bosier City minute. Rest your tonnage and have a drink."

"I could do with a glass of sherry after riding with that dreadfully unclean taxi driver." She curled a bejeweled finger at someone in the foyer. "Stop dawdling and come into the drawing room to greet Miss Justicia, Phoebe. She may nibble, but she won't bite."

The girl who entered the room did not appear frightened, but merely reluctant, an attitude I could appreciate. She was the antithesis of Maxie—tall, thin, and almost chinless. Her hair, a utilitarian brown cap, framed her face with no concession to style. Her sallow complexion, devoid of makeup, matched her pale yellow dress. What light there was glinted off the round lenses of her glasses, disguising her eyes.

"Hello, Miss Justicia, and happy birthday," she said without enthusiasm.

"Cousin Phoebe," Ellie said from the sofa, "now that you and Cousin Maxie are here, we can get on with the party. You will stay off the chandelier this year, won't you?"

Phoebe crossed her arms and stared. "I cannot imagine why you'd say something so absurd, Cousin Ellie. Unlike others of us, I do not drink alcoholic beverages, nor do I engage in those primitive rituals you find so diverting. Is penicillin still adequate for your condition, or have you moved on to one of those trendy new Asian strains?"

"The results of the test aren't back. It's a risk one takes when one has contact with men who haven't been freeze-dried as a prerequisite for tenure."

"I have a perfectly reasonable social life, when time

permits," she said with a sniff. "I have a significant relationship with someone at the moment. Unlike your invariably imprudent choices, he is not covered with matted hair and obscene tattoos."

"And you didn't bring him along so we could meet him? Oh, I am so very disappointed with you, Cousin Phoebe! What does he do for a living—rob graves?"

"It's hardly any of your business, but he happens to be in the transportation industry."

"A grease monkey at a truck stop?" Miss Justicia said with a short laugh. "At last you've found someone who'll take a shot at deflowering you, although I wouldn't put any money on the outcome. Come over here so I can take a look at you, my dear child. You're so thin, I lose you in the lamps. Don't they feed you at that college you've been attending for what? The last ten years?"

"A doctorate requires both time and diligence. I'm currently working on a dissertation that I've been assured is of publishable quality. It focuses on the complexity of management's bilateral relationship with—"

"I'll be sure to keep a copy by my bed," Miss Justicia interrupted.

Phoebe's voice dropped half an octave, and only her mouth moved as she said, "Then I'll make a note to send one to you, Miss Justicia."

"And to me, too," Ellie chirped, clapping her hands. "I'm having a terrible time with insomnia."

"You sleep in your bed, too?" Phoebe permitted herself a small smile, then sat down beside Pauline and began to talk quietly with her. Ellie scowled but said nothing.

Maxie went to the cart and poured herself a glass of sherry. She then noticed yours truly, who'd been trying to hide in the upholstery in case the cozy reunion escalated from verbiage to violence. "You must be Cousin Carlton's widow," she said, studying me as if I were a potential arsonist. "I'm Maxine Rutherford Malloy-Frazier."

"I'm Claire," I admitted.

"It's so nice of you to visit after all these years. It must mean so much to Miss Justicia to finally meet you. What a shame you wouldn't come while Carlton was still alive. Are you interested in genealogy?" Before I could manufacture a reply, she continued. "I've done extensive work on the family's genealogical charts for inclusion in the parish historical society's files. Are you aware we are in direct descendancy from the *Mayflower,* and that William Malloy opened one of the first blacksmith shops in the Colonies in 1623?"

"No," I said truthfully.

"Furthermore, your daughter is entitled to membership in the Mayflower Society, should she provide verification to the proper authorities."

"Mother's on the national board," Phoebe said from across the room.

With a deprecatory laugh, Maxie paused to pat her hair, although every strand was lacquered into position and would have handily resisted a tornado. "It's true that I have a certain amount of influence with the organization. That is not to say, however, that you yourself qualify unless you can trace your lineage independently. Our guidelines are quite strict about those who try to sneak in on another family's lineage."

"As well they should be," I murmured. "Sneaking in like that would make a debacle of the organization."

Phoebe took a small notebook from her purse and flipped it open. "Carlton's daughter is your second cousin once removed, Mother, and therefore my third cousin."

"Isn't that fascinating?" Ellie drawled to no one in particular.

"Actually," Phoebe said, settling her glasses on her nose more firmly in order to glower more darkly at Ellie, "the study of familial relationships is quite fascinating. Cultural anthropologists are able to give us keen insights into specific tribal patterns that have—"

"You must excuse me," said Miss Justicia. "I'm too frail to risk being bored to death."

"Now, Miss Justicia," Maxie began, "Phoebe's simply sharing—"

Miss Justicia banged her glass down on the wicker cart, shifted into low gear, and, with a wave, accelerated across the carpet and shot through the doorway.

After a moment, I mumbled a generic remark and went upstairs to rout Caron for dinner. The pitiful excuse for a bed was unoccupied. After a short search, I reluctantly accepted the truth that she was not lying under the bed, nor cowering in the wardrobe, nor even engaging in a pimple-monitoring session in the little bathroom. She had vanished. Her luggage was open, and clothes were scattered about, which gave me some degree of comfort. The child might bolt, but not without her new white shorts.

The degree of comfort was no more than that, however. I went back into the hall and studied the half dozen doors on either side. Caron was much too self-centered to bother snooping in anyone else's bedroom; her curiosity stopped at her epidermis.

I returned to the monastical bedroom and looked out the window at the yard. As I frowned at the unruly scene bereft of postpubescent runaways, Miss Justicia's wheelchair appeared below me and whipped across the yard at what I estimated to be a good twenty miles an hour. She rounded the azaleas at a dizzying angle and disappeared.

Seconds later, a screen door slammed and Cousin Pauline stumbled into view. She stopped to peer in all directions, clasping her hands like a true heroine in distress.

I opened the window and leaned out as far as I dared. "She went thataway," I called down.

Pauline stared up at me as if I were a gargoyle on the facade of a cathedral. "Whataway might that be, Cousin Claire?"

I pointed at the path between the azaleas. She hesitated, then took off at an admirable pace. Wishing I'd had the presence of mind to ask her to watch for Caron, I went back out to the hall once again and opened the door across from mine. It was a linen closet, filled with dingy sheets and blankets with satin hems fringed from use. The small corpses on the floor were moths.

The door next to it led to an antiquated bathroom, complete with a bathtub on claws and a cracked porcelain sink. Great-Uncle Eustice eyed me sternly as I closed the door and contemplated my next move, which might or not be the next door. I had no desire to pop in uninvited on Maxie or Phoebe, much less on Stanford, who would misinterpret my motive and, in his eagerness, fall all over me—literally.

From the main floor, I heard a gong reverberate. Ellie came out of her bedroom, now wearing a tight white evening gown, with a mass of glittery glass beads dangling into her cleavage and a white feather boa draped around her neck and down her back. My nice blue dress suddenly seemed to be of bargain-basement origin, at best.

She swept up one end of the boa and posed at the top of the stairs. "Dinner is announced, Auntie Claire. We mustn't be late, or dear Miss Justicia will have yet another fit, this one fatal. One second thought, let's both hide in the linen closet. How long does it take to probate the estate? Are they allowed to advance money before it's settled?"

"You'll have to ask an attorney," I said, unamused.

"Suit yourself." She sailed down the stairs, the ends of the boa swishing in her wake.

I glared at the top of her head until it was no longer visible, then glared at the empty hallway. Miss Justicia was volatile enough to react forcefully to cold soup; the self-perceived slight of Caron's absence might result in Ellie's vision. While I tried to decide how best to produce a facsimile of a granddaughter within a matter of minutes, the gong rang again, this time with an undertone of vexation.

Rehearsing excuses in my mind, I went down the stairs, although I certainly did not sail and the only thing in my wake was a expletive. As I reached the foyer, I heard Stanford's voice.

"Then you find him!" he commanded, not sounding in the least like a gallant Southern gentleman. "That boy is going to sit down at the dinner table or I'm going to know the reason why! You'd think he was raised by white trash in some shack along the railroad tracks." After a pause, he bellowed, "May I remind you that you were sent to Miss Garman's finishing school, at considerable expense and sacrifice on my part, so you could learn how to preside over tea parties and speak French? You are pushing me, girl, and I do not care for it. Find that sorry excuse for a brother and drag him by his ponytail to the dinner table!"

Ellie strode down the hall and went out the front door, her expression reminiscent of my missing daughter's. I chewed on my lower lip while I studied the possibilities. On my right was the parlor; that much I knew, being an observant sort who'd been in there less than fifteen minutes earlier. The hall led to the back of the house, where one might reasonably assume there would be a kitchen, pantries, a dining room, and a red-nosed, lecherous bore. That left the set of double doors. I had taken a step when a small doorway beneath the staircase opened and Keith crawled out. From what I could see of his expression—and it wasn't much—we were equally startled.

"Ellie's looking for you," I said.

The sunglasses and hair blocked whatever reaction there might have been. The thick lips did not move.

"Ellie's looking for you," I repeated more loudly, resisting the urge to rip off the headphones along with whatever hair was tangled in them.

He fiddled with the cassette player clipped on a belt loop of his jeans. Once he'd turned down the volume, he said, "What?"

"Your father sent Ellie outside to find you for dinner. She went through the front door forty-five seconds ago."

"If she has any sense, it'll be the last we see of her."

I held back an acerbic response. "The gong's been rung twice, so I suppose it's time to sit down. Is this the way to the dining room?"

He tipped his sunglasses to peer at me. I caught a glimpse of dark, distrustful eyes before they disappeared behind the shields. "Who are you?" he demanded, suddenly belligerent.

"Claire Malloy. I'm Carlton's widow."

"Yeah, okay. I thought maybe you were the Avon lady or something. I'm gonna pass on this dinner thing. The old lady gives me hives, and I'm into vegetarianism, anyway." He toyed with the cassette player, then retreated through the door from which he'd come. It closed with a click.

"He's rather like the White Rabbit, isn't he?"

Phoebe stood in the parlor doorway. She'd combed her hair and applied pink lipstick, but her efforts had done little to soften her appearance. She held her notebook and a tape measure in her hand, but when she noticed me looking at them, she tucked them in her bag.

"I've always considered him a genetic mutant," she said as she joined me. "Luckily, our branch of the family has never shown any indication of incipient insanity; otherwise, I'd feel morally obligated to have myself sterilized."

I bent down. The outline of the door was almost invisible in the dark wood; only a small wooden knob indicated its presence. I determined that it was locked from the inside, and straightened up with a frown. "What on earth is he doing in there?"

She sniffed the air. "Smoking marijuana, or *Cannabis sativa*, to be more accurate. It produces a mild euphoria, along with alterations in vision, distortion of time and space, and muscular incoordination. It has long served as a sedative or analgesic, and was first mentioned as a Chinese herbal remedy in about 2700 B.C."

I saw no reason to contribute personal observations made in the late sixties, long before this pedantic twit was born. "Imagine that," I said.

Phoebe was well into an analysis of possible therapeutic properties when the gong struck three. She ran her fingers through her hair, undoing what minimal results she'd achieved with a comb, and sighed. "We'd better go into dinner if we don't want Miss Justicia to have a stroke in the gumbo."

"What about Keith? Should we try to persuade him to come out, or just leave him?"

"I wonder if there's any way to nail it shut from the outside. It wouldn't take much more than a handful of nails, and I've become quite handy with a hammer since I moved into my apartment."

"I don't think we ought to do that," I said, alarmed at the seriousness with which she seemed to be considering her proposition. "He might suffocate."

"He's been in prison, you know." She said this as if presenting an argument for the judicious use of nails.

"Stanford mentioned something about it. We'd better . . ."

She cast a final, wistful look at the door, then nodded and said, "Yes, we'd better . . ."

We went down the dark hallway and into a room dominated by an enormous table. The gong beside the door still quivered from its final whack. Miss Justicia sat in her wheelchair at the head of the table, drumming her swollen fingers on the yellowed tablecloth. Stanford paced in the narrow space behind her. Cousin Pauline sat midway along the table, looking a bit wan from her latest pursuit. Maxie sat on Miss Justicia's left.

And on Miss Justicia's right sat Caron Malloy. She looked quite demure in white blouse with a round collar. I wouldn't have been surprised if the tablecloth hid a navy blue skirt, cuffed socks, and shiny little patent leather shoes, neatly buckled.

"Are you here to gawk or to eat?" Miss Justicia said with a sweet smile.

3

I sat down next to Caron. "Where have you been?" I said in an angry whisper.

"Out." She looked down at the daunting array of tarnished knives, forks, and spoons. "Wow, there's enough hardware to equip a small nation for hand-to-hand combat."

"The silverware is counted after every meal," Miss Justicia said. "Phoebe, you're standing there like you'd been hit between the eyes with a magnolia branch. Please sit down next to your mother. Stanford, sit down at once, on the other side of Claire. Where are Keith and Ellie?"

"Ellie went to look for him," Stanford said as he sank down heavily next to me.

"Under all the rocks?" Miss Justicia began to cackle, but, as before, lapsed into ragged coughing.

Pauline shoved back her chair and stood up. "Shall I fetch a glass of water?"

Maxie pushed the wine decanter across the table. "The water around here tastes as though it's pumped out of the bayou. The wine might be better, although I find it on the sweet side. I myself prefer a dry white wine with dinner."

"Justicia is not supposed to . . ." Pauline began.

"But I do," Miss Justicia said as the coughing spasm eased. "Maxie, pour me a glass of that stuff. Colonel Maynard Malloy bought cases of it fifty years ago from a New Orleans pimp, and it's been good enough for the family ever since."

"I find it overly sweet," Maxie insisted as she filled a glass.

While the two debated the merits of the ancestral wine cellar, I said in a low voice to Stanford, "I saw Keith a few minutes ago, crawling out of a little doorway under the staircase. He said he was a vegetarian, declined to come to the table, and went back through the same door."

"A closet vegetarian? Sweet Jesus, the next thing I know, he'll claim to be a satanist or some other assinine thing. I did my best, Claire, but it just wasn't good enough. I sent child-support money every month until they were eighteen. Maybe it would have been better for everybody concerned if I'd gone off to war like Miller and gotten myself blown up by jungle gooks."

"Miller?" I said.

"I didn't say Miller." Sweat popped out on his forehead. "If I did, my tongue was twisted. I meant to say *military*. I should have gone off to war like a military . . . person."

"Who's Miller?"

Stanford glanced warily at Miss Justicia, and then leaned toward me and whispered, "My older brother. Didn't Carlton tell you there were three of us?" He astutely interpreted my look of total bewilderment. "Miller was ten years older than me, twelve older than Carlton, so he was pretty much going about his own business when we were growing up. He joined the army, and they sent him to Vietnam as a so-called military advisor long about 1960."

"Carlton never even hinted of this brother."

"We can't discuss it in front of Miss Justicia. It . . . ah, distresses her. You and I'll just find ourselves a comfy love seat after dinner and I'll tell you the story." He took a deep drink of wine, mopped his forehead with his napkin, and began to pat my knee under the table. "Your girl seems to have grown into a fine young lady. In a way, she reminds me of Keith and Ellie's mother. She and Sharlene Anne have the same innocent face, although Sharlene Anne's eyes were as clear and blue as the early-morning sky and her hair was the color of honey. Look how sweet Caron is, sitting there listening to the adults chatter."

"Caron? Why, she's an absolute angel." I nudged the angel with my elbow. "Isn't that so, dear? Tell Uncle Stanford how nicely you waited for me in our room upstairs."

"Oh, Mother," she said, rolling her eyes in the classic adolescent style that invariably accompanies those two words, "I went for a walk, okay? I wanted to see where my father played as a child."

"And such a sentimental little thing," Stanford inserted mistily.

I gritted my teeth as his hand fondled my knee, but I ordered myself to ignore it. "How intriguing," I said to Caron. "Did you chance upon a tire swing and a sandbox?"

"No, just a bunch of weeds and bugs. I'd have totally died if I'd seen a snake or something gross like that, but I didn't." She paused. "Are you okay?"

"I'm peachy," I muttered. I brushed Stanford's hand off my knee, but it was back before I could rearrange my napkin. I eyed the forks, wondering which one would serve best to discourage him.

Ellie came into the room, draped the boa over the gong, and sat down beside her father. "My brother is not to be found," she announced. "He's not been stimulating company since his lobotomy, Miss Justicia. I don't know why you insisted he come this weekend."

"Because it's my eightieth birthday tomorrow, Ellie dear, and I want my devoted family gathered around me. I do hope you're going to surprise me, because I certainly intend to surprise the britches off all of you."

"Do give us a hint," wheedled Maxie.

"You'll have to wait, all of you. I want Keith to be here, and my lawyer, of course."

"Good ol' Bethel D'Armand?" Stanford asked jovially. "How's he doin' these days, Miss Justicia? Still going to the old folks' home every Sunday to visit his—"

"I fired him," she said.

Phoebe and Pauline broke off their whispered conversation to stare at her. Stanford mutely wiped his forehead with a damp napkin. The wineglass in Maxie's hand halted halfway to her lips, its contents sloshing perilously. Ellie raised her eyebrows and pursed her lips. For what felt like a very long time, the only sound was the rattle of pans in the kitchen.

Stanford let out a wheezy sigh. "Now why would you go and fire Bethel after all this time, Miss Justicia? He's been the family lawyer for thirty years."

"I had my reasons. Besides, you'll find this new lawyer very stimulating, in more ways than one. But not another word. Tomorrow at dinnertime, we'll have our surprise. If Keith has any wits left, he'll be here, too."

Maxie put down her glass. "I hardly imagine the boy's presence to be of any importance. He may be your grandson, but he's not a likely candidate to establish the trust and see that Malloy Manor is placed on the National Historic Register." She put her hand on her daughter's shoulder. "Luckily, Phoebe has taken several courses at the university in the preservation and management of our national resources. Isn't that so, dear?"

"Yes, and it's a complex procedure that requires in-depth knowledge and familiarity with the federal tax regulations."

"This house has significance as an example of pre–Civil War plantation architecture," Maxie said, pink with passion. "It was built by Richmond Malloy in 1853, and it once stood in the midst of several thousand acres of prime farmland. He himself was a most respected member of the community, a deacon in his church and a member of the city council from . . ."

She faltered, but Phoebe was poised with her notebook. "He served from 1884 until his death in 1891. Cholera, complicated by gout and chronic obesity. He left behind his wife, Rosalee, nee Duchampion, a very good family from the next parish, and eight legitimate children, five of whom survived the epidemic. The eldest son, Sturgis, married his maternal second cousin, thus further unifying the two lineages and—"

"What's this crap about the National Historic Register?" Ellie said, saving us from what might have developed into an all-night marathon of trivialized history.

Maxie turned to smile at Miss Justicia. "It's vital that the trust be managed by a person who is intimately acquainted with the Malloy family's glorious history. The girl would have the house bulldozed for a subdivision of tacky little houses."

"People have to live somewhere," Ellie muttered.

Stanford stopped exploring my kneecap. "Ellie's making a small and unamusing joke, Miss Justicia. She has a great fondness for this house, as do we all. She and Keith have warm memories of playing in the yard, then coming inside so Cousin Pauline could give 'em fresh cookies and milk."

"And pinch the silver when they thought I wasn't looking?" Miss Justicia cackled.

"Now, now," said Pauline, "they were dear children. Keith was always eager to help me with the chores, and I still remember his lovely curls and wide, innocent eyes." She looked across the table. "His twin sister, on the other hand, did have a bit of a temper."

"I did not!" Ellie snapped, then realized the incongruity of her response and batted her eyelashes at Pauline. "He always was your pet, wasn't he? Did you ever count the money in the sugar bowl after one of his visits?"

Stanford's hand was still twitching above my knee, but all his attention was on Miss Justicia. "They were mischievous tykes, but they loved every minute they were here." Without turning his head, he added in a cold voice, "Isn't that so, Ellie? Why don't you tell your grandmother all about it?"

Miss Justicia rang a silver bell. "It's time for food, not fairy tales." She sat back and regarded us with the complaisance of a cat with a bloodied mouse between its paws.

I was finding all of this quite dreary, and I could see from Caron's expression that she concurred. Two more days, I reminded myself as the door to the kitchen swung open. Two more tiresome days with these tiresome people, and Caron and I could go home and revise the Christmas card list.

The meal was served by a grim black woman with a few gray hairs and a badly wrinkled uniform. The food was as unappetizing as those who pretended to partake of it. The only incident of interest occurred when Caron studied a gray lump on her plate and, with a sharp intake of breath, realized what it was—or had been in the distant past.

"The taxi driver said not to eat any fish!" she said, horrified.

Phoebe frowned. "Fish is a good source of protein, low in saturated fats and high in omega-three oils, which prevent heart disease." She looked down at her plate more carefully. "Fresh fish, that is. I'm not sure about this."

"He warned us about tapeworms," Caron added.

Pauline conveyed a tiny bite to her mouth. "When they did the autopsy on Annabel D'Armand, they discovered a tapeworm that was forty-one feet long. I believe that's the parish record."

Caron was not the only one of us to put down her fork very quietly.

After we'd shoveled down what we could of dry bread pudding covered with a sticky yellow sauce, Miss Justicia threw down her napkin and switched on the motor of the wheelchair. "I'm looking forward to tomorrow, as I'm sure all of you are. Until then, my devoted family, nighty-night."

The wheelchair banged against the kitchen door as it moved backward, banged against a table leg as it surged forward, and banged against the doorsill as it disappeared.

Stanford filled his wineglass and glowered across the table at Maxie. "What the hell was all that nonsense about the house being turned into some sort of national monument?"

Maxie made a production of daintily touching her mouth with her napkin, but I could see her mind moving more briskly than Miss Justicia in third gear. "Well," she said at last, "for some time I've been trying to persuade Miss Justicia of the importance of preserving Malloy Manor as a perfect example of its architectural period."

"Which will, of course," Phoebe said, "require the establishment of a nonprofit trust to be used judiciously for upkeep, repairs, and the acquisition of antiques until each room is brought up to proper standards."

Ellie stood up and reached for the decanter. "And let's not forget the hefty salaries of the administrators."

Maxie snatched the decanter at the last moment and filled her glass. Then, with a condescending nod, she set it down within Ellie's reach and settled back in her chair. "The money is in no way as important as the obligation to posterity."

"What's the matter, dear?" cooed Ellie. "Did ex-Cousin Frazier finally quit sending those hefty alimony checks after all this time? How long has it been since he dumped you for that sweet young thing with the big tits?"

"A paradigmatic midlife crisis," Phoebe explained to me, although I hadn't planned to demand the details.

Maxie lit a cigarette. "His checks stopped about a year ago, but Frazier's temporary lapse has nothing to do with the establishment of the trust. It will be a time-consuming and demanding task, and I feel strongly that it requires the services of those members of the family who have shown a dedication to its traditions and lineage."

"All this talk of the National Historic Register is poppy-cock," said Stanford. "Sheer poppycock. You may think you can weasel up to Miss Justicia and convince her to leave all the family money to some idiotic trust to convert this mau-soleum into a museum, but I won't have it."

"You won't have it, Cousin Stanford?"

"No, ma'am, I am the custodian of the family business, and it's a damn sight more important than this transparent scheme of yours. We're undercapitalized at the moment, but with a substantial influx of cash, we can develop a gourmet line and dominate the market within the year."

"What market?" Caron asked.

"Kibble," he told her curtly, then turned back on Maxie. "Don't think you're going to get away with this, dear cousin. The money rightfully deserves to go to Pritty Kitty Kibble, and Miss Justicia agrees with me."

Ellie tapped her glass with her fork. "Hey, wait just a minute. My money isn't going into a new recipe for codfish pâté, nor is it going to be used to purchase Louis the

Fourteenths for the parlor. I have some rather pressing promises to keep, and miles to go before I sleep."

"With every biker in Atlanta," Phoebe inserted neatly.

"I do so admire your wit." Ellie snatched up her glass, drained it, and then studied it as if judging its potential as a projectile.

Cousin Pauline fluttered her hand. "Justicia assured me that the house would be mine as long as I wished to live here, along with an income from the capital."

"Come now," Maxie said with a short laugh, "you're hardly capable of doing this house justice. I'm sure we can find a suitable apartment for you once Phoebe and I become administrators of the trust."

Phoebe took out her notebook and made a notation. "One bedroom ought to be adequate, although you may have to make do with an efficiency if it proves more economical."

Pauline attempted to smile. "But I've lived here for forty years, as Justicia's companion and nurse. I put aside my personal aspirations in order to care for her. I once dreamed of being a concert pianist. As a child, I was told I had great promise. My études, in particular, were considered exquisite."

"I'm sure they were," Stanford said soothingly. "We're all aware of the sacrifices you made, and I for one am not going to see you living in some seedy apartment building. Hell, I'll find you a condominium where you can be surrounded by old people like yourself."

Pauline's face hardened. "Malloy Manor is my home. I have spent my life here. I will not be discarded."

"This is too comical for words," Ellie said. "Miss Justicia told me that the grandchildren will share the bulk of the estate. She called last week and said that if Keith and I came this weekend, we'd be pleasantly surprised with the new will. Well, both of us are here."

Maxie ground out her cigarette in a saucer. "She told me

she was committed to the preservation of Malloy Manor. The new will establishes the trust."

"With Mother and me as administrators," Phoebe added.

Stanford rapped on the table. "Hold your damn horses! I am sorry that you four are under any kind of delusion about who will receive the bulk of the estate. Last week, Miss Justicia assured me that I would realize more than enough money to revitalize the company."

"The money goes to Keith and me!" Ellie said.

"She told me I would receive the house and an income," Pauline said sharply.

"Poppycock!" Stanford roared, banging his fist hard enough to rattle the china.

I sat and wondered how best to escape the asylum now that the inmates were in control. I was toying with faking an attack of botulism when Caron poked me and whispered, "I'm a grandchild."

I glanced at my little angel, who had a calculating expression not unlike those of our dinner companions. "Forget it," I whispered back. "It's obvious Miss Justicia has more than enough would-be heirs to bicker over the family fortune. I make a decent living. You don't have cardboard soles in your shoes and dresses from Goodwill."

"I don't have a closet filled with Esprit jeans, either."

Stanford's fist regained my attention in time to hear him snarl that he was going to Miss Justicia's room to find out who all was getting what. Maxie announced that she and Phoebe would be on his heels. Ellie said she loved parades and had no intentions of missing this one. Pauline murmured that she would feel much better when the misunderstanding was resolved.

The five of them marched out of the room, although not in the precise order of their avowals. After a certain amount of jostling in the doorway, they were gone.

Caron sighed morosely. "Don't you want me to be a wealthy heiress?" she asked as her lower lip crept forward.

"No." I pushed back my chair and rose. "I think we ought to scurry upstairs while the others are occupied."

The cook came out of the kitchen. "Are you done? I got to clear the table and wash up so I can go home. I don't plan to be here any longer than I have to, not with a full moon."

"Why not?" asked Caron.

The cook leaned forward and in a husky voice, said, "Whenever there's a full moon, ol' General Malloy comes riding through the yard on a big shadowy stallion. He's dressed in his Confederate uniform, waving a saber over his head and crying out for his beloved mistress."

"I don't believe that," Caron retorted with a supercilious smile. "Creepy old legends have no historical basis."

"This one does, because the mistress was my great-great-grandmother Lavinia. She was as black as coal, with a fine figure and eyes that blazed like embers. He kept her in a shack at the far end of the bayou, and whenever the moon was full, he'd gallop down on his stallion to visit her."

"Like, sure he did," Caron said, although her smile was increasingly strained.

"But one night," the cook continued, "he rode to the shack to bring her a handsome gold necklace. When he went inside, he stumbled over her mutilated body. Somebody'd killed her with an ax, and there was blood everywhere—on the floor, on the walls, even on the fancy brass bed he'd had brought all the way from New Orleans. He went crazy with grief, and came charging up the hill to find her murderers and hack 'em to pieces with his saber. He never did find 'em, but whenever the moon is full, he tries again."

Caron marched to the door, then looked back at me. "Have I mentioned the G word lately?" With a sniff, she went down the hall.

"Ronald Colman?" I asked politely.

"And Greer Garson as the wife." The cook began to stack plates and cutlery. She noticed Caron's untouched dessert. "Is she done?"

"More than done," I murmured.

4

I left the dining room and went down the hall to the foyer. It seemed I was not quick enough, however; before I could flee upstairs, the double doors flew open and Stanford strode out. Ellie followed more slowly, as did Maxie and Phoebe. No one looked cheerful, although none of them looked as enraged as the purported ghost of General Malloy.

"This is a fine barrel of pickled herring," Stanford muttered. "I'm not opposed to a small wager every now and then, but I do not relish a game of Russian roulette—when she loads the revolver. She's more than capable of filling the damn thing with bullets so all of us can have a turn at blowing our brains out for her entertainment."

Maxie took a cigarette from a black beaded evening bag and lit it. "Nor do I, Cousin Stanford, nor do I. Perhaps it's time to form an unholy alliance. One-sixth of the estate is preferable to nothing."

"But, Mother," Phoebe protested, "she promised us."

"I know she did, but it appears that she also promised cousins Stanford, Ellie, Keith, and Pauline. I'm not at all sure which promise she intends to keep—if any. She very well may give the entire estate to a home for prodigal alligators."

"It's a shame we can't take a tiny peek at this new will," Ellie said pensively.

"As well as the old one," Stanford added. He noticed me and winked. I regretted not stabbing him with a fork.

Maxie dropped her cigarette in a vase. "Miss Justicia said she would reveal the contents of the new will tomorrow at dinner, and we must abide by her wishes." She regaled us with an elaborate yawn. "Come along, Phoebe, it's time to retire."

"Yes, Mother. I am fatigued after the day's journey. Traveling can disrupt one's diurnal biological rhythms."

Stanford pulled out an ornate silver pocket watch and harrumphed in disbelief. "My goodness, it's after ten, and I'm feeling a bit bushed, myself. How about you, Ellie?"

"I can't imagine anything more appealing," she said.

I realized it was my turn, and said, "Caron's already upstairs. I suppose we'll see all of you at breakfast?"

They all assured me that we certainly would.

No one moved.

Maxie glared at Stanford, who was glaring at Ellie, who was glaring at Phoebe, who was glaring at me. I was merely gazing at them when the double doors opened and Pauline slipped out.

"Justicia is settled for the night," she said in a hushed voice. "She insisted on a nightcap from the brandy decanter in her bedroom. Her doctor will be most displeased."

Maxie tucked her bag under her arm. "Then we can all retire, content in the knowledge that Miss Justicia is resting peacefully. Until the morning, dear cousins?"

On that note, we all trooped upstairs in a tight group. I continued to my cell and went inside with a sigh of relief.

Caron sat in the middle of her bed, dressed in a T-shirt. Her face was speckled with green cream, as if a baby with a mouthful of strained peas had sneezed in close proximity. "Do you think that painting out in the hall is of General Richmond Malloy?" she asked ever so casually.

"Does he resemble Ronald Colman?"

"Who?"

"Never mind, dear." I drew the curtains and sat down on the edge of the bed to pull off my shoes. "What a crazy group they are. No, I take that back. They're greedy; Miss Justicia's the crazy one. Why would she privately promise each one the majority of the estate? She's asking for trouble, and these people are more than prepared to give it to her."

"I think Miss Justicia enjoys it," Caron said. She crossed her legs and pulled up one foot to study its bottom. "There aren't tapeworms in the carpet, are there? I don't want to end up like that person in *Alien* whose guts exploded. Talk about disgusting . . ."

"Why do you think she enjoys it?" I asked, unable to deal with the latter part of her remarks.

"None of them ever visits her except when they want money. This is her way of getting even with them."

"Your perspicacity amazes me at times. Your father wasn't any better than—" I stopped as I heard a creak in the hall. "Sssh, someone's outside the door."

I tiptoed to the door and opened it to a slit. Keith was moving furtively down the hall. He tapped on Ellie's door, and was admitted after a whispered word from its occupant.

A second door farther down the hall opened and Stanford's head popped out. Another opened, and Maxie and Phoebe peered out, their two faces poised in totem-pole fashion. Phoebe was on top; her chinless face fit snugly into her mother's beehive. Pauline's door opened only a few inches, but I could see her elongated face in the shadows.

Various eyes met, and then all doors, including mine, closed with perceptible clicks.

"Okay, so they're crazy, too," I said as I opened a suitcase and began to rummage for my nightgown. "And the situation is becoming more gothic by the minute, in an oddly off-key fashion. We've got a creepy house, a full moon, a mysterious will, dark family secrets, at least one ghost, and carefully staged scenes that are straight out of one of Azalea Twilight's five-hundred-page bodice rippers. I might have a better grasp of things if I'd forced myself to read one of them."

"Azalea's characters are a lot more interesting than these dweebs," Caron said, still studying her foot. "In her books, there's always a handsome hulk with a dueling scar. Keith's pockmarks hardly qualify." She glanced at me. "And a poor, mistreated girl who's penniless and has to marry some sadist who keeps his other wives locked in the attic. When she learns she's actually an heiress, everybody's really sorry about being mean to her. Really, really sorry."

"Is that an erumpent pimple on the tip of your nose?"

With a squeal of terror, she fled to the bathroom. I changed into a nightgown and plumped the pillow as best I could, then took a mystery novel from my suitcase and settled in to read something entertaining rather than instructional.

After the best part of an hour, a slightly greener Caron reappeared and lay down on her bed to gaze at the ceiling. "I wonder if Ellie has anything that might help."

"Help with what, dear?" I asked distractedly, more concerned with the blizzard at the country house that had trapped a sextet of potential murderers, along with an elderly butler who dressed impeccably and served brandy on a silver salver. He did not wear sunglasses and a set of headphones, although he did glide silently in and out of the chapters.

"My complexion. I look worse than when I had the chicken pox in second grade." She yanked the sheet away and sat up. "Maybe Ellie has some cream or something I can use tonight."

"Everyone has gone to bed. Ask her in the morning." I turned the page. The electricity was out because of the blizzard, naturally, and everyone was creeping around the house with candles in their sweaty fists. I decided the butler was doing too much creeping for his station in life. Ignoring the sighs and groans from the other bed, I turned another page.

After a while, the sighs and groans became snuffly snores. I continued to read until I realized I was holding the book while I dozed. I crossed the room to switch off the light, and made it back to my bed with only a minor bit of damage to one toe. I deplumped the pillow, pulled the sheet up to my chin, and closed my eyes.

As if controlled by a thread from the ceiling, my eyelids rose. I tried again, but they refused to stay down without conscientious effort on my part. I stared at the ghostly blotches of mildew on the walls. I stared at the crouching figure made of suitcases. I stared at the sliver of moonlight on the wardrobe. Eventually, I found my watch on the bedside table and stared at it until I determined it was nearly midnight. I also determined that I was hungry—ravenously, primitively, inescapably hungry—and that I was not going to be able to sleep until I appeased the internal demons.

I eased out of bed, put on my robe and bedroom slippers, and went out to the hall. One small bulb in a wall fixture on the landing provided enough light for me to make it safely down the stairs.

As I turned to go to the kitchen, I saw a narrow line of light under the parlor door. I crept to the door and tried to peek through the keyhole, a vastly overrated technique. I caught a glimpse of movement but no face. I considered my options and opted for the obvious. As I opened the door, the figure spun around.

"Cousin Claire!" gasped Phoebe as she stumbled backward through the thicket of floor lamps.

"I came down to raid the refrigerator," I said, glancing at the tape measure in her hand. "What are you doing?"

"I had trouble sleeping, and I thought I'd look in here for a magazine."

"Any size in particular?"

She looked at the tape measure as if it were the record-setting tapeworm. "I left this in here earlier."

"I'm going to the kitchen to see if I can find some cheese and bread," I said, not bothering to point out I'd seen her put it in her bag before dinner.

"I'll come with you." She put the tape measure in her bathrobe pocket, switched off the lamp, and joined me in the doorway. "I must agree that dinner was inedible. Whatever could have been in that sauce on the pudding?"

We discussed possibilities as we went down the hall toward the kitchen. As we passed the open door of the dining room, I spotted movement. I caught Phoebe's arm. "There's someone in there," I whispered.

She unceremoniously removed my hand. "There is a great deal of moonlight, Cousin Claire. It's more likely that you saw a shadow from the magnolia tree near the window."

"Or someone looking for a magazine." I turned on the light.

Stanford was on his hands and knees under the dining table. He gave us the frantic look of a puppy caught piddling on the carpet, then hastily crawled out and stood up. His bathrobe hung open, exposing pajamas dotted with teddy bears. "I . . . came downstairs to . . . ah, to find myself a little snack."

"You're rather desperate if you're willing to settle for crumbs from under the table," I said.

Stanford snatched up a napkin from the table to wipe his forehead. "There is a perfectly good explanation for my behavior, which I'll be the first to admit looked peculiar." We waited diplomatically while he concocted it. "When I retired earlier, I realized I'd misplaced my pocket watch. It's been in the family for generations. I was too distraught to sleep. It finally occurred to me that it might have fallen out of my pocket during dinner, and I came down to search under the table." His bald lie gave him enough courage to narrow his eyes at us. "And what are you two ladies doing down here?"

Phoebe narrowed her eyes right back at him. "I desired a magazine to read, Cousin Stanford. Cousin Claire says she came down to find something to eat."

"Miss Justicia insists that the kitchen door be locked every night." Stanford dusted off the knees of his pajamas and tightened the belt of his bathrobe with a jerk that must have pained a few of the dear little teddies. "Cousin Pauline has always kept the key; she used to allow Keith into the kitchen when they thought no one was up."

I tried to imagine the two as comrades in a midnight pantry raid, then reminded myself that he'd probably been dragged to the barbershop on a monthly basis.

"I suppose I'll go back upstairs," I said.

"So will I," Stanford said. "And you, Cousin Phoebe? I see you didn't have much success finding a magazine. . . ."

"As much success as you had finding your pocket watch."

I turned off the light and we went toward the foyer. As we came through the doorway, I saw a diaphanous white figure in the darkness. Phoebe and Stanford must have seen it, too, since their gurgles of surprise echoed mine as we rammed into each other like a chain-reaction accident on a foggy freeway.

The figure turned around. I could see a gossamer gown, but the face was masked by the shadows. Bits of the cook's cinematic ghost story came back in icy dribbles down my spine. Gulping, I squinted until I could make out features.

"Pauline." I exhaled. "What are you doing out here?"

A few noises came from her throat, but I could make no sense of them. As I reached her side, I realized the front door was ajar. I pulled it open and found myself confronting not the vaporous remains of General Malloy but the pudgy white taxi driver who'd delivered Caron and me to Malloy Manor several eons ago.

"Somebody called for a cab," he said, shrinking back as I gaped at him. "Now this lady says she doesn't know who called. I drove all the way out here, and lemme tell you—it ain't no hop, skip, and jump."

Pauline found what there was of her voice. "I'm at a loss as to who would call at this hour."

"Are you positive someone called from this house?" I asked the driver.

"I didn't drive out here for my health."

"No, I suppose not." I looked back at Stanford and Phoebe. "Do either of you know anything about this?"

Stanford numbly shook his head, but Phoebe turned on Pauline with a tight frown. "Perhaps you might explain why you're in the foyer, Cousin Pauline?"

"I . . . I thought I heard voices down here, and felt it only prudent to see who was up and about. Justicia oftens wakes at the slightest sound. As I came down the stairs, I heard a knock on the door, and I subsequently discovered . . . the gentleman on the porch."

I gnawed on my lip for a moment, and then resorted to surreptitious twitches of my fingers as I mentally counted. "There are only nine of us in the house. I can vouch for Caron's innocence; she's sound asleep. If none of us called, it must have been Miss Justicia, Ellie, Keith, or Maxie. Why would any of them want to leave in the middle of the night?"

"It is most puzzling," said Pauline. "I'll peek into Justicia's room and make sure she's asleep." We waited while she went across the foyer, opened one of the double doors, and closed it carefully. "She does awaken so easily," she whispered as she joined us. "However, she is in her bed under her comforter. The brandy decanter is no longer on her bedside table, which I fear indicates she . . . well, she polished it off once I'd settled her down for the night."

Stanford shook his head. "So Miss Justicia is drunker than a skunk and passed out, as usual. We'd better ask the others if one of them made the call for some bizarre reason."

"I can assure you it wasn't Mother," said Phoebe.

Pauline timidly touched my shoulder. "What shall we do about the taxi driver, Claire? I don't think we should require him to wait on the porch. Shall I send him on his way?"

"Oh, no," I said. "Take him into the parlor and chat with him while I get to the bottom of this."

She clutched her collar. "I'm not dressed to entertain gentleman callers! I would never dream of sitting in the parlor in my nightclothes. People would talk."

I pointed my finger at the driver, who was halfway down the porch steps and no doubt hoping to disappear into the night. "Come back here. Someone called you, and I'm going to find out who it was. Was it a male or a female?"

"I dunno. The voice was low and whispery. This place's rumored to be haunted. Maybe it was a ghost."

I gave him an icy look. "Nineteenth-century ghosts are

not familiar with the concept of calling a taxi. The call was made by a person who either will climb in the backseat of your taxi or reimburse you for your time and gasoline."

"It's not a big deal, lady."

"No, I suppose not," I said, gesturing more emphatically for him to come into the house, "but it's a curious deal. Would you mind waiting in the parlor for five minutes?"

"Okay, okay." He went past me, his head lowered, and continued into the parlor as if it was the principal's office.

I turned on the light for him, closed the door, and regarded my three cosleuths. Given my druthers, I would have preferred the company of the driver to that of Stanford, Phoebe, and Pauline. I clearly had no druthers.

"Well," I said, "let's find the person who called the driver and let him or her do whatever he or she has in mind. This is peculiar, but I don't intend to stay up all night because of it."

"Maybe we ought to forget about it," Stanford said with a sigh. "We're getting ourselves all stirred up over what may have been a little misunderstanding on his part."

Phoebe frowned at the closed door that led to the parlor. "Cousin Stanford's apt to be right. Why don't I tell the driver to run along?"

"No," I said firmly to squelch the palace revolt brewing in the foyer. "It's a very small mystery, but I'm wide-awake now and I'm going to solve it before I go back to bed."

I started upstairs, but before my foot touched the third riser, my band of Malloy Manor irregulars (in all senses of the word) fell into line.

At the top of the stairs, we halted for a conference. After a great deal of hissing and gesturing, I shushed them and crossed the hallway to tap softly on Ellie's door.

Keith opened it, still dressed and wearing the sunglasses. "Isn't this a little late even for the Avon lady?"

"Someone in this house called for a taxi," I told him. "The driver is waiting downstairs. Did you call him?"

"Why would I want to split in the middle of the night?"

Stanford nudged me aside. "Why would anyone wear dark glasses in the middle of the night? With that disgraceful hair and those ratty clothes, I wouldn't speak to you on the street. You look like a two-bit hoodlum."

"Or a junkie," Phoebe contributed.

"It's *my* hair," Keith muttered, brushing even more of it in his face for emphasis. "I'm like into heavy metal, and all the guys in the band have long hair. I got a tattoo on my butt. Wanna see it?"

"Your mother, may she rest in peace, reared you to show respect for your elders," Stanford said in a sputtery voice. "Remember how I used to take you outside and tan your bottom for sassing me? I ought to—"

I decided we were merely rehashing old hash. "What about Ellie?" I asked Keith. "Is she planning to go somewhere tonight?"

"Naw, she's in the bathroom putting mud on her face."

I glanced at the closed bathroom door behind us. Light glinted beneath it, and I heard running water and the faint sound of someone conversing with her perfect complexion in the mirror.

"She's got a car, anyway," Keith added. "Why would she need to call a cab?"

"Why would anyone?" I said, making a face.

While Stanford grumbled at his hirsute offspring and Pauline made tart remarks about the risks of infection from tattoos, Phoebe went down the hall, slipped inside her room for a moment, and returned to inform us that her mother was asleep. "As well we all should be," she concluded.

"I suppose so," I said. "I'll go downstairs and dismiss the driver, and we can all try to get some sleep."

A door banged in the foyer below. I peered over the banister, wondering if our driver had fled farelessly into the night, but I saw nothing. After a minute, however, I heard an ominously familiar droning sound.

In the bathroom, Ellie stopped murmuring compliments and began to sing "Claire de Lune."

5

Pauline joined me at the banister. "This is terrible, simply terrible. Justicia promised to give up these childish pranks, but she persists at every opportunity. It's dark, the grass is wet and slippery, and all sorts of animals are in the yard at night. I could just kill her." She hurried into the bedroom and tugged at the window until it opened with an abrupt squeal. "Perhaps we're mistaken," she added without optimism. "We might have heard the taxi as it left."

We crowded around her. Moonlight softened the raggedness of the yard and gave it a certain deceptive tranquillity. The inky water of the bayou glittered, as did the leaves of the tangle of trees beyond it. Several mosquitoes took advantage of the open window to zoom in for a midnight snack. Their buzzing competed with the increasingly insistent drone that was not the taxi's departure, to our collective regret.

The wheelchair came around the corner of the house, its white-haired driver bent over the controls. She narrowly missed a tree, teetered precariously on one wheel, and then, at the fateful second, regained her balance. With a triumphant cackle, she shifted into high and shot into the shadows.

Pauline snorted angrily. "I must find her before she causes herself serious harm. All that wine at dinner, and then the brandy . . ." She squirmed through us and ran out the door.

We waited mutely at the window. Bedroom slippers flapped down the stairs like soft applause. A door banged. Seconds later, Pauline came into view and trotted away in the direction Miss Justicia had taken. It was much the same scene as I'd observed earlier, although the white gown that Pauline was wearing gave this version a macabre air.

Keith whistled softly. "Did you catch the look on her face? She's so far off her rocker, she couldn't find it, much less sit in it."

"Don't speak of your grandmother like that," Stanford said, leaning over my shoulder to get a better view. His hand rested on my fanny, and, after a moment, began to explore its planes and curves. Keith and Phoebe jostled for position behind us, pinning me to the windowsill.

I froze, unable to believe Stanford would take advantage of his mother's potential peril to resume his advances. I then regained my sensibility and elbowed him hard enough to elicit a muffled grunt, but no respite. I was preparing to punch him in the nose when Pauline reappeared from the bushes.

"I can't find her," she said. "I've looked all along the paths she usually takes, but there's no trace of her. I don't hear the wheelchair."

"We'll help you search the grounds," I called down. I gave Stanford one last jab, a truly vicious one, and pushed my way through the group. "Well? Are you coming to find Miss Justicia before she runs into a magnolia tree?"

Stanford gave me a wounded look, although I didn't

know if I'd offended his superficial sense of decorum or his rib cage. "Of course we are," he said grimly. "All of you, step to it. Poor Miss Justicia's out there in the dark, and we have a responsibility to find her before it's too late."

Phoebe sniffed. "It seems to me it's Cousin Pauline's responsibility. It's part of her job description."

She caught my glower and reluctantly came across the room. Keith opened the bathroom door, tersely described the situation, and joined us with a smirky expression. "Ellie'll be down as soon as she can chip off the mask," he reported. "With that gook on her face, she'd give Granny a heart attack. I thought only kids were into mud pies."

I could think of one kid who'd be delighted to dabble in mud—if it was guaranteed to ward off pimples. I ascertained that said kid was asleep, then trooped downstairs with the others. As we went through the foyer, I considered inviting the taxi driver to join in the fun, but decided to leave him in isolated ignorance. As it was, his opinion of the clan was already less than flattering. Miss Loony Tunes herself, he'd said. No rebuttal came to mind.

We halted on the porch to assess the situation. A cloud drifted across the face of the moon, briefly blotting out the eerie white light. Tree frogs competed with distant bullfrogs. Mosquitoes and gnats buzzed in my ears. Birds squawked at us from deep within shadowy tunnels of foliage. Amidst this bucolic cacaphony, I did not hear the wheelchair.

"I suppose we need to fan out," I said unenthusiastically.

Stanford nodded sharply, now assuming the mantle of a battlefield general. "Phoebe, you come with me. We'll cover the area by the old barn Claire, you and Keith go around that side of the house and work your way along the bayou. Gather up Cousin Pauline."

I doubted Keith would be of much use should we encounter one of the less appealing denizens of the bayou, but I didn't relish the idea of wandering into the yard on my own. "Let's go," I said to him as I went down the steps and to the driveway to check for wheelchair tracks. There were none.

We went around the corner of the house, past a ramp at the end of the porch, and into the vast wasteland of the backyard, where we found Pauline peering under a bush.

She let the branch fall. "I cannot believe Justicia would do this dreadful thing," she said as she fell into step with us. "She's in frail health, and this can't be good for her."

"Hey, the old girl just wants to have fun," Keith said.

Pauline made a small noise of exasperation. "That's easy for you to say. You're not responsible for her well-being, nor are you particularly concerned about it. How long has it been since your last visit—ten years?"

"Something like that," he muttered.

"Then again," she continued mercilessly, "how could you visit when you've been engaged in involuntary residence behind a fence topped with barbed wire?"

"So what? This place gives me the heebie-jeebies."

I tried to ignore them as I squinted into the shadows. Miss Justicia was a tiny woman, but her wheelchair could not easily be hidden. I glanced at Pauline. "Has she ever vanished like this before?"

"I'm afraid so. Several months ago, the police picked her up more than nine miles from here and returned her. One of the officers indicated he might charge her with reckless driving and resisting arrest. She was very . . . indignant at the time. Luckily, he was a local boy and I was able to dissuade him from taking action that might disgrace the family."

"She was heading this way," I said as we walked toward the guilty bushes. I rubbed my temples and reminded myself Caron and I now had less than thirty-six hours left. It was possible I was going to spend a lot of them poking around a swampy yard for an old lady in a wheelchair, but like dental surgery, labor, and televised football games, this, too, would pass.

"Drunken driving in a wheelchair," Keith said admiringly. "You know, that's a class act."

Pauline stiffened. "I do not think it proper for you to snicker at your grandmother, despite her propensity for immature behavior and overindulgence."

"All I said was—"

"You snickered. I distinctly heard you snicker when—"

"Shall we continue the search?" I interrupted. Both subsided, and we arrived at the edge of the bayou without further analyses of Miss Justicia's propensities. We followed the bank at a prudent distance. As we came around a clump of shrubbery, I saw a glint of silver in the water that was not the elusive glitter of moonlight.

I stopped in mid-step and took a deep breath. "You'd better wait here, Pauline."

She must have seen the glint, too, because her face turned chalky. "Is that . . . is that . . . ?"

"I'm afraid it might be." I patted her on the shoulder, then gestured for Keith to accompany me. We halted at the edge of the odiferous water. As I'd suspected, the glint came from the rim of a wheel. The back of the wheelchair was visible, indicating the water was no more than a foot or two deep.

Keith took off his sunglasses and gulped. "Do you think she pushed it in here for some screwy reason?"

"Let's hope so. Go find your father and Phoebe." Once he was gone, I gave myself a minute to dredge up some courage, then stepped out of my slippers and into the water.

It was as tepid as discarded tea as it lapped against my calves. My feet sank in several inches of silky mud that oozed between my toes. A submerged branch scraped one leg, almost eliciting a bloodcurdling scream that would have brought Stanford at a run. On the far side, something slithered into the water with a soft plop. Two fierce red eyes regarded me from within a burrow. I ordered myself not even to speculate on what might consider the mud to be its home, sweet home.

When I reached the wheelchair, I grasped the handles on the back. The thing weighed more than I'd imagined, and my footing was not what I would have preferred. It took a great deal of puffing and slipping to wrestle the chair to one side. It relented with a drawn-out slurp and a splash that caught me in the face.

Whispy white hair floated to the surface. I yanked the chair the rest of the way over and grabbed Miss Justicia's shoulder. I dragged her to the bank, laid her in the grass, and crouched beside her to listen for any sign that she was alive. Muddy water dribbled from her mouth as her jaw fell open, exposing sleek pink gums. Her eyes were flat and unseeing. Her concave chest was still.

Pauline approached, her hands clasped. "Is Justicia dead?"

"Yes," I said gently. I sat back on my heels and tried to let the horror of the moment drain off me like the water on my legs and forearms. "It's been at least fifteen minutes since we saw her drive across the yard. She could have been in the bayou most of that time." I looked up as Stanford, Keith, and Phoebe came out of the bushes. "I'm afraid there's been an accident," I told them. "Miss Justicia must have become disoriented in the dark. She went off the path and drove into the bayou. Although the water's not very deep, the wheelchair held her down."

Stanford walked past his mother's body and stared at the wheelchair. "The damn contraption's heavier than a refrigerator, considering it's mostly a collection of hollow metal tubes. I told her time and again to get a smaller model, but she insisted on state-of-the-art technology, maximum horse-power, and front-wheel drive." He turned back with a misty smile. "She did enjoy her wild rides around the yard. We can all take comfort in knowing she died while having a mighty fine time."

Pauline sank to her knees and began to rock back and forth as if she was on the porch in a cane-bottomed chair. Phoebe gave me an enigmatic look as she went to Pauline and bent down to comfort her. Keith came over to the body, his hands in his pockets and his sunglasses once again hiding his eyes.

"What do we do now?" he asked.

Stanford had recovered from his nostalgic mode. "I'll call the funeral home and have them send some boys to—ah, handle the situation in a discreet fashion. Cousin Pauline, did Miss Justicia ever mention a favorite funeral home?"

Pauline continued to rock mindlessly in the grass.

Pencil and notebook readied, Phoebe frowned at her. "You really must pull yourself together, Cousin Pauline. We're all aware that this tragic accident could have been averted if you'd noticed the wheelchair when you first searched for Miss Justicia, but I'm sure none of us intends to hold you fully responsible. If you can tell us Miss Justicia's preference in funeral homes, I'll take it upon myself to contact them. Otherwise, we'll simply be forced to select names at random from the Yellow Pages and discuss the various package rates."

"Wait a minute," I said when I could trust myself. "The first thing we have to do is call the police and tell them what happened."

"I don't believe that's necessary," Stanford said, crossing his arms as he peered down at me.

"Of course it's necessary. The local authorities have to be informed in the event of a fatal accident."

He took the napkin from his pocket and wiped his forehead. "We're not going to get all carried away with calling in any damn-fool authorities. In these parts, we're accustomed to dealing with tragedy in a calm and dignified manner befitting our family's position in the community. I don't want my dear, departed mother being disturbed by some policeman she never met, much less allowed in the parlor." He stuffed the napkin back in his pocket and said to Phoebe, "What say we stick a pin in the Yellow Pages, accept the best deal they offer, and get on with it?"

"It would be the most expedient method," Phoebe said, looking a bit disappointed as she retired her notebook and pencil.

"And cut down on delays," said Keith. "I can't hang around this place while the cops poke poles in the bayou and run blood tests to determine how drunk she was. I've got things to do."

I stood up to stare at them. "You are the strangest people I've ever met, and I've met some real doozies in my day. Listen very, very carefully: The law says that the police must be called in on an accidental death. It doesn't matter if it's expedient or not—it's the law."

Stanford mulled this over for a few seconds. "I've got it," he said brightly. "How about we take her back to the bedroom, dress her in some nice dry pajamas, and put her in bed? The doctor can have a quick look, then fill out a death certificate saying she died peacefully in her sleep."

"There have been very few documented cases of drowning in bed," I said, still battling with myself to stay calm in the midst of this incredible scene. Miss Justicia gazed blindly at the moon while her intimate family debated how best to expedite her interment. I wouldn't have been overwhelmed with shock if Stanford had ordered Keith to fetch a shovel and Phoebe a prayer book. Pauline was the only one evincing any grief. The others apparently had internalized theirs and moved on to more pressing concerns.

"I suppose not," Stanford admitted.

"I knew a smack freak who drowned in his water bed," Keith said. "Nobody knew he was dead until the water started dripping from the ceiling of the apartment below, and that was four, maybe five days later. It was summer, too, and the dude didn't have an air conditioner."

Stanford gave him a sharp look, then resumed his discussion with Phoebe. "I don't know if the doctor would cooperate with us on this or not. He may be able to tell that there's water in her lungs. As Claire was so eager to point out, no one drowns in bed."

"That junkie did," protested Keith.

"Just hush!" Phoebe snapped at him. "Your father and I are trying to determine how best to deal with this problem. Your drug-induced fantasies are not worthy of notice, much less serious consideration."

"Hey, it really happened. The guy punched holes in the plastic mattress with his needle, and then passed out."

I had had enough. I urged Pauline to her feet and put my arm around her trembling shoulders. "Stanford, you stay here with Miss Justicia's body. Pauline is in shock and needs a cup of tea. Phoebe, you can see to that while Keith lets Maxie and Ellie know what happened."

"And you, dear cousin?" Phoebe said.

"I am going to telephone the police and tell them about the accident. They'll want to examine the scene before they write an official report."

Stanford assessed me for a moment, then conceded with a shrug. "All right, all right. I don't see why that should take a whole lot of time. What'll they say, anyway? The fact that

Miss Justicia had these urges to overindulge in beverages of an alcoholic nature, then go whipping all over God's green earth in her wheelchair is . . . why, I'd say it was a legend in the parish. The whole state, for that matter. Pauline can just remind them of a few unfortunate incidents from the past, and we'll be done with the police before we know it."

"It seems we have no choice," Phoebe said as she took Pauline's arm and tugged her forward. "Come along, Cousin Pauline. We'll pour a pot of tea into you, with a nice slug of brandy. You're going to have to pull yourself together so that you can relate all that to the police."

"But it's so . . ." Pauline said dully. "I don't know if I can remember all . . ."

"Don't worry about it," I began. Despite the fact I was holding Pauline's other arm, Phoebe managed to dig a hard leather heel into my bare foot. I bit back a snarl, took a breath, and said, "No one's going to pressure you to tell the police anything."

Phoebe gave the older woman a smile meant to be sympathetic. "That's correct. No one's going to pressure you, Cousin Pauline."

The slight emphasis on the *you* gave the reassuring words quite a different message. It was received, but not appreciated any more than the incipient bruise on my foot.

We moved slowly toward the back door of the house. Stanford remained beside the body, his hands on his hips. Keith caught up with us as we guided Pauline through the back door and down the hall to the dining room. Phoebe briskly demanded the kitchen key, and after a few moments of fumbling, Pauline took it from her robe pocket and handed it over.

Once Phoebe had departed to make tea, I asked Keith where I might find a telephone. He mumbled a response and turned to study the dark oil paintings of dead, featherless fowl and mottled fruit. I once again patted Pauline on the shoulder, then went down the hall toward the parlor, which seemed as good a possibility as any.

As I entered the foyer, Ellie stepped out of the parlor and carefully closed the door. Devoid of makeup and with her hair hidden by a turban, she looked appreciably less glamorous. She hurried over to me, her satiny pink robe rustling, and grabbed my arm. "I was just coming outside to help you find Miss Justicia, but I discovered the most amazing thing in the parlor!"

"You did?"

She pulled me farther away from the door and lowered her voice. "There's a man in there, an unclean and unattractive man. He's lying on the sofa, and snoring away as if he lives here and fell asleep watching the late movie. You know, this place has always been a madhouse, but lately it's been downright peculiar."

"Has it now?" I said dryly. I gave her a short explanation of what had occurred, from the midnight prowlers to the discovery of the body in the bayou. I concluded with a request for the location of a telephone.

"The man in the parlor is a taxi driver?" Her fingernails bit into my arm. "Is that what he told you?"

"I suspected as much when he actually drove the cab from the airport this afternoon."

"But why would anyone in this house want to be picked up at midnight? And who?"

"We don't seem to have any confessions as of yet, and other things have taken precedence. I do need to call the police before your father concocts some scheme to transfer Miss Justicia's body to a health club and leave it in the hot tub."

"There aren't any hot tubs in this parish. Trust me." Ellie looked nervously at the parlor door, but she did have the courtesy to remove her claws from my arm. "Did you ask everyone abut this call to the taxi driver? Everyone?"

"A telephone, please?"

"God, I'm sorry, Claire. I must be in shock or something. This accident is so tragic, and I feel awful about Miss Justicia. She was a harridan, but she was my grandmother, and in our own way, we got along pretty well. I suppose that implies something less than charming about my personality, but I'll save it for my shrink." She gave me a rueful, if somewhat manic, smile. "There's a telephone in her bedroom, on the desk by the window. I'll get a couple of glasses from the kitchen and we can have a nip of brandy. I could use one, and you must be a basket case after discovering the body . . . like that."

If I was, I was not the only one, I thought as I went into the library. Stanford, Phoebe, and Keith had stood over a corpse in the moonlight, debating their chances of claiming she drowned in bed. Ellie was more distraught over a cabbie on the couch than the death of her grandmother.

Dearly hoping Caron had avoided any of the family's aberrant DNA, I went to the telephone, dialed the operator, and requested to be put through to the police. The operator told me I could dial direct, and thanked me for using AT&T. I told her it was an emergency. She asked in a hushed, almost reverent tone for details. I declined to share them and repeated my request that she ring the police. She told me I could dial direct, etc.

I would have taken a drink from the decanter, but if it was in the room, it was not within my sight. I barked at the operator, who, with a sniff of disapproval, at last connected me with the police department. The officer sounded bored as I began, but his voice rose in both pitch and volume as I mentioned names and arrived at the unpleasant conclusion of the story.

I was told to wait right where I was, ma'am, and not touch anything at the scene of the accident. Although it was a little late in the game for that, I acknowledged his instructions and replaced the receiver.

Ellie came into the room with two glasses. "Where's the decanter, Claire?"

I remembered an earlier remark, and said, "Pauline told us that Miss Justicia finished off whatever was in the decanter. I could use a drink, myself. Let's avail ourselves of a little something from the cart in the parlor."

"That man is in there."

"Indeed he is," I said as I started for the door. "We need to rouse him and give him a brief idea of what's happened. He'll have to stay until the police arrive."

"You said he claimed someone called him from here, but that's absolutely crazy. Maybe he came to case the joint in hopes of lifting an heirloom or two."

"He knocked on the front door, Ellie. That's hardly standard procedure when planning a burglary. I'd like to hear a more detailed version of the call, however. We were all so stunned that no one asked him for the exact wording." Which, I admitted to myself and myself alone, was pretty damn stupid. On a more charitable note, the oversight was salvageable in the immediate future.

Or so I'd thought. The parlor was devoid of snoozing taxi drivers. Ellie gave me a bewildered look, then checked behind the drapes while I searched the shadowy caverns under tables and between sofas and walls. We met by the wicker cart.

"He was here not ten minutes ago," Ellie said defensively. "I stood over him for I don't know how long, trying to figure out who the holy hell he was and what the holy hell he was doing in here. Look, there's a smudge of mud on the arm of the sofa where his feet were propped."

"You don't have to argue with me. I stuck him in here in

the first place." I fixed a drink, then sat down on the sofa under discussion. "He probably grew tired of waiting and simply went away. I can't see how he could be involved in what happened, but, in any case, the police should have no difficulty finding him tomorrow. He was parked at the airport when Caron and I arrived. It's most likely his regular stand."

Ellie poured a full glass of bourbon and sat down beside me. "You know, Claire, maybe we ought to do him a favor and not mention anything about his being here tonight. After all, he's just a dumb jerk trying to make a living, and as you said, he couldn't possibly have anything to do with Miss Justicia's accident. He was on the sofa the entire time she was . . ." She slumped back and covered her eyes. "Jesus H. Malloy," she added softly.

"Was there one of those, too?" I heard myself ask.

"You'll have to ask Maxie, but I wouldn't be surprised. She can trace the family all the way back to Adam Malloy and his lovely wife, Eve, who was a third cousin twice removed from a very good family in the next garden."

Our attempted diversion dwindled into a long silence. I studied the amber liquid in my glass, doing my best not to compare it to the quickening waves in the bayou when I'd struggled with the wheelchair. When I'd struggled with the body. I realized I was about to splatter my robe, and put the drink on the coffee table.

The doorbell rang.

"That must be the police," I said to Ellie. "Phoebe's in the kitchen making tea for Pauline. I have no idea if your brother bothered to wake Maxie and tell her what happened. Caron can sleep through this, but Maxie needs to come downstairs."

When we reached the foyer, she turned and went upstairs, and I opened the front door. A uniformed officer stood there, his hand resting on his holster. He must have been in his twenties to have graduated from an academy, but he had a boyish face dotted with blemishes, twitchy eyes, and the uneasy bravado of a playground bully. He was so thin that his uniform hung on him like a saggy elephant skin, presuming the existence of blue elephants.

"You the woman who called?" he asked.

"Yes, and I'm also the one who discovered the body. Let me tell the others you're here, and then I'll take you down to the . . . scene of the accident."

His eyes left mine to meander down my body, which was less than fashionable in a terry-cloth robe. He lingered on its muddy hem for a moment, then flinched as he noted my bare feet.

"Where are your shoes?" he demanded accusingly.

"I took off my slippers when I waded into the water."

"Why'd you wade into the water?"

"To pull Miss Justicia from under her wheelchair."

"Why'd you tamper with the scene?"

"Because I didn't know it was 'a scene' at the time."

"Then why'd you wade into the water?"

I thought of numerous clever responses, most of which were likely to result in the necessity of raising bail in the morning. I even caught myself wishing Maxie would swoop down the stairs to deal with this boneheaded excuse for a policeman, or Stanford to come forward brandishing his handkerchief to defend me. Ellie with a mud pie. Keith with his headphones. Caron with her capital letters. Even Phoebe with a sharp pencil and a sharper frown.

After less than twelve hours in residence in Malloy Manor, I was in a very sorry state—and I don't mean Louisiana.

6

I asked the officer to wait, then went to the dining room to check on Pauline. She was slumped at the table, her head bowed and her fingers playing with the frayed cuffs of her peignoir. There was no cup of tea in evidence, much less a medicinal shot of brandy. I asked her where Phoebe was and received a numb look in response. I asked her where Keith was and received another.

I continued into the kitchen, a large and awkwardly arranged room, the primary function of which, I suspected, was to provide a habitat for nocturnal insects. Beyond the stained sink and peeling countertops, I found a metal pot whistling forlornly on a black cast-iron stove. A cup, saucer, flowered teapot, and several tea bags were laid out on a tray. It seemed Phoebe had lost her zeal, tut, tut (this from a woman who was fairly sure she herself had lost her mind).

Once I'd gotten Pauline marginally interested in tea, I went back to the foyer and the policeman, who was peering suspiciously into the umbrella stand. He had been joined by a colleague, although this latest arrival was a slightly more mature man who'd been stuffed into his uniform only by the grace of God. Name tags identified the thin one as J. Dewberry, the pudgy one as L. Puccoon. What can I say? I read the backs of cereal boxes and the fine print on airline tickets, too.

As we walked across the yard toward the bayou, J. Dewberry asked me to describe the events that led to the accidental drowning. When I reached the point at which Miss Justicia raced through the bushes in her wheelchair, cackling satanically, they both began to chuckle.

"So she was drunk," J. Dewberry said, punching L. Puccoon on the arm. "I personally don't have a lot of trouble believing that. How about you, Lester?"

"You know me, Dewey; I'll believe most anything. I always set out cookies and milk on Christmas Eve. 'Xactly how much did she drink this time, ma'am?"

"She consumed several martinis before dinner, a quantity of wine during dinner, and a decanter of brandy after dinner," I said with nary a chuckle. "I think it's probable that she was more than minimally intoxicated, but the lab report will establish the precise level of alcohol in her blood."

Dewberry punched Puccoon again. "Hey, Lester, we can find out the precise level of alcohol in her blood just by sending it to the lab. Ain't that good to know?"

"Gee, Dewey, we don't have a lab."

"We don't?" Dewberry slapped his forehead. "I must have forgotten. For a minute there, I was thinking we were in New York City, New York, or Los Angeles, California, or even in one of those big plastic buildings in Florida with palm trees out front and cops what dress in pastel shirts."

"Sorry, Dewey, we don't got anybody what dresses in pastel shirts. All we got is you and me on this shift, and Bo and Cap'n Plantain on the other one. Do you think we ought to get ourselves pink shirts?"

"And look like a pair of flamingos? Wouldn't the boys over at the diner be im-pressed!"

If I'd held one itty-bitty Uzi in my hand, the two would have ended up splattered over the magnolia blossoms. As it was, I was obliged to bite my lip while they amused each other. I stalked around the azaleas and along the bank of the bayou to where Stanford stood guard. He was down to his pajamas, having covered the body with his bathrobe.

"The police have arrived," I said sourly.

"Why, Dewey Dewberry and Lester Puccoon!" Stanford said as he came over to slap them on their respective shoulders (others of us would have aimed higher). "You boys still going out on Saturdays nights in that rusty ol' johnboat to shoot gators? How's that little bride of yours, Dewey? She as perky as ever? And Lester, you still goin' to night school to get your equivalancy certificate? I must say I have unflagging admiration for that kind of dedication to self-improvement."

"Thank you kindly," said the purported student, shuffling his feet. His cohort would have tugged his forelock, had his receding hairline not precluded it.

Stanford nodded graciously. "Boys, I want you all to know how deeply, how very deeply, I appreciate your coming all the way out here at this time of night. We've had a terrible tragedy this evening. Knowing you boys will do everything you can to help us through this time of grief and mourning is a great comfort to us all."

"It's the least we can do for your family," Dewberry said obeisantly.

Puccoon squatted next to the body, pulled back the bathrobe, and sniffed. "Oh, Lordy, she must have been really plastered when she took off in the wheelchair. I can still smell the booze through the swamp water. I think it's clear what happened, Mr. Stanford. You have the condolences of all of us in the department."

"And we'll do our best to keep it quiet," Dewberry added. "I don't see any reason to make things worse by making public a lot of irrelevant details. We'll just say it was dark and she lost her sense of direction while taking a small drive around the yard."

Stanford put his hand on his chest and bowed ever so slightly. "I'm very moved, boys. So very, very moved by your sympathy and understanding of what some might see as an uncomfortable, not to mention potentially embarrassing, situation for the Malloy family."

I wasn't moved one centimeter. "Don't you intend to investigate the accident? For one thing, there's a lot of moonlight tonight, and Miss Justicia's lived here for decades. For another, we all know she's had some experience driving while under the influence."

"Meanin' what?" Dewberry said, giving me a beady look.

"I don't know," I admitted. "I just don't think you should write up a report without making some effort to determine exactly what took place."

Stanford put his arm around me and squeezed my shoulder. "Now, now, Claire, it's clear that you're in a state of shock from having found poor Miss Justicia's body the way you did. It was an act of heroism I shall always admire. But don't you think it might be wise for you to go back to the house and have a bracing cup of tea with Cousin Pauline while the boys and I work out the minor details? I hate to see you all upset like this and saying wild things you're apt to regret in the light of day."

I removed his hand. "No, Stanford, I think it might be better for me to stay right here until these clowns agree to conduct a proper investigation of the accident."

"The accident," Stanford repeated emphatically. "That's

exactly what it was—a straightforward accident with a tragic conclusion. I've known these boys since the day they were born, and I played poker with their daddies before that. I can assure you they'll proceed in a professional manner befitting our fine, upstanding police department. We'll take care of things here. I'd be most grateful if you run along and have that tea with Cousin Pauline."

The policemen were looking displeased by my characterization of them, and Dewberry was once again fingering his weapon. I realized there was nothing to be gained by arguing with them. Stanford had pulled the undeniable rank of an old, established, moneyed family, and the local serfs had bought it. To add to the problem, I wasn't sure why I was disturbed by the accident.

As I trudged back to the house, I searched for a crack in the scenario. Miss Justicia did careen around the yard in her souped-up wheelchair; I'd seen her doing so three times since my arrival. I had no doubt she was an habitual offender who did as she damn well pleased. She had consumed enough alcohol to pickle the occupants of several fraternity houses. Pauline had settled the old woman into bed, and had remarked on the emptiness of the decanter when she'd peeked into the room later.

At that point, we'd all been preoccupied with the inexplicable appearance of the taxi driver. Everyone was accounted for: Phoebe, Stanford, Pauline, and I had been questioning Keith when we heard the door slam and the wheelchair race across the yard. We'd stood together at the window and watched Miss Justicia disappear. Ellie was in the bathroom. Maxie and Caron were asleep. The cook had left for the night, and the driver was in the parlor, hoping to collect at least a portion of his fare if we could determine who'd called him.

It must have been an accident, since no one had the

opportunity to manipulate the situation. Motive, however, was an entirely different matter, courtesy of Miss Justicia's threatening remarks at dinner. Excluding the cook, the driver, Caron, and myself, the house was waist-deep in people with motives. Maybe. No one claimed to know the contents of the old will. No one claimed to know the contents of the new will. Therefore, no one could be sure he or she would profit more from the status quo or from what might transpire at the birthday dinner.

But a brief unauthorized reading of either would be illuminating for any of the would-be heirs. It was obvious from the earlier antics that at least a few mendacious souls were searching for one or both wills. Magazines, pocket watches, and voices in the dark. Right. And do let me show you the prospectus for some prime beach frontage in Wyoming.

I sat down on the back porch for a moment to rub my foot and curse Phoebe. I could hear low voices from the area I'd just left; Stanford was winning over the cops with words as silky as the silt in the bayou. Maybe it was an accident, rather than some ominous puzzle with too many pieces missing to even guess at its solution. Stanford, Phoebe, and Keith had opined as much within seconds of arriving at the scene. Ellie concurred. Maxie would leap onto the bandwagon as soon as she heard the tidings. The two so-called professionals were no doubt jotting down suggestions from Stanford as to how best to phrase the official report.

And I had to admit that I myself had described it as an accident. Paranoiacs could have enemies, hypochondriacs could have medical problems, and manipulative old women could have accidents. Motives did not a murder make. It also took opportunity, and no one had that.

I told myself to stop brooding over something that lacked definition, and continued into the house and the dining room. Pauline was in the same chair I'd left her in, but the cup of tea was nearly empty. At one end of the table, Phoebe and Maxie were whispering to each other. They broke off as I sat down next to Pauline and refilled her cup from the teapot.

"So here you are, Cousin Claire," Maxie said without warmth. "Phoebe has told me the dreadful news, and how you insisted the police be called in to investigate what might have been quietly dismissed as an accident. Our family can be traced back to the *Mayflower*, and many generations before that, as I told you earlier. There is a distinct possibility of a connection with William of Orange. Although there have been a few scalawags in the lineage, we've rarely produced a branch that was involved with the police. The Malloys prefer to handle their private problems with dignity."

"The Malloys are off the hook," I said. "Stanford has already persuaded the police to write up an unadorned report that handles things ever so discreetly."

Phoebe smirked at me. "If you were a Malloy by birth, you wouldn't have been so mulish about it. Breeding shows, doesn't it?"

"I can trace my family back to the Bordens of Boston," I said, doing my best to look as if I had an ax in my bathrobe pocket—and the willingness to wield it. "Borden was the spelling we adopted when we came to the United States. Before then, we went by Borgia."

Maxie peered at the teapot for a moment, then whinnied. "How witty you are, Cousin Claire. Especially at this tragic time when it might be more appropriate to express grief for poor Miss Justicia."

Pauline gulped down the contents of the cup, then banged it down and hiccuped. "Poor Miss Justicia. That's what they'll all say. She was a screwy old bitch, you know. Never could stand her. Just stayed 'cause I had no place else to go. Parents died when I was seventeen. Miss Justicia's family took me in and pretended I was one of them, but she never let me forget who was the wealthy, prissy lady of the manor and who was the scrawny orphan. Prissy, pissy Miss Looney Tunes."

Her hand was unsteady as she refilled her cup and took another gulp of what I'd assumed was tea. The slurring cadence of her voice, coupled with the rhythmic hiccups, made it clear I'd aided and abetted in the consumption of a liquid of a similar color but vastly different genre.

"How difficult for you," I murmured—as I reached for the teapot.

She snatched it up and huddled over it protectively. "I never married, you know; it could not be. But I've known passion—lustful, steamy, sweaty passion. I'm not the withered virgin you think I am. The cruelty of others kept us from proclaiming our love to the world, but not from countless nights of mindless sex at the Econolodge."

"Cousin Pauline, dear," Maxie said in a shocked voice, "it's clear you're upset about Miss Justicia's death, but I—"

"Upset?" Pauline giggled. "I can't tell you how many times I wanted to push the old bitch and her wheelchair down the stairs. *Bumpety, bumpety, bumpety, bump.* Fine sound, doncha think? *Bumpety, bumpety, bumpety, bump!*"

Maxie stood up. "I don't think it's prudent for the police to find dear Cousin Pauline in this unseemly condition. Help me with her, Phoebe, and we'll tuck her in bed. Claire, should the police desire to have a word with her, tell them she was overcome with shock. They'll have to return at a more convenient time."

Once they'd escorted a hiccupy woman gleefully shouting, "*bumpety, bumpety,*" down the hall, I sagged back in the chair and resisted the urge to polish off the contents of her teacup. The evening had begun dreadfully, and we'd been going downhill ever since then. Acrimony, accusations, an accident, and a pair of accommodating cops. It was by no means a cozy case for an amateur sleuth who wanted nothing more than a few hours of sleep and an early-morning flight. I had no illusions that I would get my wish. Caron and I were stuck in this contorted Southern gothic plot, complete with a cast of characters from a B-grade movie and enough wrinkles to drive the mildest of us to polyester.

I wrenched myself out of what was, in my opinion, justifiable self-pity and considered this newest development. Cousin Pauline was not the meek, long-suffering sort I'd assumed her to be. In truth, it seemed she'd been nursing a grudge for nearly forty years—long enough to work herself into a murderous rage. As much as I hated to even entertain the thought, she was the only one among us with a shred of opportunity. "I could just kill her," she'd said. It was an unfortunate comment.

It might play, I thought glumly. Miss Justicia heads off down one of her favorite trails. Pauline dashes off in pursuit, and seconds later catches up with Miss Justicia, who makes a typically brutal remark. Pauline grasps the handles of the wheelchair and gives a mighty shove. *Bumpety, bumpety, bumpety . . . splash.* She then returns to tell us she's unable to locate Miss Justicia. Fifteen minutes later, we find the body. Pauline collapses, but out of remorse rather than grief.

If she hadn't had a nip or two, none of us would have suspected how deeply she hated her benefactress, who'd promised her the house and an income, and then jerked it away with a cackle. Perhaps Miss Justicia had named her heir by the bayou, and the knowledge had sent Pauline over the edge . . . and the wheelchair into the water.

I blinked at the teapot. I'd filled it and poured one cup before going outside with the policemen. Unless we were into religious miracles (and we weren't), how had the innocuous tea been transformed into noxious booze? Pauline could have emptied the teapot, gone down the hallway to the parlor, refilled it with scotch, and then returned to the dining room. It didn't seem likely, though. No matter what had transpired beside the bayou, the woman was thoroughly stunned.

Maxie and Phoebe certainly hadn't done the little errand out of compassion; they were as startled as I by Pauline's inebriation. Stanford had been outside the entire time. Neither Ellie nor Keith seemed the type to worry about an elderly cousin's pallor.

I bent down and looked under the table, expecting to see a bottle. For my effort, I was rewarded with a view of scattered bread crumbs and a lump of bread pudding.

I was in this pose when I heard voices in the hall. The back of the chair must have hidden me, because there was no intake of breath or acidic comment as Ellie and Keith came to the doorway.

"I saw Daddy out front with a couple of cops," she said. "He was telling them all the details of the tragic accident, and they were bobbling their wee heads and scribbling notes."

Keith snickered. "Of course it'll be written up as an accident. We saw the wheelchair and heard that gawdawful cackle. We were all with somebody until we found the body, except for the few minutes when Pauline stumbled off in the dark. Only a certifiable idiot would think for a second that Pauline's got the balls to murder the old girl."

"What about the guy in the parlor?"

"I don't know what the hell his game was, showing up like that at midnight and saying someone called him. Damn crazy stunt. Hey, the kitchen's open. Let's find something decent to eat."

"Now if Cousin Pauline will just keep her mouth shut . . ." Ellie's voice faded as they went into the kitchen and closed the door.

The certifiable idiot stayed in the silly posture, scowling at the lump of inedibility and wondering if the blood rushing to her head might invigorate a few brain cells. Why was the taxi driver pulling a crazy stunt? What did Pauline need to keep her mouth shut about? If she hadn't done the dirty deed, then what could she possibly know that might implicate someone else?

The brain cells remained dormant. I was about to both give up and sit up when more travelers came down the hall. It was not the most dignified position for eavesdropping, but it did seem to work well, and by this time my sense of scrupulosity was history. To put it mildly.

"That was a close call," Phoebe said with a sigh.

"It was indeed," said Maxie, sounding no happier. "With Cousin Pauline in this disgraceful condition, she might have blurted out almost anything. I shall have a quiet conversation with her in the morning and point out the necessity of propriety. This ranting about . . . intimate relationships at a motel is . . ."

"Enlightening?" Phoebe suggested.

"To say the least. When she smiles, she is not unattractive, but I was under the impression she spent her evenings practicing the organ at the church."

"You were partially correct."

"Phoebe!" Maxie said. "That sort of innuendo is not appropriate. We must concern ourselves with the issues at hand."

I held my breath on the off chance she wished to list them. She did not. As they came into the dining room, I was treated to an interesting perspective of their ankles and feet, which they could undoubtedly trace back to a Scottish thane or a mundane pope. They were both wearing white satin slippers, although one pair was pristine and the other grass-stained. This in and of itself was not especially fascinating. It did, however, remind me of something I'd noticed earlier.

In jack-and-the-box fashion, I popped up and said, "When did you change back into your slippers, Phoebe?"

Phoebe braked so suddenly that her glasses slid down her nose. She caught them at the last minute and, with a nervous laugh, settled them back into position. "Good heavens, Cousin Claire, whatever were you doing under the table?"

"I felt faint," I lied smoothly. "Actually, I'm not really intrigued by when you changed back into your slippers. I'd like to know when you changed out of them earlier."

Phoebe turned the color of her slippers. Maxie grabbed her arm and propelled her to the chairs they'd occupied previously. "I must say you're acting in a most peculiar way, Cousin Claire," she intoned in a stern display of disapproval. "Why on earth does it matter what Phoebe chooses to wear on her feet?"

"At this moment, it doesn't matter," I replied. "When I encountered her in the parlor at midnight, she was wearing slippers. Eventually, we went upstairs and stayed together until we split up to search for Miss Justicia in the yard. Phoebe was still in slippers, as were we all. But when we found the body fifteen minutes later, she as wearing shoes with very hard heels." I held up my foot and wiggled my toes at them. "See? I have a bruise to prove it."

"So?" Phoebe said, averting her eyes and squirming as if the chair were wired to the nearest outlet. "I was concerned that the wet grass would ruin my white slippers. Although I was frantic about Miss Justicia's whereabouts, I realized I could search more efficiently if I were shod in an appropriate manner."

"I fail to see anything suspicious about that," Maxie contributed. "And I find this inquisition most unamusing, Cousin Claire." The final two words could have come from a machine gun.

I shook my head. "No one promised to amuse you, Cousin Maxie. When we went outside, Keith and I found Pauline. We then stayed together until we found the body in the bayou. I'd assumed Phoebe and Stanford did likewise. This appears to be erroneous. Unless Phoebe had her shoes stuffed in her pocket with the tape measure and notebook, I would offer the hypothesis that she went back into the house."

"For a minute." Phoebe was watching me from the corner of her eye as if leery of an attack on her person. We certifiable idiots garner more than our fair share of mistrust.

I flashed my teeth at her. "That means you were by yourself for an unknown portion of the fifteen minutes."

"What difference does that make?"

"You might have chanced upon Miss Justicia beside the bayou and given her an unsolicited shove," I said levelly.

"How dare you!" gasped Maxie. "How dare you accuse my daughter of such a heinous crime? This is an outrage! I insist you retract that absurd statement this moment and offer Phoebe an apology! I demand it!"

Phoebe's reaction was quite the contrary. She swiveled her head to gaze thoughtfully at her blustery protectress. "It also means that Cousin Stanford was out there by himself, Mother. When we first divided into search parties, I told him I'd be back shortly and went inside to change into my shoes. But when I did return, I looked all over that half of the yard and couldn't find him anywhere. I must admit I was not comfortable being out there alone, and I distinctly remember thinking that even Cousin Stanford would be better than no one. I finally found him only a few seconds before Cousin Keith came crashing through the shrubbery."

"He said he was going toward an old barn," I said. "Was that where you encountered him?"

"No, he said he'd already been down that way. We were

fairly near the bayou at the time." She stretched her thin lips into a semblance of a smile. "Cousin Stanford's company is in chaotic financial shape, Mother. I inadvertently came across the reports he sent to Miss Justicia. He's on the brink of bankruptcy, and the only thing that can save him is a major infusion of capital."

"Do you think he found the will?" Maxie demanded, clutching Phoebe's arm and spewing flecks of spittle. She then noticed my brightly curious look and managed to compose herself. "Not that I would entertain for even one instant the possibility that Cousin Stanford would do such a dreadful thing to his beloved mother. I'm sure he had nothing but the deepest devotion to Miss Justicia, as did we all."

"Damn straight I did," Stanford said as he stomped into the dining room. "And furthermore, I was coming up the path from the barn when I spotted Cousin Phoebe." He pointed at her with the fervor of an evangelist on the opening night of a tent revival. "She was coming from the direction of the bayou. At the time, I wondered why she'd gone that way when I'd told her as clear as branch water that I was going to the barn. Oh, yes, I wondered about it."

"You were coming from the bayou," Phoebe said firmly. "I was not!"

"You were too! I saw you creeping along like some species of aquatic mammal."

"You, missy, were doing what creeping was done!"

"I beg your pardon," Maxie inserted, perhaps bored from the lack of attention. "If Phoebe says you were creeping, then you were creeping. Did you creep up behind poor Miss Justicia and push her into the water?"

Stanford snatched up a napkin and swished it across his forehead. "Miss Justicia was my dear mother. I may have needed some money, but I didn't have my greedy, beady eyes on the house and the entire estate. I didn't see myself as some snooty matron escorting garden-club ladies through the parlor!"

Maxie paused to light a cigarette and consider her rebuttal. "Some money, Cousin Stanford?" she said mockingly. "From what I've heard, you needed a bit more than that. All the money might be more accurate, don't you think? One small push for Miss Justicia, one giant push for Pritty Kitty Kibble?"

"I could say the same for the matron of the manor—or her daughter." Stanford snapped.

I raised my eyebrows and said, "Then you're not certain Miss Justicia died in an accident, after all?"

That stopped everyone in mid-accusation. Stanford blotted his neck, tossed the napkin on the table, and took a noisy breath. "Now don't you start getting yourself all stirred up like a spider on a hot stove, Claire. Due to the grief we share, we may have exchanged a few thoughtless remarks here, but we're all certain in our hearts that Miss Justicia met her Maker in an accident. A very sad and senseless accident brought on by her own irresponsible actions. An accident that none of us could have prevented. The police have satisfied themselves, and arranged for some boys from a mortuary to help us in our hour of need. All we can do is prepare ourselves for the mournful ordeal we must face over the next few days."

Maxie put out her cigarette and rose. "Indeed, Cousin Stanford, indeed. The shock must have overcome us. I would never accuse you of harming so much as a tiny hair on Miss Justicia's head."

"Nor I," Phoebe added. She joined her mother, and as the two swept out of the room, attempted to toss her chin at me. The effect was minimal.

Stanford smiled benignly at me. "There, you heard them. None of us would dream of accusing a member of the family of causing harm to Miss Justicia. She may not have been all that easy to get along with, and at times was downright trying, but she was the head of the family and we were all devoted to her." His smile deepened as he continued to regard me. "I must say, that robe is most becoming, Claire, although it certainly doesn't begin to display your deliciously feminine attributes to their fullest."

I instinctively retreated, then ordered myself to stop. "Let's get one thing clear, Stanford. I will not tolerate any more nonsense from you and your roving paws. You may outweigh me by a ton or two, but I won't hesitate to punch out your lights if you lay so much as a finger on me."

"I think pastel pink might be a better color for you," he continued, his eyes almost salivating. "With a few ruffles and a lace collar to frame your face, why, you'd be the belle of the ball."

"And you'd be a dead ringer." I left the room.

7

Despite the cruel foray into the bedroom of the dawn's early light, I managed a few hours of sleep. Caron, who had slept through the night in the hospital nursery and had rarely missed a night since, was still snoring when I came out of the bathroom and dressed. I went downstairs for breakfast, which I hoped would be an improvement over the preceding evening's meal. Gravel, for instance, would easily qualify. As I arrived in the foyer, I cast a wistful look at the door of Miss Justicia's bedroom, motivated not by grief but by the presence of a telephone beyond it.

I suspected I could predict Peter's reaction. We'd first met during a murder investigation, when he'd had the audacity to imply I had both the motive and the means to strangle a romance writer (I had, but I hadn't). He'd also implied that I was meddling in his official police business, despite avowals that I was merely doing my civic duty. Our relationship had grown more complex, to the point of allusions to matrimony, but I wasn't yet prepared to turn over half the shelf space in the bathroom, much less issue a permanent invitation to my bed. This isn't to say he wasn't welcome on occasion. Very welcome.

Grinning at my impure thoughts, I settled down at the desk, dialed the number, and waited impatiently until he answered.

"Guess what?" I began brightly.

"This is my morning off, and I'm not permitted to sleep late?"

"Try again."

"If you were here, I wouldn't want to sleep late," he murmured, his tone conveying what he might want to do instead. He proceeded to elaborate on several possibilities (most of them in compliance with the telephone company's encouragement to reach out and touch someone), and I must admit they appealed.

It was not the time for heavy breathing, however, so I waited for him to finish, assured him that when I returned home I would not be immune to his charms, and jumped right in with the recitation of the events of the previous afternoon, evening, and midnight hours.

The transition may have been too much for a sleepy mind. After a moment of silence, he said, "Repeat all that, but very slowly."

"This is long distance, you know," I pointed out, then once again began with our arrival and ended with my return to bed only a few hours earlier.

"But the local police determined that it was an accident, right? You have nothing to go on except your instincts and your unwillingness to accept their professional opinion?"

"My instincts are very good," I said, ignoring the latter half of what amounted to an accusation. "And there were several things that failed to fit in neatly. Miss Justicia may not have worn a seat belt, but she's been cruising the yard for years and knew the paths, Why should she lose control last night—after those vaguely threatening hints at dinner? Don't you agree it's an odd coincidence?"

"I'll agree the police officers may have bought the family line. And it may not have been a coincidence. Perhaps she chose to stage a so-called accident at a time when most of the family might feel guilty. Or look guilty, anyway."

"But something's missing." I wrinkled my nose and tried to decide what it was. The wills, certainly. The taxi driver. A decent meal for approximately twenty-four hours. And not least of all, several hours of sleep. It struck with the intensity of a hunger pang. "The brandy decanter's missing," I said excitedly. "It was in this room when Miss Justicia was settled in bed, but later Pauline mentioned that it was gone. Where could it be?"

"In the bayou," Peter replied without hesitation. "She had it in her lap when she rolled into the water. It filled with water and sank."

I sighed. "And is buried in several inches of mud."

"Don't get involved in this, Claire. Let the family proceed with the funeral and the battle over the estate—and let the police deal with any further questions about the accident. If your instincts are wrong, you're only going to create trouble. If they're right, you and Caron might be in danger."

"From these people?" I laughed merrily despite the prickles running along my spine.

He failed to sound convinced of my invincibility. "When are you leaving?"

"I suppose we'll stay for the funeral, and fly out as soon as possible afterward. I can hardly wait to tell Caron the news; she's been counting the minutes, not the hours." We exchanged a few pleasantries and I told him I would call when I had an update on our travel plans.

After we'd disconnected, I sat for a long while, hoping I could come up with the significance of the missing decanter. My lack of success was enough to send me on to the dining room for a dose of caffeine. I was not pleased to find a few members of the dear family around the table.

Maxie and Phoebe sat in their usual seats, both somberly dressed to confront any upcoming challenges to the family honor. Ellie was draped over her chair, dressed in a skimpy blouse, shorts, and sandals. Stanford's teddy bear pajamas had been replaced by the white suit and pink bow tie. No one offered me a cheery good morning. In that we'd all been up most of the night, I hadn't been holding my breath—or planning to waste it on any efforts to brighten their respective days.

I went into the kitchen, poured myself a cup of coffee, opened the refrigerator, and sadly determined the only thing available to eat was the sinister fish from the previous night's dinner. I returned in time to hear Ellie say, "This whole thing's a bummer. When do we find out what's in the will?"

"I suppose I could call that lawyer fellow this morning," Stanford said. "The damn thing's likely to be in his office. Knowing lawyers like I do, I wouldn't be surprised if he was charging a storage fee."

Maxie noted my arrival with a frown, then looked at Stanford. "We don't know who he is. Miss Justicia failed to mention his name, and there are at least half a dozen lawyers in LaRue and three times that many in the parish."

I chose a chair well away from Stanford and tried the coffee. It had the viscosity of pea soup, and a vileness all its own. I made myself take a few more sips, then put down the cup and looked around optimistically for something to eat.

Ellie pushed a plate toward me. "Blackened toast," she murmured. "Cajun style. Daddy made it himself from the last of the bread."

I did not groan, although I suspected my shudder was visible to anyone watching me. No one was.

Phoebe blinked owlishly at her mother. "Bethel D'Armand might know the identity of the new attorney. Miss Justicia may have asked him to transfer files and documents."

"You are too clever for words," Ellie drawled. "This display of ingenuousness is simply too dazzling for poor little me so early in the day. You will perform a second act after lunch, won't you?"

"Certainly. Surely by then you'll have had a chance to do something about your hair. You must be ever so distressed by it at the moment."

"What's wrong with my hair?"

"The roots. They seem more . . . shall we say, dominant this morning." She turned back to Maxie. "Shall I call D'Armand and see if he has the pertinent information?"

Ellie was licking her lips in preparation for a retort, but Stanford intervened, saying, "Now, let's not rush into this like stampeding cattle. We may not know this new fellow, and I'd hate to get off on the wrong foot with him. Miss Justicia's not even cooled off yet, much less planted."

"A good point," Maxie conceded as she lit a cigarette. "We do want to speak with him as soon as possible, but we don't want him to think we're more concerned with the estate than with the tragedy." Smoke snaked from the corners of her mouth as she gazed at me. "The tragedy caused by the accident, that is. You do feel differently this morning, don't you, Cousin Claire? You do realize what complications your hysterical remarks might have caused, had they been overheard by some lower-class sorts blessed with simian mentalities?"

"That's precisely who overheard them," I said, considering my chances with the burned toast. Somewhere in the back of my mind, I seemed to remember it could function as an emetic in cases of poisoning. "But don't worry about me, Cousin Maxie. Caron and I will stay in our room until the funeral, and then immediately leave for home. The rest of you can chop up the furniture or dredge the bayou until you find the old will, the new will, or William of Orange."

"'Will you, won't you, will you, won't you, will you join the dance?'" Ellie added.

Stanford ignored all attempts at levity. "I can tell you all one thing—there's no will hidden in this room. I checked real carefully"—he winked at me—"while I was hunting for my pocket watch."

"It's not in the parlor," said Phoebe. "I took the opportunity to measure for secret drawers while I looked for a magazine."

Ellie lifted her foot to admire her pink toenails. "Nor is it in Miss Justicia's bedroom, unless it was tucked in the brandy decanter. And later last night, Keith and I searched the kitchen and pantry without any luck."

"This is highly frustrating," Maxie said, putting out her cigarette on a triangle of toast. "As Cousin Claire so obligingly pointed out, we don't even know how many wills there are floating about like scraps of paper. Miss Justicia was rather fond of signing new ones."

Stanford blew his nose, although I doubted he was overwhelmed with grief. "I suppose we're gonna have to go through his lawyer, whoever the hell he is."

"I'll call D'Armand," Phoebe said. She left the room at a brisk gait.

"This is so exciting," Ellie said as she trailed after her at a more leisurely pace. Her voice drifted back to us as she said, "My goodness, Cousin Phoebe, I do believe all that sedentary research has added a couple of inches to your hips."

Maxie nodded at me. "I'm so glad you've come to your

senses, Cousin Claire. It's so much better for all concerned if we present a dignified family front. We are Malloys, after all. How is your daughter this morning? Was she so distressed that she felt unable to come downstairs for breakfast?"

I was too interested in the rumblings of my stomach to produce an explanation, or even a polite lie. "Something like that," I said. I raised my voice to cover the sounds of a germinal ulcer. "Is this all there is to eat? No cheese grits? No biscuits and red-eye gravy?"

"The cook will stop at the market on her way to the house," she said, continuing to reward my avowed penitence with a charitable smile. "You must tell me all about Carlton and his career at the college, Cousin Claire. He and I lost touch many years ago, and I often wondered how he and his little family were getting along." I opened my mouth to reply, but I was not quick enough. "I spent my childhood summers here, you know. Stanford, Carlton, and I used to have such fun playing in the yard, climbing trees, riding bicycles into town to buy candy, and even venturing out into the bayous in a flat-bottomed boat."

"Remember how you squealed when Carlton put the leech down the back of your pretty white pinafore?" Stanford contributed genially. "You peed in your pants, and the two of us laughed so hard, we damn near tumped the boat."

She stiffened. "Miss Justicia failed to share your merriment, if I recall. Wasn't there a little scene on the back porch with a hairbrush?"

"And a bullfrog in someone's bed that very same night?" he said, entwining his fingers on his belly and twinkling at her.

All this good-natured reminiscing reminded me of my conversation with Stanford at dinner. "Was Miller around when you came to visit, Maxie?"

She and Stanford exchanged quick looks. From their expressions, it was clear that I'd found a nerve, or at least a sensitive spot. Maxie lit another cigarette, aligned the pack and her lighter next to her saucer, and then said, "I saw him every now and then. He was quite a bit older than we were, and usually off with his friends."

"And he was killed in Vietnam?" I persisted.

Maxie stared at Stanford until he bestirred himself to say, "They sent him over there long before those yellow-bellied hippies started marching in the streets."

"So Miller wasn't drafted?" I asked. "He enlisted voluntarily?"

This time, the look they exchanged was longer, more intense—and equally impossible to decipher. I was preparing to repeat my question when Pauline came into the dining room. She wore the same plaid housedress, but the jogging shoes had been replaced with loafers. Her face was the shade of wet concrete. Her eyes were bloodshot and ringed with red puffiness. Either blinded by her hangover or unwilling to acknowledge us, she drifted across the room and into the kitchen.

"She looks worse than death warmed over," Stanford said in a gloating voice. "Guess she'll think twice before she goes swimming in the scotch again."

"I hope so," Maxie began, "because discretion is—"

"I have his name and telephone number," Phoebe said as she entered the room, her notebook in hand. "However, I was unable to arrange an immediate appointment with him, despite my repeated expressions of urgency. His receptionist was extremely rude, not to mention incompetent and uneducated. I doubt she graduated from high school, or even elementary school." She resumed her seat, threw down the notebook, and pulled off her glasses to rub her eyes. "She has no idea about the Malloy family's historical significance in the parish, none whatsoever. I had to spell the name for her. Twice."

"So what's the fellow's name?" Stanford said, cutting short what might have become an entertaining display of indignation.

Phoebe picked up the notebook and squinted at it. "Rodney Spikenard . . . a truly tasteless name. I was not at all surprised to discover his receptionist is named Florine."

Maxie snorted under her breath. "Did Bethel D'Armand tell you anything regarding this Spikenard person?"

"He wasn't very helpful. Spikenard claims to hold a law degree from Yale. He moved to town and opened his practice less than a year ago. He doesn't participate in any civic organizations, nor does he socialize with fellow members of the bar. That's all D'Armand would tell me."

"I'm not real comfortable dealing with this unknown factor," Stanford said. "I wish Miss Justicia'd seen fit to stick with ol' Bethel. I could call him up right this minute, and he sure wouldn't give me any nonsense about being too busy to see me. No sir, he's worked for the Malloys so long he probably knows the first names of all our family skeletons, along with their birthdays and preferences in ice cream flavors."

Maxie dismissed the heresy with a dainty laugh. "As if Malloy Manor harbored any family skeletons. When will we be able to see this Spikenard, Phoebe? Were you able to make an appointment for later?"

"Florine," Phoebe said, making the name sound like a disease characterized by pustules, "said he had clients all morning, but he would return my call when he was free."

Stanford put down his napkin and pushed back his chair. "Then we'll have to occupy ourselves making arrangements for the funeral until this character sees fit to call. I'll check with the mortuary, see what all we need to do. Anybody have any suggestions for hymns?"

Pauline opened the kitchen door. "How about 'Row, Row, Row Your Boat'?"

I decided it was time to rouse Caron. Mumbling something to that effect, I left the dining room and went upstairs. The bed was empty, but the bathroom door muted the sound of shower water running. I brilliantly deduced her whereabouts, and wandered over to the window to look down at the scene of the—I gritted my teeth and made myself continue—accident.

I was repeating aloud the word, emphasizing the different syllables each time, when the bedroom door opened and Ellie came in. Even in her casual clothes, she radiated more confidence than I'd ever felt, even in graduate school when we'd sat in coffeehouses and condescendingly analyzed the failings of the bourgeoisie.

"Has Malloy Manor finally gotten to you?" she said as she made herself comfortable on Caron's bed. "First making faces at Great-Uncle Eustice, and now talking to the bayou?"

"Very possibly," I said. I doubted she'd dropped by for a girlish giggle, but I was not in the mood to cooperate by inquiring into her motives. What I was in the mood for contained scandalous amounts of cholestoral and calories, alas.

"I want to ask you something. You're sort of a disinterested party in this whole thing. The others would start snorting and harrumphing, and I'm simply too stressed out to deal with them."

I sat down on my bed and attempted to smile encouragingly, although my mind was far, far away, at a stainless-steel counter beneath an expansive plastic menu. "You're welcome to ask, Ellie."

"I realize you're not a lawyer or anything, but you did have to deal with Uncle Carlton's estate. Suppose Miss

Justicia's will divides the estate among the six of us. If one of us was already dead, would the shares increase to fifths?"

"Who's dead?" I asked sharply, visions of special sauce banished in an instant.

"I said *suppose*. No one's dead . . . although Cousin Pauline did look rather gruesome this morning." She arranged the pillows and leaned back. "I just wondered what would happen, that's all. Another question: What if one of the heirs turned out to have murdered Miss Justicia? Would he—or she—still receive a share, or would we then be at fifths instead of sixths?"

"I thought we all agreed it was an accident," I said. The water was turned off in the bathroom. I held up my hand, and in a lower voice, said, "Caron doesn't know what happened last night. Somehow or other, she managed to sleep through the entire thing. This is not a good time to continue our discussion of hypotheticals, Ellie."

"What? Oh, sure, I understand." She gnawed on her lip for a moment, then sat up and clapped her hands. "I have a wonderful idea! Why don't we run into town and drop by the library? They've got scads of books; surely some of them have legal information."

"Are there any restaurants in town?"

"There used to be a café with the greasiest cheeseburgers in the state," she said, lapsing into her sugary drawl as she regarded my famished expression. "French fries, onion rings, homemade pie."

"I'll meet you downstairs in half an hour," I said without hesitation. Ellie gave me a little wave and sailed out of the room.

Seconds later, Caron came out of the bathroom, wrapped in a towel and with her hair dripping, and gave me one of her darkest looks. "What is Going On, Mother? It's bad enough to be dragged into this remote area and forced to converse with weird people and sleep on a mattress that ought to be standard issue in a penal colony, but then to—"

I battled an impulse to fling a pillow at her and said, "If you'll stop shrieking, I'll answer your question."

"I should hope so." She stalked over to an open suitcase and began to throw clothes over her shoulder in the direction of the bed. Each missile was accompanied by an indictment. "First everyone goes to bed, then everyone stomps around, then everyone vanishes, then everyone starts jabbering downstairs. Cars in the driveway. Doors slamming. Someone chanting, '*bumpety-bump!*' About the only thing that Didn't Happen was for some grandfatherly ghost to charge through the bedroom. It's utterly impossible to get any sleep around here!" Her lower lip shot forward until I doubted she could see over it.

"Are you finished?" I waited until she nodded. "I know that anything that happens that does not have a direct effect on your immediate comfort and welfare is of minimal concern, but—"

"All I said was it was impossible to get any sleep. I didn't say I was some sort of egotistical monster."

Her cheeks were flushed, although I wasn't sure whether out of anger or repentence. I gave her the benefit of the doubt and gently told her about Miss Justicia's death.

She looked away, silently studying the wall for a long while. "I'm sorry about it," she said in a small voice. "I didn't know my grandmother very well, and I wasn't sure I liked her very much, but still . . . it's too bad. I feel like some invisible thread has been clipped, just like when Dad died. When I was born, there were all these threads that linked me to people all the way back in history. They went through you and Dad, through my aunts and uncles and grandparents. Maybe all my ancestors are watching to see if I do okay, maybe even cheering for me, but they feel farther away when someone dies."

I was surprised by her philosophical response. For a brief moment, I wondered if the last three years of hormonal turbulence was abating and she was within sight of maturity. Her analogies in the past had focused on her best friend Inez's lack of discernment or her arch enemy Rhonda Maguire's thighs.

Caron then obliterated my flicker of sanguinity by widening her eyes and adding, "Do you think Miss Justicia left me anything? Not necessarily the house or a lot of money, but maybe one little diamond ring or some old-fashioned brooch with rubies and emeralds?"

"You are not the only would-be heir lost in speculation," I said as I picked up my purse. "I'm running an errand with Ellie. Get dressed and go downstairs for breakfast, and then amuse yourself until I return."

"With Those People?"

"Those people happen to be your uncle and your cousins. You know, the threads."

I hurried downstairs and out to the porch. Ellie was leaning against the sports car, her hand lightly stroking its side as she stared at the ground.

"Oh, good," she said as I joined her. "It's absolutely morbid inside. Daddy's on the telephone bickering about casket prices, Pauline's humming, and Maxie and Phoebe are rummaging through Miss Justicia's closet for something suitably dignified for her to wear. Malloys wouldn't be caught dead in inappropriate clothing, you know. Nothing less than the best will do at a funeral."

"When's the funeral?" I asked unenthusiastically. Caron and I had reservations for the following afternoon, and as much as I wanted to look down at the cemetery from several thousand feet, I wasn't sure I could bring myself to do it. Miss

Justicia had been Carlton's mother, I reminded myself. Caron's grandmother. And, if I could bring myself to admit it, my mother-in-law.

Ellie climbed into the driver's side and patted the adjoining leather seat. "As soon as Daddy can get it on the schedule, I'm sure. The service has already been edited down to three hymns, a quick obit, and thank you all ever so much for coming."

I arranged myself beside her, and after a moment of piercing character analysis, put on the shoulder belt and made certain it was firmly engaged. A sheen of perspiration formed on my forehead as I noted the array of gauges, flashing buttons, and obscure digital messages. This was not the family station wagon. Ordering myself to continue coolly, I said, "Will the funeral be tomorrow or Monday?"

I couldn't hear her reply as the engine roared into action like a 747 and we shot out of the driveway like a 748 (or even a 750). The blast of humid wind flung my hair in my eyes and left me gasping for breath. What I gulped down was thick with dust and grit.

We arrived at the highway long before the dust had settled in front of the house. The stop sign was not worthy of our attention. With an eerily familiar cackle, Ellie slammed into a gear I would have termed *fatal accident* and accelerated. Trees melted away as we sped along a mercifully straight and empty road. Billboards were blurred streaks. Normally unflappable crows abandoned lumps of roadkill as we swerved around them. My hair was not only slapping my eyes but also attempting to tear itself free of my scalp. My face felt as if it had been splashed with scalding water.

"Isn't this great!" Ellie yelled. She switched on the radio, and explosive rock music began to compete with the howling wind and the ear-shattering sounds of the beleaguered engine.

"Just great!" I yelled back. I slumped down in the leather seat, covered my face, and, with admirable stoicism, awaited death.

When the car stopped, the sudden silence was almost as alarming as the previous deluge. I felt Ellie's fingertips on my shoulder. "Are you feeling ill?" she asked solicitously.

"A bit of a headache," I said as I forced my hands away from my face and looked up.

We were parked in front of a squatty brick building, artfully landscaped with bleached grass and a solitary, leafless tree. A sign proclaimed it the LaRue Public Library. LaRue itself appeared to be a moderately prosperous town of perhaps ten or so thousand residents. One- and two-story buildings lined either side of the main street. There was a fair amount of traffic, predominantly of the pickup truck persuasion, but with a well-seasoned sedan every now and then. Pedestrians moved slowly but steadily along the sidewalks. A bench outside one establishment was lined with elderly men in caps. It looked a great deal more civilized than I felt.

"I'm going to pop in here," Ellie said as she removed the keys and opened the car door. "The café's in the next block. After you've had something to eat, why don't you come back and read legal textbooks with me? We can pretend we're college students boning up for a big test."

"How entertaining," I said, then got out of the car, waited until my knees stopped wobbling, and walked up the sidewalk. The department store promised incredible deals on back-to-school clothes, and the drugstore abutting it promised as much on notebooks and pencils. The occupants of the bench, which proved to be in front of the barbershop, eyed me suspiciously despite my smile.

I gradually became aware of scrutiny from within stores, from within vehicles on the street, and even from within the occasional offices. I paused in front of a window to check my hair; it was slightly aboriginal but hardly worthy of more than a sneer. My pants and shirt were unremarkable. My lipstick had been sucked off during the drive, and I still looked pale, but I found nothing in my general appearance that alarmed me.

A trio of women stopped on the opposite sidewalk and gawked with the subtlety of malnourished refugees. A carload of teenagers almost came to a halt in the middle of the street, and only the blare of a horn propelled them back into motion. A stout male clerk came to the doorway of a record store to stare at me.

It was disconcerting, to say the least. My steps faltered as I contemplated a retreat to the library, where I might cower between the shelves while Ellie pored over laws of intestacy. My stomach protested such a craven act. I continued on numbly, feeling as if I were Lady Jane Grey transversing the lawn of the Tower of London—for the last time.

Moments later, I found the café. A faded menu with curled edges and the residue of many generations of fly droppings was taped in the window. A bell tinkled as I opened the door. Much like the shrill cadence of a burglar alarm, the sound was enough to cause conversations to be cut short and all eyes to turn to determine the identity of such a bold intruder.

The stools along the counter were occupied, as were the booths along the wall and a few tables in between. Saturday mornings at the café were obviously as busy as Saturday nights at trendy New York bistros—where the patrons enjoyed a certain amount of anonymity. Here, I did not.

Rather than an oily maître d', an obese waitress approached me. "He's in his regular booth," she told me with enough of an accent to give each word roughly twice it's assigned syllables.

I felt a mischievous urge to mock her, but I managed to

squelch it. For all I knew, I might be interrupting the weekly meeting of the Ku Klux Klan. "Who's in his regular booth?" I asked.

"Why, Lawyer D'Armand, honey. That's why you're here, ain't it?"

"I'm here to have something to eat."

"Then you just settle in back there in the corner and I'll fetch you a menu." She put her hands on her hips and waited impatiently. All around us, heads nodded and eyes darted from my face to the farthest booth. The consensus seemed to be that I needed to quit stalling and do as I was told.

"I'll have a cheeseburger and fries," I said, "and an order of the same to go in a few minutes." I then found a path through the tables to the booth occupied by Bethel D'Armand, the ex-family retainer.

He stood up as I approached the table. Based on what I'd heard, I assumed he was of Miss Justicia's generation. His silver hair was thin but neatly styled; in contrast, his bristly white eyebrows shot out as if he'd been struck by lightning. His face was covered with hairline wrinkles, and his teeth were much too even to be original. His white suit was dotted with cigar ashes, the origin of said ashes smoldering in his hand. Despite the smoke, I could smell cologne from several feet away.

"Mrs. Malloy," he said, extending a manicured hand, "I am delighted to meet you, although my pleasure is diminished by the tragedy that has settled like a heavy fog upon all of us." Still holding my hand, he looked past me and raised his voice. "As I'm sure you all know, this is Mr. Carlton's widow. She and her daughter came all the way down here to LaRue for Miss Justicia's eightieth birthday, which would have been this very day, had she not been snatched from us and carried aloft to the waiting arms of her beloved husband, Hadley Malloy."

The ladies and gentlemen (using the terms charitably) of the jury offered a smattering of applause, but when he failed to continue the eulogy, they resumed eating, drinking coffee, and no doubt doing their best to overhear whatever might be said in the immediate future.

"I wasn't aware we had an appointment," I said as I sat down across from him.

"Neither was I, Mrs. Malloy. Even though I've retired, I still like to drop by the café every morning to visit with my friends." He put down the cigar to pat my hand. "I do hope you'll consider me a friend. I knew Carlton from the day he was born, and I watched him grow up. I must say I was secretly pleased when he defied his mother by choosing to stay in the realm of academia. If he hadn't had such an untimely death, I'm sure he would have outshone us all."

"I'm sure he would have," I murmured, keeping an eye out for the food I'd ordered, "or at least have been awarded tenure."

"And I was so distressed to hear about Miss Justicia, for whom I had nothing but the deepest admiration and respect. She was the epitome of Southern gentility."

I forgot about my hunger pangs and gazed through the smoke. D'Armand was playing the role perfectly, from his eloquent pronouncements to his mournful smile. With a small cough to express my distaste for either his habit or his facade (he was welcome to choose one), I said, "Was she the epitome of Southern gentility when she fired you?"

"Fired me? I'm afraid you're mistaken." He stopped as the waitress arrived with my food, then continued in a quieter voice. "I informed her that I intended to retire within a few months, and suggested she find a younger attorney who would be able to handle her affairs for years to come."

I resisted the urge to stuff the cheeseburger into my

mouth in the manner of an ill-bred chipmunk. "Did you personally recommend the new man?"

"Rodney Spikenard? Why, I seem to recall passing his name along to Miss Justicia, but I didn't recommend him per se. He does have impressive credentials, however, and I certainly did nothing to discourage her in the matter. He's young, hungry for work, and . . ." D'Armand picked up the cigar, and, with a faint look of amused complacency on his face, inhaled deeply.

"And what?" I said.

"Interested, Mrs. Malloy, interested. He has a solid background in the field of wills and trusts. He was somewhat alarmed when I mentioned the quantity of documents, but he seemed eager to tackle them and familiarize himself with the family's affairs."

A man in overalls approached the table and asked D'Armand about a lawsuit that involved fences and heated remarks made over them. I grabbed the cheeseburger, which well might have been the greasiest in a state that thrived on offshore oil rigs, and managed a few ladylike mouthfuls. Once the man left, I swallowed and said, "The family's already attempted to contact Spikenard. They're in an uproar about the estate. No one seems to know what was in the previous will—or if a new one supercedes it."

"I'm sure they are concerned," he said blandly. "I would be."

"Do you have any idea if indeed Miss Justicia revoked the will of"—I thought for a moment—"five or six years ago that settled the bulk of the estate on a sperm bank?"

He gave me a shocked frown. "I am an adamant believer in the sanctity of client-attorney communications, Mrs. Malloy. Even if I felt it would prove of benefit to the probation and eventual dispersal of the estate, I would never betray that confidence."

"I just thought I'd mention it," I said as I crammed a few french fries in my mouth.

"I'm sure Rodney will enlighten all of you when the times comes." D'Armand seemed in awe of the velocity with which I was eating but was too polite to stare openly. He gave me a few minutes to finish wolfing down the food and licking my fingers, then said, "Have the date and time of the funeral been settled as of yet?"

"You'll have to ask Stanford," I said as I wiped my chin with a napkin and leaned back against the seat. "I'm merely the widow of the prodigal son, and no one feels compelled to keep me informed."

"I assume I'll be asked to be a pallbearer. It seems to happen more often these days, although it's not unexpected. Most of my friends have passed away, and I keep glancing over my shoulder, waiting for my turn."

"It's unexpected for a mother to outlive two of her three sons," I said casually. "Carlton died ten years ago, but Miller's been dead for more than thirty years, hasn't he?"

"Miller?" D'Armand croaked. His hand shook as he took a drink of coffee, and when he replaced the cup, it rattled in the saucer.

I waited, wondering why he looked as if the Grim Reaper had just walked through the door.

8

Ellie Malloy walked through the door, spotted us in the last booth, and continued across the room, nodding graciously at a selected few who mumbled condolences. "Why, Uncle Bethel," she said as she sat down beside him and kissed his cheek, "I haven't seen you in a coon's age. What have you been up to, you sexy ol' scoundrel?"

He beamed at her. "And you're prettier every time I see you. How long has it been since you brightened us with a visit? Five years?"

"Not long enough," she said, laughing. "Doesn't anything ever change around here, Uncle Bethel?"

They lapsed into a conversation about people I did not know and recent local events about which I cared even less. The waitress refilled my coffee cup, and I listened idly to them while I pondered D'Armand's reaction to hearing Miller's name. Stanford and Maxie had reacted in an odd way, also. And the man I'd married until death did us part had not once mentioned the existence of an older brother.

Maxie had pooh-poohed the possibility of family skeletons, but I suspected I'd chanced upon one hidden deep within a closet of Malloy Manor. I tried to piece together what I knew about the elusive Miller. He'd been twelve years older than Carlton, which meant he was born circa 1939. He'd died in Vietnam in 1960, at the age of—I dipped my finger in my coffee and did a bit of calculation on the tabletop—twenty-one (circa, that is). Had he died in disgrace, court-martialed for some reason? The atrocities committed against civilians were news in the late sixties and early seventies, but that did not preclude an earlier existence. The same applied to fragging, or the less interesting commission of an ordinary crime.

Even if that was so, I told myself, thirty years was a long time to remain worried about it, or to act as though I'd suggested we dig up the body and prop it in a chair at the dining room table. Miss Justicia's death might be nothing more than an unfortunate accident, but the mystery surrounding Miller's life/death seemed worthy of my attention.

Ellie and D'Armand stopped their conversation while she ordered lunch. Once the waitress was gone, I said, "Did you find any answers at the library?"

"It was absolutely muddlesome," she said, sighing. "Louisiana's blessed with some silly system called the Napoleonic Code. Every time I came across something promising, there'd be a footnote that said it didn't apply here. All I wanted was a little enlightenment about wills and things like that. What's a girl to do, Uncle Bethel?"

"I have all the law books you could ever want. You're welcome to come by the office and look through them."

"You're a sweetheart, but I really do think Auntie Claire and I ought to get back to the house. I haven't decided what to wear to the funeral, and I can almost hear Maxie's snorts this minute. Why don't I just ask you a few questions?"

I already knew the questions, and I wasn't sure the

answers would interest me. "Ellie," I said quickly, "I think I'll have a look around town. Why don't I meet you in front of the library in about an hour?"

"Doing a little research yourself, Mrs. Malloy?" D'Armand said as he studied me with a shrewd expression. The amiable Clarence Darrow pose slipped for a moment, and I felt a chilly breeze from across the table.

"Panty hose for the funeral," I said. I took my bill to the front counter, paid it, and waited until a sack with Caron's lunch was brought from the kitchen.

Thus armed with provisions, I left the café and started back toward the library to see what I could dig up—in the newspaper files rather than in the cemetery. As I walked past the stores, however, the *circa* drifted into my mind and I realized I had no definite dates, nor did I have an entire day to work my way through an entire year.

My facetious thought about the cemetery evoked one of my more brilliant flashes of inspiration. I halted in front of the toothless wonders on the barbershop bench. "Would one of you be so kind as to give me directions to the local cemetery?" I asked.

I assumed I'd spoken in perfectly reasonable English, but their blank looks did not reassure me. "The cemetery?" I repeated, dearly hoping we wouldn't be reduced to a round of charades (four syllables; first one rhymes with 'dim' as in witted).

"Down that way a piece," one of them finally conceded. He spat in the direction of the side street next to the shop.

I winced. "How far is it?"

"A piece. Not what I'd consider a far piece, but a piece," he said after a moment of what was clearly pained thought. The other three nodded with equal animation, and one mouthed *piece*, as if it was an unfamiliar word.

I thanked them and took off down the indicated street,

not sure how they differentiated between a "piece" and a "far piece." I went past several small shops, a school with a haunted air about it, and shabby houses set increasingly far apart. Then, to my dismay, I found myself at what I perceived to be the edge of town. I shaded my eyes from the glare and strained to see anything in the distance that could be the cemetery. Beyond the pasture was a mobile home, and beyond it, a stretch of brush and scraggly trees that hinted of swampland. On the other side of the road was an endless field dotted with small green bundles.

My watch was on the bedside table, but I figured I had at least forty-five minutes to find the cemetery and Miller's tombstone. "Not what I consider a far piece," I told myself as I headed down the road.

As I may have mentioned in previous narratives, I do not care to perspire, and I never do so voluntarily. I am opposed to the very concept of sweat. I have never owned a sweatshirt, and I rarely wear sweaters. I will admit that Lieutenant Peter Rosen has elicited a glow on more than one occasion, perhaps even a damp flush. That was an entirely different matter, and one in which I was a willing participant.

Striding along what soon became a dirt road, however, was hardly in that category. My brisk pace was causing dribbles to run down my back, salt to flood my eyes, and an intolerable stickiness to spread beneath my arms. The local population of mosquitoes must have been dieting for months; they more than compensated as they swarmed in to feast on every patch of exposed skin. My scalp began to tingle moistly and my curls to droop in a most unattractive manner. The corners of my mouth followed.

It goes without saying that I was not in a cheerful mood when I finally found a rusty wrought-iron arch with paint-flecked letters. "I might consider it a far piece," I growled as I went under the arch.

To my initial surprise, I was not confronted by a grassy expanse of rows of tombstones. Here the caskets were placed in concrete and marble vaults above the ground, giving it the illusion of a vast field of scattered blocks. Vague recollections of the more renowned cemeteries in New Orleans provided me with an explanation. We were at sea level. Interment below ground was unthinkable; the omnipresent seepage precluded it.

The vaults were of all sizes, from the starkly compact to the expensive affairs with coy cherubim and simpering angels, and of all states of maintenance, from pristine to mossy and corroded. Based on the dates on the nearest vaults, the residents of LaRue had been in need of eternal housing for more than 150 years. There seemed to be dozens of vaults down every row, and dozens of rows confronting me. The Malloy family could be stashed anywhere, I thought bleakly.

I used the hem of my shirt to blot my face, then squared my shoulders and went down the row in front of me, scanning names. When I reached the end, I headed up the next one. By now, I'd left Ellie at least an hour ago, and still faced the interminable walk back to town.

"So what?" I said aloud, hoping to startle the mosquitoes into allowing me a brief respite. I sat down on someone named Marileau and wiped my face again. The worst scenario was that Ellie would grow tired of waiting and drive back to the house. I would be forced to call and request that someone pick me up. I might even end up with a chauffeur who observed the speed limit and shunned the radio.

It would also give me time to find out what I needed from the library files, that being the point of what had evolved into a mission of madness—and sweat. Feeling much better about standing Ellie up, I stood up. Seconds later, I heard a pinging noise. I glanced down at Mr. Marileau, wondering if my modest weight had caused the marble to crack. Another ping sounded louder, and a puff of dust exploded from a neighboring monument.

I cannot say if the third ping caused a puff, because I dove to the ground and squirmed my way between two vaults. The ground was as unrelenting as concrete. A noseful of dust elicited several sneezes that made my eyes water and my head reverberate. It was certainly the appropriate place for one's life to pass before one's eyes, I thought as I peered around the base.

No sniper stood at the top of the row, but that did little to relieve me. There were more than a hundred dandy places of concealment between the arch and me. I retreated to consider the situation, and concluded it was quite grim. I was several miles from town, and with the exception of the gnarly men on the bench, only one person knew where I was—and that person possessed a gun and a very bad attitude.

I had two choices. One was to stand up and find out if I was still a target. The other was to remain where I was indefinitely. After all, in a mere eight hours, it would be dark. I was still clutching the carryout order. As long as my unseen stalker was willing to wait, I certainly was. But would he be so accommodating? Although I was by now drowning in sweat, I began to shiver as though I was in a blizzard.

The sound of a car door slamming interrupted my bleak analysis of my chances. A querulous female voice demanded assistance, and a male voice answered soothingly. I wiggled forward, wondering exactly how painful a bullet between the eyes might prove to be, and poked my head out.

An elderly woman, dressed in black and using a cane, was being escorted beneath the arch. A younger man held her arm and carried an arrangement of flowers. Neither looked especially threatening, nor at all interested in terminating me.

I rose cautiously. The two seemed startled by my dramatic entrance, but after a moment of hesitation and a brief conference, they continued on their way. I wasn't yet ready to find out whether the sniper was crouched behind a vault and willing to sacrifice a pair of witnesses, but as I waited, I heard a car engine come to life. I stepped forward in time to see a flash of canary yellow as the vehicle drove down the road. It was the same color as the taxi that had brought us from the airport.

I sank back down on Mr. Marileau. The driver had disappeared, but now it seemed he had rejoined in the game. His arrival the previous night was mysterious; this was totally bewildering. Was he so eager for a fare that he was prepared not only to claim the existence of one at midnight but also to shoot one in broad daylight?

The woman and her companion were several rows away. She was issuing orders about the placement of the vase, while he moved it accordingly. I smoothed down my hair, wiped my face, and tried to smile as I walked toward them.

"Did you happen to notice the taxi when you arrived?" I said in as normal a tone as I could manage.

"No." She pointed a gloved finger at the flowers. "Over that way, but just an inch or so. Oh, you are such a dolt. I want them centered properly. No, no, no, now you've moved them too far. Do try to listen, Spencer."

"Sorry," the man said, shrugging at me. He made a minute adjustment to the vase of flowers and waited for a critique.

"Then could you please tell me where to find the Malloy family?" I said.

The woman halted her harangue long enough to suggest I search the back row in the farthest corner, then resumed with renewed peevishness. I left Spencer to his Herculan task and zigzagged among the vaults to the corner.

The Malloys surrounded an impressive monument with

phallic overtones. They'd been inhabiting the cemetery for well over a century, I determined, and in vaults of all sizes and degrees of adornment. Carlton had made known his desire to be cremated in Farberville rather than to be shipped home to the family plot. I could understand why. Here one did not sense the biblical admonishment of "ashes to ashes, dust to dust." It was difficult not to visualize the remains of bodies forever held in abeyance from the earth by marble boxes. There could be no transition back to nature.

I grew gloomier and gloomier as I searched for Miller's vault, and felt only a twinge of triumph when I finally found it at the edge of the plot. I brushed a patina of dust off the bronze plaque. Miller Randolph Malloy had been born on July 17, 1939, and had died on December 16, 1960. Purportedly, he was Resting in Peace.

My mission accomplished, I headed for the arch and the long walk back to LaRue. I'd learned the date of Miller's death, and I'd also learned that someone was so vehemently opposed to my well-being that he would indulge in the extreme behavior of shooting at me. The someone was likely to be the taxi driver, but it was impossible to imagine what his motives could be. I'd paid the fare and given him an adequate, if not astronomical, tip. I'd arranged for him to provide us with transportation back to the airport. As far as I was concerned, we'd both conducted ourselves properly for what was nothing more than an ephemeral professional relationship.

I stuck my hands in my pockets and began to walk along the side of the road. I was more lost in confusion than engrossed in thought; nevertheless, I almost stumbled into the ditch when a voice said, "Are you in need of a ride?"

Spencer smiled from the interior of the car. The woman sat in the backseat, staring forward with tight-lipped disapproval.

"Thank you," I said, getting in the front seat before she could counteract the offer. "I didn't realize the cemetery was so far from town."

"May I assume you're a Malloy?" the woman asked icily.

I glanced over my shoulder. "I'm Claire Malloy, Carlton's widow."

"So I see. When is Justicia's funeral to be?"

"I'm not sure," I said, struggling not to be intimidated by her hostility. "Stanford was making arrangements when I left this morning."

"I shall attend, but only out of respect for the family's prominence. Justicia behaved scandalously these last few years. Many of us became unwilling to call upon her, or to welcome her into our homes."

"Mother," Spencer said warningly, "there's no need to speak ill of the dead. The Malloy family served the community generously over many decades. Miss Justicia herself donated money to the hospital and was a pillar in the church until she became . . . dehabilitated by arthritis and the deterioration of her mental faculties." He gave me a faint smile. "Where may I take you, Mrs. Malloy?"

"The library, please."

"What were you doing at the cemetery?" he asked, doing his best to drown out the grumbles from the backseat.

"Verifying a date," I said.

"Oh, really?" Spencer glanced nervously in the rearview mirror, and his hands tightened on the steering wheel. "Did you find what you were looking for?"

"I saw you at Miller's tomb," the woman said accusingly.

"He was my husband's oldest brother," I said, "and I was curious about him."

"About his life—or his death?"

I gestured weakly. "About him."

We arrived without further conversation, but as I climbed

out of the car, the woman in the backseat said, "Allow me to apologize for my disparaging remarks about Justicia. We were friends for many, many years, and it was most difficult for me to accept the recent changes in her personality. I shall see you at the funeral service, Mrs. Malloy."

"Of course, Mrs. . . . ?"

"D'Armand, Mrs. Bethel D'Armand." She nodded dismissively at me, then poked the back of Spencer's head with her cane. "This is not our final destination. Do stop gawking."

I was the one who was gawking, but I closed my mouth and stepped back as the car pulled away. As I went up the steps to the library, I asked myself why I'd found her identity so amazing. I was unable to answer myself.

The library was cool and quiet. The rows of books were encased in dark wooden shelves, and the tables were antiques. Sofas provided seating for the patrons who thumbed magazines and newspapers. Two teenage girls giggled as they jostled each other to read what I presumed was a racy passage, despite the grim scrutiny of a woman hunched over a seed catalog.

A pleasant young librarian listened to my request for newspapers from the last month of 1960, settled me at a microfiche machine, and returned shortly with a canister. "At the time, there was only a weekly paper," she whispered. "What precisely are you looking for?"

"An obituary," I whispered back. She frowned but left me alone. I fed the film into the machine and located the issue from the third week in December. The front page contained little of interest, the pressing concerns of the week being a slump in cotton prices and a fire in a feed store. I moved on to the second page, and found what I was searching for—but not at all what I'd expected. Miller's obituary was several paragraphs long. He was the son of . . . He'd attended . . . He was survived by . . . And he'd died a hero, the recipient of the Purple Heart and the Bronze Star, among other medals.

How very odd, I thought as I leaned forward and reread the final paragraph. Sergeant Miller Randolph Malloy had not died in disgrace; he'd been killed by an enemy mine while on a training maneuver with a South Vietnamese unit. Several of the medals had been awarded posthumously.

Why had the family decided to hush up the existence of a hero? It was right up Maxie and Phoebe's ancestoral alley; they should have delighted in it. Stanford had no reason to choke on the name, nor Carlton to fail to mention his brother. Bethel D'Armand had blanched when I'd asked him an innocent question, and his wife had implied I'd done something dastardly at the cemetery.

I replaced the film in the canister and returned it to the desk, then went outside to stand on the top step.

Nothing out of the ordinary was taking place in LaRue. Pickup trucks and cars were still moving in the main street, and pedestrians were still doing the same on the sidewalks. My chums on the bench in front of the barbershop were sitting where I'd left them, and, from all appearances, had not moved even an inch. The sun was higher and hotter, and the sky perhaps paler, but it all looked depressingly normal to someone who was finding everything, as Ellie would say, muddlesome.

"Miz Malloy!"

I wrenched myself out of my befogged state. A car had stopped, and the two policemen who'd been at the scene of Miss Justicia's accident were regarding me. Dewberry, the skinny one, was in the driver's seat. Puccoon sat beside him.

"Good afternoon," I said.

"Had a call about you over an hour ago," Puccoon said with a smirk. "Miss Ellie reported you missing, and asked us to keep an eye out for you. Guess she thought you were in some sort of trouble, rather than merely catching up on your reading in the library."

"I went for a walk earlier, and misjudged how long I'd be gone. As you can see, I'm not missing anymore." I stopped and tried to decide whether to tell them about the incident in the cemetery. "I had a frightening experience, though, and I suppose I ought to report it."

"Tell you what, Miz Malloy," said Puccoon, "why don't you get in the backseat and tell us all about it while we run you out to the house?"

I was surprised by the invitation, but not so much that I declined it. Once Dewberry pulled into the traffic, I said, "Thank you for the ride, Officers."

"It was Miss Ellie's idea," said Puccoon. "We're hardly in the business of delivering people all over the parish. But what with Mr. Stanford being who he is and all, I told the little lady we'd oblige her, since we're going out there, anyway. What did you want to report? More suspicions about the accident?"

"Someone took several shots at me in the cemetery. When a pair of potential witnesses arrived, he left in what looked like a taxi."

Dewberry swiveled his head to stare at me. "Bright yellow?"

"It was the same color as the one I took from the airport yesterday. I only saw it as it left, and I couldn't see the driver."

"Who were those witnesses? They see anything?" demanded Puccoon.

I had not expected them to take my story seriously, in that I knew I was not high on their popularity list. "The witnesses were Mrs. Bethel D'Armand and her son, Spencer. I asked them if they'd noticed the taxi, and they both implied they hadn't. Surely you know the identity of the driver. It shouldn't be too difficult to find him, should it?"

"We already found the taxi driver," Puccoon said.

"You did?" I said excitedly. "Did he have a gun in the taxi?"

"He wasn't in his vehicle, ma'am. He was in an irrigation ditch several miles past the airport. Been shot in the head several times."

"But I was at the cemetery a little more than an hour ago. How'd you find his body so quickly?"

"One of the other officers found him about three hours ago. The driver's name is Baggley, and he's been driving that same cab for fifteen years, maybe more. What he hasn't been doing is taking shots at you out at the cemetery. In fact, he hasn't been doing much of anything except bloating up for the best part of two or three days."

I leaned forward and grabbed onto the back of the seat. "I don't understand. If he was already dead, then who was driving the taxi? And what about last night?"

Dewberry hit the brakes and we came to an abrupt halt in the middle of the road. "What about last night?"

I told them about the driver's appearance and disappearance during the search for Miss Justicia. They both began to rumble unpleasantly, forcing me to point out that they themselves had opted to conduct only the most cursory of investigations.

Dewberry thanked me for the criticism, although he seemed to miss its constructive potential. Beside him, Puccoon cursed under his breath, then said, "Describe the man who was driving the taxi when you arrived at the airport."

"Young, pale and fleshy, and dirty," I said. "He knew the area, or the location of Malloy Manor, and he expressed some familiarity with the family's reputation." I closed my eyes and ran through the scene in the foyer. "He must not be local, however. No one recognized him."

"Miss Justicia and Miss Pauline hardly ever came into town," said Puccoon. "The others, like Mr. Stanford and his two, only come back to visit every once in a while." He scratched his head. "She's sure as hell not describing Baggley, Dewey. What about that stranger we picked up for brawling last week?"

"Fifty years old and his face carved up worse than a school desk," Dewberry said as he resumed driving. "Other than that, and the snake tattoos all over his hands, it might be a positive ID."

I uncurled my fingers and sat back, although I was far from relaxed. "So this person, identity unknown, killed the owner of the taxi and decided to make a little money picking up fares at the airport. Later he realized he wasn't making enough and came to Malloy Manor with the story that someone called. Today he dropped by the cemetery and decided to engage in a bit of target practice. Who is he?"

"We're looking into it, ma'am," Puccoon said. "We don't know that he murdered Baggley, but we'd sure like to hear his side of the story. Odds are we're dealing with a psychotic. We'll pick him before too long, in any case. There ain't a whole lot of places to hide a bright yellow taxi. I don't want to be snoopy, but just why were you at the cemetery?"

I considered lying, but at the last moment adopted a different ploy in hopes that candor would beget candor. "I was curious about Miller Malloy, and I went out there to ascertain the date of his death. When I returned, I found the obituary at the library. He was quite a hero when he died thirty years ago. Full military honors and lots of medals." I held my breath and willed either of them to offer information.

"Before my time," said one.

"Mine, too," said the other.

9

As we entered the house, Officers Dewberry and Puccoon pulled off their hats. Their expressions were befittingly respectful (or toady, some might opine) as they asked me to find Mr. Stanford and inquire if they might have a word with him.

While I was debating which way to go, Pauline glided out of the parlor. Her face looked less puffy than it had earlier, but the only signs of color were two asymmetrical circles of rouge. The plaid housedress had been discarded for a dark gray dress. "Oh, here you are, Cousin Claire. We've all been worried about you." She began to sag as she saw the policemen by the door, but stiffened herself and inclined her head. "Good afternoon, gentlemen. Is there something you wanted?"

"They want to speak to Stanford," I said. "I was just going to look for him."

"He's using the telephone in the library. I shall be happy

to convey any messages to him," said Pauline, attempting to seize the role of mistress of the manor and run with it.

A stumbling block came out of the hallway. "Yes?" Maxie said to the policemen. "I thought we'd passed beyond the necessity of police intervention in this most stressful period of mourning. Has Cousin Claire"—ping, ping—"brought you here for a purpose?"

"They gave me a lift," I said, then went into the library before she could get out a single incredulous snort.

Stanford was indeed on the telephone, barking as furiously as a hound that had treed a raccoon. "Don't give me this crap! What do you mean we can't have the service until Monday? Are you telling me that some old cleaning woman's more important than Miss Justicia Malloy?" He paused. "I don't care how long that old woman's been dead! Three days, five days—so what? You've got a refrigerator, don't you?" His cheeks ballooned as he paused again. "So pack some dry ice in the coffin, for pity's sake. Nobody'll notice, anyway. If she was a hundred years old, she started to decompose a long time ago. You listen up, and listen up good, buddy boy—my great-great-grandfather practically founded this parish, and not once since then has the Malloy family been treated with such disregard! You either reschedule that other service or be prepared to kiss your overpriced casket business good-bye!"

He slammed down the receiver and wiped his forehead, all the while cursing most creatively. When he spotted me, he spread his hands in apology. "I don't believe I heard you come in, Claire. I was havin' a slightly heated conversation with an ol' friend about funeral arrangements."

"And when is the funeral to be held?"

"Not till Monday morning at eleven, damn it. He's got some mummified woman who died early in the week, and he was trying to act as if she was more important than my dear, departed mother." He wiped his eyes, and, in a ragged voice, added, "May she rest in peace as soon as possible."

"The two police officers would like to speak to you," I said, unimpressed by his emotionalism and dismayed by the knowledge Caron and I were stuck in Greedy Gulch for another forty-eight hours.

"They do? What about?" He moved toward me, his eyes narrowed. "I understand from Ellie that you disappeared in downtown LaRue this morning. I'd like to hope you didn't go to the police station and try to persuade them to reconsider their report, Claire. It'd be like poking a hornets' nest with a short stick." He loomed over me until his face was inches from mine. "A real short stick."

He brushed past me and went into the foyer. I listened to him slapping backs and welcoming the two, but I was too unnerved to follow immediately. Peter had warned me that if my instincts were wrong, I would stir up trouble—and if they were right, I'd put myself and Caron in danger. At that moment, I regretted possessing any instincts, except for those concerned with survival. They were likely to come in handy.

As I came to the doorway, Dewberry was saying, "I am sorry to have to disturb you all, but the captain wanted me to let you know what the acting coroner said in his report."

Maxie nudged Pauline aside to vent her outrage on Dewberry. After a series of huffs and puffs that would have leveled a subdivision, she said, "Are you telling us that poor Miss Justicia was subjected to an autopsy?"

"Yes, ma'am," he said unhappily.

Puccoon attempted to save him. "But you'll be comforted to know we had Fred Spies do it, rather than our regular coroner, on account of he was out of town visiting kinfolk in Mississippi. The regular coroner—not Fred."

"And why are we to find comfort in that?" demanded Maxie, giving each word maximum impact.

"At least Fred's an anesthesiologist. Gordie's . . . well, he's what you might call an animal doctor."

"A veterinarian? If this person had not been out of town, he would have conducted the autopsy on Miss Justicia?" Maxie sat down heavily on the bottom step and began to fan herself with her hand. "Pauline, see if there are smelling salts in the bathroom cabinet. I'm feeling quite dizzy."

Pauline hesitated, then went upstairs.

"Why, Dewey," said Stanford, "I must say I'm a might disappointed, particularly after our conversation last night, that you'd involve the coroner in this sad, sad business. I thought we'd agreed that a substantial donation to the police benevolent fund in Miss Justicia's honor might suffice?"

"Cap'n Plantain didn't see it that way, Mr. Stanford. He's been in a bad mood since he started his sessions with a proctologist, and he ordered me to hunt up somebody to do the autopsy. None of us thought Spies would find anything. I didn't think it would matter much, to tell the truth, and I'd like to let you know Cap'n Plantain says he'll be most grateful for that donation you mentioned."

Stanford stalked into the parlor. A bottle clinked against a glass as he said, "You tell Plantain I'll send a check about ten minutes after the bayou freezes over. You can use it to buy yourselves some ice skates."

Maxie struggled to her feet. "And what, Officer Dewberry, did this small-town doctor have to say about Miss Justicia Malloy, a leading lady of the parish for eighty years?"

"It wasn't as bad as you think, ma'am," he said, blanching under her beady gaze. "In fact, it'll probably help you through this terrible time to know Miss Justicia didn't suffer while drowning. Fred said in the report that the back of the wheelchair must have busted her on the head hard enough to crack her skull, which was as thin as parchment paper due to her advanced age and all. There wasn't any water in her lungs."

"'Water, water everywhere, but not a drop to drink,'" Pauline chanted from over the banister at the top of the stairs. With a giggle, she disappeared into the shadowy recesses of the hallway.

"She is still feeling the shock," Maxie said in the ensuing silence.

Puccoon shook his head. "Most understandable. We'll send you a copy of the report, but basically we can say the investigation is completed. You can commence with the funeral arrangements whenever you want." He thrust a plastic bag at me. "We don't need these anymore."

I took the bag, which contained my white terry-cloth bedroom slippers. The mortal remains of them, anyway. Not only were they stained and muddy, they were also badly frayed, as if I'd shuffled through low-lying thorns. They were deserving of a few kind words and a decent burial, but in a trash can rather than a marble vault. "Thanks," I said unenthusiastically.

"There was no indication of a heart attack?" came another voice from the top of the stairs. Ellie was leaning over the banister at a perilous angle.

"No, ma'am," Dewberry said. "Just the one blow from the back of the wheelchair. The damn thing's heavy enough to knock the socks off a full-sized man. It took us better than half an hour to drag it out of the water."

"Thank heavens," Maxie said, now recovered enough to light a cigarette and send a stream of smoke into Dewberry's face. "I speak for all of us when I say it is a great comfort to know that Miss Justicia did not suffer the indignity of drowning in her own bayou. Don't you agree, Stanford?"

"A great comfort," he rumbled from the parlor.

She raised her voice but not her face. "And, Ellie, aren't you heartened to know that your grandmother felt no moment of panic, and that it was over in a single moment?"

"Very heartened," she answered.

"As am I," Phoebe said from farther down the banister. "So is Cousin Pauline, who's gone to lie down for a while."

Maxie had found her rhythm. "And even you, Cousin Claire, must be relieved that you can put aside your silly ideas and join the family in our time of mutual grief and mourning."

I crossed my arms and leaned against the doorsill. "Oh, absolutely, Cousin Maxie. Absolutely."

The two officers might have intended to ask about the taxi driver, but this unified front was too much for them, and they left with a few mumbles. The rest of us stayed put like garden statuary.

At last, Maxie dropped her cigarette in a vase, and said, "I do believe I'll lie down for a few minutes. Like poor Cousin Pauline, this whole thing has simply twisted me inside out and left me as limp as last night's salad. I shall see you all in the parlor at four o'clock." She began to ascend the stairs.

"What's happening at four?" I asked.

She turned back, and her elevation allowed her to make it clear she was looking down at me in more ways than one. "Phoebe has arranged for Rodney Spikenard to come to Malloy Manor to provide us with information about the dispersal of the estate. You're more than welcome to sit in on the discussion, but if you'd prefer to remain in your room, I'm sure none of us will object too strongly."

"I wouldn't miss it for all the fish in the refrigerator," I said sweetly.

Shortly thereafter, I was alone in the foyer. I could hear clinks and curses in the parlor, but I would have crawled into

Keith's hole before I joined Stanford. The presence of Maxie, Ellie, Pauline, and Phoebe on the second floor made my bedroom seem less a haven.

It occurred to me that Caron had missed this latest familial meeting. I was till clutching the sack from the café, although its having been squashed, dragged through the dirt, toted all over LaRue, and even taken for a drive in a police car had diminished its visual appeal. On the other hand, it might be more edible than anything she might have encountered thus far.

I darted upstairs, tiptoed to our room, and ascertained that she was not there. I dropped the bag containing my bedroom slippers in a corner and went back down to the foyer. Yesterday Caron had vanished, and her story of wandering around the yard had not rung true. I finally went down the hallway to the dining room to see if she had materialized at the table.

Crumbs were scattered on the tablecloth, but the table itself had been cleared, and not even the ghost of Miss Justicia presided over it. In that Caron's prime motivation was self-gratification, I continued into the kitchen.

She was perched on a stool, listening to the cook with all the wide-eyed amazement of a child half her age. She must have suspected as much, because she sniffed at me and said, "I've decided to do a paper for social studies on the folklore of the region. This woman has been providing me with some of the more infamous legends."

The cook stood in front of the sink, her hands buried in soapy water. "That's right," she murmured.

"Did you know, Mother," Caron continued, "that this woman's great-great-grandmother was a *femme de couleur libre* and was chosen at a quadroon ball by General Richmond Malloy to be his *placée*? Before the Civil War, she kept a boardinghouse in New Orleans, but afterward, during Reconstruction, she had to come back here and live in a shack on the bayou? Isn't that the most tragic thing you've ever heard?"

"Except maybe getting herself murdered," the cook inserted dryly.

"Well, yeah, that was pretty tragic, too." Caron stuck out her lower lip just enough to warn me not to think for one second that she'd been giving serious attention to a ghost story.

I valued my winsome looks too much for that. "I'm sure your social studies teacher will be impressed." I held out the sack. "Cheeseburger and fries, if you're interested. They've had a few adventures in the last couple of hours, but—"

"Where have you been? You told me you were going into whatever that town is with Ellie, but then Ellie came back and said you'd just gone poof! I had to hang around this dreary place all morning, and there was absolutely nothing to eat. I thought I would faint. I Really Did!"

"Do it now," I suggested. "Make my day."

"I fixed her up just fine," the cook said. "I made her some biscuits and a nice cheese omelet."

The teary-eyed martyr realized her case was weakening. "But that wasn't until nearly noon, Mother."

I found a biscuit in a pan on the corner and began to nibble on it. The cook had finished with the dishes and was now scouring a pan. Although she appeared to be engrossed in her work, I figured she wasn't so engrossed that she was missing a single word. To Caron, I said, "Last night at dinner, I learned of the existence of an uncle of yours. He was your father's oldest brother and his name was Miller."

"Be still my heart. Speaking of which, we don't have to stay for Miss Justicia's funeral just because she died while we were here, do we? I heard Uncle Stanford say he didn't think it would be until Monday. I promised Inez I'd be back tomorrow afternoon. She's supposed to find out if Rhonda and that other dumpy cheerleader are really having a pool party, or if they were just saying that so we'd feel left out."

My masterful ploy was doing no better than Caron's essayed claim to martyrdom. "We'll have to stay for the funeral. It might be useful for your social studies report. I went out to the local cemetery, and—"

"Mother, didn't you hear what I said? Rhonda told Inez that Louis Wilderberry and some of the other guys were coming to swim, but she didn't know"—Caron switched to a simper—"if her mother would let her have anybody else."

I gave it one last try. "I found Miller Malloy's vault, and later learned from his obituary that he was a highly decorated hero during the first years of the Vietnam involvement."

"It's not like Rhonda's mother cares how many guests she has. On her birthday, she must have had a hundred people. Now she says"—resorting to the simper—"that her mother doesn't want too many kids around because she's worried that some of them might start groping each other in the pool." Caron's cynical laugh was so polished that she must have practiced for hours before the bathroom mirror. "Barracudas wouldn't touch Rhonda, even though she's a floating chunk of cellulite. Her thighs jiggle when she walks."

"We're staying for the funeral," I said. "Why don't you call the airlines and see what flights we can get on in the middle of the afternoon on Monday?"

"I cannot believe you're Doing This to me." She slid off the stool and left the room, although her words of condemnation seemed to hover like a haze of acid rain.

The cook's head was lowered, but her shoulders were twitching and portions of her body were jiggling just a bit. I took Caron's seat and said, "I don't suppose you're old enough to remember Miller, are you?"

"Oh, I remember him. He was a year or two older than me, and he used to come by my grandpa's grocery store and drink beer. I liked to see him out there on the porch. He'd prop his feet on the rail just like the old men, and listen to their stories. Always seemed to have his share of jokes to tell."

"He hung out at this place when he was a teenager?"

She chuckled. "The store was real popular with the white boys, because they could buy beer. Some of 'em were smart-mouthed and meaner than gators, but Mr. Miller was always respectful."

We were making progress, although at this point it could be measured in millimeters rather than in leaps and bounds. "But then he enlisted in the army," I prompted her.

"In a manner of speaking." She removed a dripping pan from the water and reached for another. "I should have soaked these last night," she grumbled. "I knew better than to leave them, but I wanted to get away early. Now I'm paying the price for the sin of slothfulness, and I got nobody to blame but myself."

I attempted to divert the digression. "Why in a manner of speaking? He did enlist, didn't he? The draft wasn't until 1968."

She turned around and looked at me, not angrily but with a trace of coolness. "The truth is, Miz Malloy, my folks didn't much mix with the white boys, partly because it wasn't done and partly because we didn't give a rat's ass about 'em. We were more concerned with the poverty in our community, with the unemployment and piss-poor schoolhouse, with the occasional truck with drunken rednecks dressed in sheets. Mr. Miller bought beer from my grandpa, but not because of any deep friendship. He listened to the stories because he thought they were quaint. He sat on the porch late at night because he didn't want to come back here and watch his family pretend they were living in middle of the nineteenth century, surrounded by loyal darkies singing spirituals by the light of the moon."

Not for the first time in the last two days, I was at a loss for words. I wasn't sure how I'd accomplished it, but somehow I'd managed to insult the woman. "I'm sorry," I said sincerely. "I was simply trying to get a picture of Miller. No one seems willing to talk about him, and I was beginning to wonder if he'd done something ghastly."

"You want a picture of Mr. Miller? Go upstairs and look at the portrait of General Richmond Malloy. Mr. Miller was the spittin' image of him." She turned back and bent over the sink.

The conversation was over. I murmured a farewell and wandered back to the foyer, which was still unpopulated. There were no clinks from the parlor; Stanford either had departed or regained control of unsteady hands. No one peered over the banister from the second floor. No one scratched from inside the tiny closet.

Sunlight splashed through the narrow windows on either side of the front door, illuminating drifts of dust and exposing deep scratches on the hardwood floor. A fat fly settled on the lip of a vase and began to explore it; both of us were going in circles.

I heard a nervous laugh from behind the double doors of the library. It was difficult to imagine Caron enjoying a chat with an airline-reservations operator, but she was frantic enough to go home to have done what I'd asked her to do . . . for once. I went into the library and was not especially surprised to find Ellie on the telephone.

In contrast, she seemed very surprised to find me in the room. "Hold on," she said, then covered the mouthpiece of the receiver with her hand. "It's personal, if you don't mind." She hesitated, her forehead furrowing, and, as if in response to my nod, added, "I'm talking to my boyfriend in Atlanta. I promised him I'd call today."

"Have you seen Caron?"

She shook her head and stared at me until I retreated, carefully closing the doors behind me. This time, I took a wicked pleasure in riding the elevator seat to the second floor. It lacked the exhilaration of a roller coaster, but in its staid way, it was modestly entertaining.

All the doors were closed. I found the portrait of General Malloy in his Confederate finery, but I doubted Miller Malloy was the "spittin' image" of the old man with the dour face and button-popping belly. Maybe he would have become so, I thought as I went into our bedroom, but it would have required an additional forty years of overindulgence.

The bedroom and bathroom were empty. If I had unwittingly been invited to engage in a game of hide-and-seek, I was at a disadvantage, in that Caron had a half-hour's head start on me. I looked out the window. The yard was a sea of weeks, bushes, and mossy branches, and the only activity came from indolent insects. The water of the bayou did not so much as ripple; if Caron had decided to follow Ophelia's example, she'd left no telltale traces.

On this hot summer afternoon in the rural Deep South, it seemed as if everyone and everything had shut off. We weren't talking slow motion; this was no motion. The urban areas weren't gripped with this suffocating sense of lethargy, perhaps, but here, it was time to take to one's bed with a fan and a glass of iced tea. In Miss Justicia's case, it might well have been something more potent, but I could easily envision her on the plump mattress, plotting revisions in her will as she awaited the passing of the midday heat.

Resisting the urge to collapse on the bed, a victim of tradition, I took a shower and changed into clean clothes. Caron had not returned to further analyze the extent to which I had ruined her life forever. I was disappointed. Her flair for melodrama was rivaled only by her capacity for indignation, and even a recitation of Rhonda's perfidy could have livened up what was closing in on me like a marble vault.

I had another hour before the gathering in the parlor. I had no intentions of missing it, either. Miss Justicia may or may not have been technically demented, but she certainly had a devious sense of humor. It was no wonder that the family members were finding it necessary to take to their beds to await the revelations to come. Who was in and who was out? Sixths, halves, all of it—or none of it? Would the televangelist be able to construct a new broadcasting tower? Would the sperm bank be able to take new deposits?

I was grinning as I glided downstairs. The library was vacant, and I called the airline to find out about changing our reservations. Admittedly, I was ambivalent. If they refused to allow a deviation, then Caron and I would be forced to return to Farberville as originally scheduled. I practiced a look of regret and composed a few pious sentences to explain how disappointed we were to leave before the funeral.

The brittle voice at the opposite end of the toll-free number told me that the airline always accommodated those travelers who'd experienced family tragedies. She confirmed us on a flight late Monday afternoon. My response may have lacked genuine gratitude, but I choked it out and replaced the receiver with a sigh.

I went outside, on the off chance I might find my fugitive offspring cooing over a baby gator or measuring tapeworms.

Ellie's sports car and Stanford's Mercedes were in the driveway, indicative that Caron had not yet descended to grand theft auto. As long as she hadn't called for a taxi—and been driven away by a psychotic to the nearest irrigation ditch, she had to be around somewhere.

The previous night, I'd been assigned to the right side of the house. Being a mildly curious sort, I headed around the left side to discover what botanical delights I had missed. The path I chose was wide and well marked with narrow ruts, clearly one of Miss Justicia's favorite racetracks. Although I preferred my encounters with nature to be on PBS, I benignly regarded the shrubs, clumps of wildflowers, tiny butterflies, and even the masses of Spanish moss hanging from the live oak trees.

Options presented themselves occasionally. This was hardly a maze in a palace garden, but I was rapidly losing my sense of direction as I followed the winding paths. The sun was blocked by the foliage above me, and the land was level rather than sloping toward the bayou. This was in no way alarming, however; even though I was not of the Daniel Boone school of trailblazing, I was in the yard surrounding Malloy Manor and apt to find something of interest before too long.

And I did. As I rounded a mass of bushes, I saw a weathered gray structure. It was not the shack inhabited by the *femme de couleur libre*, but merely the old barn that had been mentioned by Stanford and Phoebe. Barns were known refuges for rodents, both ambulatory and winded, along with spiders, snakes, and other stars of those PBS documentaries.

If Caron was in there, she'd been dragged in by both heels and everyone within the ambit of the parish would have heard her squeals. I was toying with the idea of taking a quick look when Keith came out of a door. Despite the sunglasses and headphones, he spotted me and came up the path. His hair looked dirtier, if possible, and his clothes more tattered. I wondered whether he might be able to use my bedroom slippers.

"Yo," he said with a vague smile. "Another body in the bayou?"

The redolence of marijuana that accompanied him gave me a fairly astute theory as to his activity in the barn. I wrinkled my nose slightly as I said, "I dearly hope not. I'm looking for Caron."

"Who?"

"My daughter. The girl who was beside me when you opened the front door yesterday," I said. "Red curly hair, green eyes, probably pouting or ranting about cellulite."

"Oh, yeah," he said, running his fingers through his long, greasy hair. "A real spooky little kid, that one. Why would she be in the barn?"

"I have no idea." I considered asking him the same thing, but I was worried that he might answer truthfully, thus giving me information I preferred not to have.

"I didn't see her here, but . . ." He began to walk away from me, his hands flapping as though he was conducting an orchestra of his own making.

"But what?" I demanded as I caught up with him. "Have you seen her this afternoon, Keith? Is she somewhere in the yard?" His shoulder blades rippled, but he continued to walk at an increasing rapid pace. "Did you see her?"

I managed to crunch down on his heel hard enough to stop him. He gave me a wounded look as he rubbed his heel, then said, "I thought I saw someone by the bayou. That's where we're going, right?"

"Of course," I said.

We arrived at the bayou with a minute, but there was no sign of anyone lingering in the area. The place where Miss Justicia had been pulled from the water was easy to locate.

The bank was a mess of muddy footprints and flattened grass. Two brown furrows indicated where the wheelchair had been pulled from the water.

Keith went to the edge of the water and shook his head. "That was really weird, wasn't it? One minute she's acting like she's in the Indy Five Hundred, and the next she's gator bait."

"She being your grandmother," I pointed out acidly.

"Yeah. I hadn't seen her for a long time. Nor my old man, for that matter. All he'd have done is yap about my hair and about how I should get a job. A job's a bummer. You have to show up every day, listen to some moron telling you what to do and when to do it, and all for a measly paycheck."

"You're playing in a band?"

"Bass guitar for Satanic Slimebuckets. If we had the dough to cut a demo, we'd make it big, but it hasn't happened. Every time we get a little cash, it ends up going for bail."

"Hmm," I said sympathetically. "So you could make it big if you could cut a demo. Perhaps Miss Justicia understood your dilemma and left you enough money to"—I had to force the words—"realize your dream?"

"She better have," he said, turning back to stare at the place the body had reposed. "This whole thing's been nothing but a pain in the butt. She insisted that her precious grand-children be here in person to collect the dough. Ellie totally lost it and spent forever moaning and groaning like she was having a baby. You'd have thought she had to shave her head or donate an organ or something. Sheesh! All she did was miss a day of work at that stupid television station. The Slimebuckets had to cancel a gig that would've paid a couple hundred bucks."

I lacked the depth of character to offer further sympathy.

"I'm going to the house," I said. "The lawyer's coming at four o'clock, in theory with information about Miss Justicia's will."

"About goddamn time," Keith said as he fell into step with me.

Although I wouldn't have expressed it in quite that way, I had to admit to myself that I agreed with him.

10

Keith and I went through the back door and down the hallway to the foyer. Ellie came down the staircase, now dressed in a demure skirt and blouse, and mutely followed us into the parlor. Stanford was straightening the bottles on the cart. I had no idea if he'd been there for the last hour, or had returned in honor of the upcoming event, but the faintly unfocused look he gave us implied the former. He nodded approvingly at Ellie and me; Keith's less formal attire elicited a quick scowl. We settled on various sofas and awaited developments.

Maxie and Phoebe drifted in and sat down, and moments later Pauline took a seat near the window. No one seemed in the mood for conversation, or even eye contact. I wasn't sure if they were drowsy from naps or so taut that a single word might shatter their facades like so much plate glass.

It was tempting to test my theory, but I instead crossed my legs and sat back to watch the fun. The ambience grew more oppressive as watches were checked discreetly, mouths pursed, exhalations carefully regulated to avoid attracting attention. The silence not only could have been sliced, it could have been run through a food processor and served on crackers.

Stanford finally cracked. "If we're going to have to wait for this fellow, we might as well make ourselves comfortable. May I offer any of you a drink?"

Five minutes later, we were fortified but no more animated than the furniture on which we sat. I was about to suggest a game of charades when the doorbell rang. Facades did not shatter, but they certainly slipped far enough to expose simmering avarice.

"That must be Mr. Spikenard," Phoebe said. She licked her lips, then stood up and smoothed her skirt. "I'll . . . uh, let him in . . ." As she left, she closed the door behind her.

Maxie examined her diamond wristwatch. "He's nearly fifteen minutes late. I, for one, am unaccustomed to being kept waiting as if I was a common housewife. I do hope we're not going to continue to be treated quite so casually by this young man."

Staring over her head at the door, Stanford said, "I am truly sorry that we're not dealing with Bethel. However, there's no call to be down on this young fellow because he's running late, Cousin Maxie. I'm sure he has a perfectly good excuse for keeping us waiting." He turned his head sharply. "Has he been to the house before, Cousin Pauline?"

"Once, I believe," she said, "last week while I was handling some bank chores for Justicia. I myself have never met him."

We could hear voices in the foyer, but the words were not audible. Everyone was watching the door as if expecting something to crash through it with the fury of a freight train.

"Whatever are they doing?" demanded Maxie. "What

can they be discussing, and why doesn't Phoebe escort him in here immediately? Cousin Stanford, I really do think you ought to find out the cause of this interminable delay."

Ellie put her feet on the coffee table and carelessly swirled the contents of her glass. "Maybe he's single and terribly attractive, Cousin Maxie. Phoebe may be so starved for sex that she's willing to do it with a lawyer. I myself would never sink so—"

"Ellie!" Stanford snapped. "How many times have I warned you that these . . ."

He halted as the door opened and Phoebe slipped into the parlor. She made sure the door was closed completely, then moved her mouth as she struggled to form words. She was not successful.

Maxie stood up. "Where is Mr. Spikenard?"

"I—I asked him—Mr. Spikenard—uh, to wait in the foyer," she stammered. "I just thought—I thought it might be—well, I wanted to—"

"Please cease this unbecoming behavior and have him join us," commanded Maxie.

"But I do—I really do think—" Phoebe said, her hands clasped tightly as if pleading for her life.

"Nonsense," said Stanford. "We've had enough of your thinking to last us the rest of the month. Hop to it, gal, and bring him in here."

Phoebe's throat rippled, but she nodded and opened the door. "Mr. Spikenard, the family will—oh, yes, they will see you now."

I had no idea what to expect. Phoebe was acting as if she were ushering in an alien life-form, resplendent with antennae and malformed appendages. What appeared in the doorway was strictly an earthly apparition in a three-piece suit.

"How do you do," he said gravely, nodding.

Behind him, Phoebe grimaced and said, "This is Rodney Spikenard, Miss Justicia's lawyer."

He looked at each of us in turn, his smile widening as he took in the varying degrees of shock. His suit was pale gray, and his tie dark red and knotted impeccably. His shoes were polished, his briefcase expensive, and his appendages ordinary. His mustache was trimmed and his hair short and unremarkable. The few words he'd spoken had been melodious, with only a faint Southern accent.

What was creating the impact on the Malloys was the undeniable tint of his skin. It wasn't ebony, by any means, but it was several shades darker than any late-summer tan. It went nicely with his facial features, which mildly hinted of a classic Afro-American heritage.

"I'm Claire Malloy," I said as I crossed the room and offered my hand.

"Yes," he said, raising his eyebrows as he shook my hand, "then you're Carlton's widow. I'm pleased to meet you, Mrs. Malloy." He waited for a moment, then said, "Miss Justicia told me about the family, but I'm not quite sure who's who."

Neither were they. Although I found this newest development highly entertaining, I took pity on them and pointed at them one at a time, murmuring names. Ellie responded with a smile and a flip of her hand, and Pauline nodded. Keith whistled softly. Maxie and Stanford, in contrast, were gaping as if they were guppies confronting a higher denizen of the food chain.

"Would you like a drink?" I asked.

"A glass of soda water, please," Spikenard said. "Is there any place in particular where you'd like me to sit?"

Before Maxie could mention the back of the bus, I took his arm and led him to an unoccupied sofa. Once I'd fixed his drink, I sat down beside him and said, "I understand you're a Yale graduate?"

To my regret, Stanford came out of his trance. "Basketball scholarship?"

"An academic scholarship," Spikenard replied easily. "I did my undergraduate work at Duke, and was at the top of my class. I had several offers, but I chose Yale." He gave Stanford a puzzled frown. "Does the Yale law school have a basketball team?"

Stanford muttered a reply as he replenished his drink, and in a spurt of sympathy, Maxie's, as well. Phoebe sank down near her mother, who'd landed on the cushion like a load of topsoil.

Spikenard set his briefcase on the coffee table and opened it. "Miss Justicia engaged my legal services within the past week, and I'm still not familiar with all the details of the trust. The trust itself is of a highly complex nature, having been in existence throughout several generations. The administrator of record, Mr. D'Armand, has agreed to send over the documents, but I've received nothing thus far. To complicate matters, Miss Justicia had instructed me to—"

"What about the will?" drawled Ellie.

"All this twaddle about the trust can wait," Stanford said. "Stick to the point—sir." He'd stopped himself before he said *boy*, but we'd all seen the initial consonant on his lips, and the beads of sweat on his forehead when he'd choked out the *sir*.

"It is my understanding," Spikenard said, "that Miss Justicia revoked the previous will. She did so in the presence of Mr. D'Armand, by verbally stating her intentions and subsequently destroying the document itself. As long as she had capacity and freedom from undue influence and fraud, this revocation would appear to be valid."

Stanford drained his glass. "Can't you lawyers get out a simple answer? What's in the new will?"

"Beats me," Spikenard answered with eloquent simplicity.

Maxie managed a bloodless smile. "Miss Justicia revoked her old will. I assume you were hired to write the new one, and to keep it for her. Please stop spouting off legal gobbledygook and produce the document."

"I fear you have made a false assumption, Mrs. Malloy-Frazier. Miss Justicia made an appointment for me to come to the house to provide her with certain legal information. At no time did she ask me to prepare a will, nor did she tender a document of that description to me for safekeeping."

"Would that have been last Tuesday, Mr. Spikenard?" Pauline asked.

"Yes, Miss Hurstmeyer. I believe you were out of the house at the time. Miss Justicia met me on the front porch. I was impressed with the agility with which she operated her wheelchair."

Stanford refilled his glass. "This ain't the time for compliments about her driving prowess. Are you telling us that Miss Justicia died without signing a new will?"

"I don't believe it," inserted Ellie. "She wouldn't do that, not after all her promises and threats."

"I have reason to think she did not die intestate," Spikenard said, shifting through papers in his briefcase.

"Now look here," Stanford said, beginning to bluster like a winter day, "first you say she tore up the old will, then had you come out here but not write up a new one. I don't know what this 'intestate' business means, but I do know when someone's talking through both corners of his mouth!"

"She didn't die intestate," Ellie insisted in a thin voice. Her face was pale, and she was twisting a curl around her finger so tightly that it cut into the flesh. "She must have signed a will."

Stanford noticed her distress, and a crafty look crossed

his face. "Just what would happen to the estate if Miss Justicia died before she made out a will, Spikenard?"

"The estate would be divided among the heirs."

"And who might that be?"

"Her descendants. In this situation, the first generation of issue who did not predecease the intestate, and the issue of those who did."

Maxie's hand shook as she tried to light a cigarette. "Is there any hope that you might speak plainly?"

"As you wish," he said, acknowledging her with a grave nod. "If Miss Justicia died without a will, the estate would be divided among her three sons. Thus, one-third of the estate would go directly to Stanford Malloy. The remaining two shares of one-third each would go to any offspring of Carlton Malloy and of Miller Malloy."

"That's it?" Maxie said, stunned. "But . . ."

Pauline put her face in her hands and began to snivel. Ellie prodded Keith with her foot, and, when he looked at her, gave him a dispirited shrug. Phoebe seemed relatively calm, but Maxie was still struggling to regain control of her flaccid jaw.

I was sorry that Caron was not present. Her reaction would have enlivened the room, if perhaps enraging certain occupants in the process. I was watching Rodney Spikenard closely, in that I seemed to be the only one who'd heard the emphasis on the *if* at the beginning of his sentence. He was trying to appear professionally disinterested, but he was keenly attuned to each and every person in the room. As his eyes met mine, I gave him a wink intended to disconcert him. I was disconcerted by his flicker of warning.

"But Miller's dead," Stanford said cheerfully, "and he didn't have any offspring. I guess that means little Caron and I get to divvy up the estate fifty-fifty, right?"

"If that was a correct assessment of the situation," Spikenard said.

As mother of the heir, I decided to jump in. "Oh, come now, Stanford, how can we be sure Miller didn't marry a nice Vietnamese girl and have children?"

"Miller wouldn't do a fool thing like that, and we'd have heard something if he had."

"We'll make inquiries through the military," Spikenard said. "However, we're by no means in a position to concern ourselves with that at this time." He tugged at his collar, and then glanced at a legal pad on which he'd made notes. "As I mentioned previously, Miss Justicia arranged for an appointment for several reasons. One was to request that I begin the process to become administrator of the trust, since she no longer wished Attorney D'Armand to serve in that capacity. She also asked me a great many questions concerning the construction of a valid olographic will."

"Way to go, Miss Justicia!" Ellie said, brightening.

"Olographic will?" Stanford said. He took out his handkerchief, wiped his neck, and gazed suspiciously at Spikenard. "What's that?"

"I've heard of an holographic will," Maxie murmured.

"It's this Napoleonic code thing," Ellie explained, still sounding much improved from a few minutes earlier. "The *h* fell off along the way. But this is so exiting, Mr. Spikenard—or may I call you Rodney?" He nodded, amused. "This means that Miss Justicia wrote up her own will, and it's just as good as one fancied up by a lawyer. I knew she wouldn't let me down!"

"Hush, Cousin Ellie," Maxie said coldly. "Mr. Spikenard, be so kind as to elaborate on your remark."

"My pleasure, Mrs. Malloy-Frazier. Miss Justicia asked me to explain what was necessary for a valid olographic will. I assured her it was not at all complicated, that she needed to date the page at the top, spell out her desires as carefully as possible, and sign it at the bottom. The courts are fairly lenient about their interpretation of the intentions of the testator, as long as it's written by hand and has the components I mentioned."

Stanford looked as if a stack of money had been placed beneath his nose and then snatched away, leaving only the scent to tantalize him. "But why would she go to the trouble of writing out this olographic will? Why didn't she tell you what she wanted and have you write it up?"

Spikenard hesitated, then said, "I'm afraid that falls into the realm of client-attorney confidentiality, Mr. Malloy."

"Bethel was throwing that phrase around, too," Ellie said. "I think it's a cop-out, a way to avoid answering sticky questions."

Phoebe cleared her throat. "The concept has its origin in English common law, actually. But are you implying, Mr. Spikenard, that Miss Justicia did write an olographic will and that it now delineates the division of the estate?"

"Poppycock!" Stanford said, spinning around to glower at her. "Even if she'd thought about writing up some will, you know her arthritis was something fierce. She couldn't hold a pencil, much less write a whole mess of who-gets-what."

"You're mistaken," Pauline said from the sideline. She took a folded paper from her pocket. "I found this under Justicia's desk some days ago."

"Is it . . . ?" said Stanford, retreating, as if she'd brandished a lethal snake.

"No, it's a very curt letter to Bethel D'Armand, telling him to"—the pink blotches on Pauline's cheeks seemed to throb—"get his fat ass out here before her birthday. It's dated Tuesday. Although the handwriting is unsteady, I did recognize it as Justicia's."

"Proving," Ellie said with a chuckle, "that she was still of sound mind, if not body. So what next, Rodney? I'm assuming Miss Justicia labored over a new will, ever mindful of the needs and desires of her adoring grandchildren. Did she send it to you or what?"

"No; she implied that she wished to read it aloud on the occasion of her birthday dinner. One thing she was most curious about was the possibility of setting out conditions in this olographic will. The condition she seemed to find most interesting was to disinherit any heirs not present in Malloy Manor on that occasion."

"Then we don't have to worry about any bastards from Miller's branch," Stanford said. "Let met see if I've got this straight—if Miss Justicia died without writing this new will, then everything's divided between little Caron and me. If she did write it, then nobody knows where it is, so it really doesn't matter either way. Am I right, Spikenard?"

"As an officer of the court, I am obliged to make known that Miss Justicia intended to make an olographic will. A proper search must be conducted, but if it cannot be found, the court will be forced to conclude it does not exist and probate accordingly."

"Hot damn," Stanford said, chortling. "How about a bottle of champagne so we can drink a toast to Miss Justicia Malloy of Malloy Manor?"

Maxie put out her cigarette and clamped her hand around Phoebe's arm. "I think not, Cousin Stanford. Phoebe and I have much to discuss, and we shall do so in private. Mr. Spikenard, it was very kind of you to come to the house. It must have been inconvenient for you, however, and I'm confident that any future conferences can best be conducted in your office."

"I invited him for dinner," Phoebe said, her chin nearly flat against her throat. "Earlier, on the telephone, before . . ."

Stanford grinned. "And why not? How about it, Spike?

Maybe the cook can rustle up some chitlins and blackeyed peas."

"It sounds delightful," Spikenard murmured. He rearranged the contents of his briefcase as Maxie and Phoebe left the room. After a moment, Ellie grabbed Keith and herded him out of the room. Pauline followed silently.

I studied Spikenard as he continued to shift papers and notebooks. His mouth was set in a rigid line, not to prevent an angry retort but to hold in a smile. I'd seen a similar expression only the evening before, when Miss Justicia had dropped her verbal bomb at the dining room table. Then, I'd wondered why the engagement of a new lawyer had amused her. Now I knew.

"Miss Justicia was quite a character," I said. "It's unfortunate that I never had a chance to get to know her. She must have had a . . . capricious sense of humor."

"I would agree," said Spikenard, glancing at me. He closed he briefcase and put it on the floor. "It's fairly obvious she did not warn the family of—shall we say, the extent of my credentials."

"So you went to law school up North," Stanford said. "I find that real interesting. Only last year, I myself had to go to a trade show in New York City, and I was downright scared for my life by the time I left. I stayed at a dumpy little hotel that still cost a bundle, and from my window I could see drug dealers and prostitutes. They didn't even look up when the police drove by. The doorman, a colored fellow like yourself, kept an eye on me. One night, he had to pull me out of a taxi and kinda roll me into the lobby. I gave him a dollar the next morning."

"Oh," Spikenard said wisely. "Now that we've finished with business, perhaps I might have a drink?"

"Sure thing. Any lawyer of my dear, departed mother is always welcome to have a drink in the parlor and dinner in the dining room. You just name your poison, and I'll fix it myself."

Stanford was in such an expansive mood that the drink was liable to end up in Spikenard's lap. I hastily took both glasses and went to the cart. "Allow me, Mr. Spikenard," I said. He admitted to a mild preference for bourbon, and I took the opportunity to do some additional fortifying for myself. "Did you hear about the Baggley murder?" I asked as I sat down.

Spikenard nodded. "It was all over town by noon. The man was somewhat of a fixture at the airport, and left behind a wife and several children, some of whom were actually legitimate."

Stanford stopped gloating long enough to frown at us. "He a colored boy, too? Get hisself knifed in an alley or something?"

"He was shot several times in the head and left in an irrigation ditch on the far side of the airport," said Spikenard. "He was a white boy, about your age, and a taxi driver."

"Isn't that peculiar?" Stanford said as he sat down, although not across the room from the cart by any means. He shook his head solemnly. "I guess we're talking about that fellow from last night, huh? He didn't strike me as the kind to get himself killed, but you never know. Maybe Ellie was correct when she said he was a criminal who was casing the house to burglarize it at a later time. Must have had a falling-out with his partners or something."

Spikenard looked mystified, as well he should have. I explained what had transpired at midnight, which only deepened the creases in his forehead. "What's more," I said, including Stanford, "I think this impostor took several shots at me this morning at the cemetery."

"At the cemetery?" Stanford said, apparently less concerned with my continued well-being than with my itinerary.

"What were you doing out there, Claire? Ellie mentioned that you'd gone off on your own in town somewhere, but she didn't say anything about you going to the cemetery."

Spikenard took a slim gold box from his pocket and lit a cigarette several shades darker than his complexion. "Did you find it of historical significance, Mrs. Malloy?"

"I found more significance in being a target, to tell the truth. It rarely happens, and I'm just not sophisticated enough to laugh it off. The police took it seriously, too."

"I am deeply relieved that you were unharmed," Stanford said. "I feel responsible for you, since you're my baby brother's widow, and I'd be unable to forgive myself if so much as a single hair on your lovely head was disturbed."

"Are you sure he was shooting at you?" asked Spikenard.

"No," I admitted. "I heard gunshots, and something did strike a monument near me. I flung myself behind a vault, and a couple of witnesses frightened him away. All I saw was a flash of yellow; I'm not even sure it was the taxi."

Stanford leaned back, and after a false start, he managed to get his ankle on his knee and give me a speculative look. "So you might have heard something and you might have seen this taxi, right? Have you considered the possibility that you're still so agitated from the recent tragedy that you were imagining things?"

I shook my head, albeit indecisively. "Someone did fire a gun at the cemetery, but he may have been doing so randomly rather than attempting to shoot me." I thought for a moment. "Or merely to frighten me, which he certainly did. He didn't follow me to the cemetery. I would have noticed any cars along the road, which was depressingly flat and empty. Unless Mrs. D'Armand had a rifle concealed in her cane—"

"Say what?" Stanford said, startled enough to slosh part of his drink onto his leg.

"Mrs. D'Armand was with you?" Spikenard asked with a frown.

I tried to envision the elderly woman aiming her cane at me while Spencer steadied her arm. It wouldn't play, not even in the most contorted gothic plot. "When Mrs. D'Armand and her son arrived, the sniper fled," I said. "They left some flowers and offered me a ride back to town. I did some research in the library, and when I went outside, the policemen appeared and brought me back here."

Stanford was wiping at the wetness, but he still caught what he felt to be the pertinent word. "Research?"

I fluttered my eyelashes at him. "Maxie has inspired me to take an interest in the Malloy family history. I hadn't realized what splendid contributions the Malloys have made to the parish, all the way back to General Richmond Malloy."

"Cousin Claire!"

I looked over my shoulder at this suppositional source of inspiration. Everything about her quivered, from her chins to her clenched fists. At best, she could have inspired an apoplectic fit.

"Cousin Claire," she repeated, "I must speak to you immediately."

"Oh, really?" I said.

"It's about your daughter."

Oh, really, I thought as I finished my drink.

11

I accompanied Maxie to the foyer, where a gunmetal gray storm system had rumbled in from the west. Although there was no flicker of lightning, no reverberation of thunder, no smell of ozone in the air, there might as well have been. Caron Malloy stood by the stairs, and she was not a happy child.

Maxie was equally grim. She glowered at Caron, then turned on me. "Do you know where I found your daughter? Do you?" When I admitted that I didn't, she paused for a stifling moment, then jabbed an ornate finger at the ceiling and said, "In the attic. She was in the attic."

"Goodness gracious," I said, "the child's incorrigible. Boarding school's too good for her; reform school's the only solution. A few years on bread and water and she'll mend her wicked ways."

Caron failed to appreciate my wit. "I wasn't Doing Anything, Mother. I was just messing around up there so I wouldn't be exposed to these people while in my impressionable teenage years." She stuck out her lower lip at Maxie. "Besides, there's not a lock on the door or a sign that says to stay out."

"Furthermore," Maxie continued, caught up in her self-imposed role of prosecuting attorney (and if she prevailed, executioner), "she was playing with some of the family's most treasured heirlooms. Playing, mind you. I was appalled."

"Well, since she's likely to be an heir," I said, shrugging, "she ought to be allowed to play with the looms."

Caron gave me a shocked look. "I am?"

"We'll discuss it later." To Maxie, I said, "Okay, what exactly was she doing in the attic?"

"She was playing . . . with the dolls." She narrowly missed a capital letter or two in the pronouncement, which clearly was intended to horrify me. I waited politely. "The dolls have china heads, and many of them are more than one hundred fifty years old. Those of us with knowledge of antiques realize the value of these heads is incredible, yet this girl was using them to stage a tea party." Her ensuing shudder jangled most of her jewelry.

Caron was devastated with embarrassment at having been caught in such an activity. Her ears were pink and her cheeks scarlet. The pimple on her chin pulsated. Her lower lip was well beyond the tip of her nose and headed for a personal-best record. Refusing to meet my eyes, she said, "I wasn't playing with them. I arranged them to create a historical setting."

"Is this where you were yesterday afternoon?" I asked. I did so without a hint of mockery or amusement in my voice, thus earning a plus mark on the maternal tally card.

"So what?" she said, flopping down on the bottom step.

Phoebe came down the stairs, a spiral notebook in her hand, and flipped to a page covered with squiggly pencil marks. "I'm so glad I thought to bring along the appraisal figures. One of the Rohmer dolls had been appraised at over five thousand dollars—in mint condition, that is. Once chip or scratch and the value decreases dramatically."

Maxie clutched at her heart. "I didn't stop to examine them. When I chanced upon this child rooting through the trunk in which the dolls are stored, it was all I could do to restrain myself."

"I wasn't rooting," the accused said sullenly.

Maxie was unswayed. "I saw you rooting."

Ellie came out of the library. "What are we rooting for? The olographic will? If it'll help us find it, I'll gladly lead a few rounds of hip-hip's and hoorays."

"This is hardly the time for levity, Cousin Ellie," Phoebe said. "There is a possibility that Cousin Caron has damaged valuable antiques."

"Half of them are hers," Ellie said as she sat down beside Caron and patted her knee. "If Daddy dies anytime soon, I'll make sure you get all the toys, little cousin, along with the house and furniture and any other souvenirs your heart desires. The dull ol' money will suit me just fine."

"What is she talking about?" Caron asked me. She had recovered from her initial discomfiture, and I could see tiny little dollar signs glinting in her eyes as she began to piece together the references to her status. Her eyes were as green as I'd ever seen them. Mint green, that is—and not the kind of mint one puts in juleps.

"I shall return to the attic to examine the dolls," Maxie said. "For the child's sake, I hope there's been no chippage."

Ellie clapped her hands. "Oooh, let's all go together. I haven't been up there for years, but I seem to remember all these old trunks filled with funky clothes. I used to spend hours and hours up there on rainy afternoons." She fluffed back her hair and gave us a view of her profile. "It's what inspired me to follow a career in the theater, dahlings."

Maxie and Phoebe were stomping up the stairs. As Caron, Ellie, and I followed them, I said, "I thought you worked for a television station."

"I do, but I'm hardly the weather girl. The noon talk show, commercials, and for a fleeting time, the star of Peppy the Clown's Cartoon Circus. I think one of the requirements for the children to be on the show was a yucky nose. It was dreadful, but at the same time very challenging."

"I'm sure it was," I murmured.

We arrived at the second floor, and in parade formation, went past the portraits and bedroom doors to a door at the end of the corridor. It was open, and beyond it was a steep flight of narrow wooden steps. Our footsteps echoed noisily, as did acidic remarks about the age of the dolls and the consequences of chippage.

The attic was an interesting arrangement of angles and recesses. The main room was large, with two alleys leading to filth-encrusted windows. A second room, partially visible behind a rack of clothes, appeared to be a newspaper burial ground. Trunks and cardboard boxes were stacked haphazardly, some listing and others reduced to shadowy rubble. Hatboxes formed slender columns, suitcases more substantial barriers along the walls. Chairs with splintery seats were crowded next to three-legged tables and drawerless dressers. The only light came from a bulb at the end of a cord; its pale glow reminded me of the moonlight that had made the backyard a surreal stage for Miss Justicia's death.

In the middle of a cleared area was a child's table, with four chairs populated by unblinking, unsmiling (and I dearly prayed, unscathed) dolls dressed in ruffled gowns. In front of the dolls were mismatched cups and saucers, and in the center of the table was a vase with a handful of droopy flowers.

"Oh, dear," Maxie groaned as she and Phoebe bent over the dolls. "This one is the Rohmer, isn't it?" She continued to mutter as they examined each hard china head for scratches.

Caron watched the scene with her arms folded, her expression flat. Only a person with a death wish would have commented on the childishly charming scene.

I did risk a closer look, however, and let out a whoosh of surprise. Pulling Caron to a corner, I whispered, "Where did you find that decanter?"

"Don't start on me," she said coldly. "I've had more than enough people howling at me already. Besides, I haven't the faintest idea what you're talking about, and, in any case, I don't appreciate—"

"The vase on the table. Where'd you find it?"

"The old glass thing? It was cracked, and someone had thrown it away. I didn't steal it from the china hutch, Mother. Despite what Some People say, I'm not some sort of criminal. How was I supposed to know those dolls are worth zillions of dollars? Personally, I think they're pathetically old-fashioned, especially in those dreary, moth-eaten clothes. Barbie wouldn't be caught dead in an outfit like that!"

"Where did you find it?" I persisted.

"In the yard, if you must know. It was half-buried in the leaves under a bush by the library window. But it was broken, so I really don't see what the big deal is."

All this sibilant murmuring had attracted the attention of the other three, who were now staring at Caron and me.

"Something is broken?" Maxie said in a tight voice, no doubt gripped by the specter of a plummeting value. "What else has this dear little cousin put her hands on?"

I shook my head. "Caron found something that was already broken, and brought it up here to hold flowers."

Ellie squatted beside the table. "Would you look at this! It's the brandy decanter from Miss Justicia's room, or a damn good replica. Where did Caron find it?"

"Outside Miss Justicia's room, in the shrubbery," I said.

Maxie squatted next to Ellie, although it clearly was more of a physical challenge. "It's cracked," she said grimly, "and there's some sort of brownish stain. Isn't this . . . ?"

Phoebe flipped open the ubiquitous notebook. "Yes, Waterford, valued at three hundred fifty dollars, perhaps more in a private sale. Now, of course, it's worthless."

"I didn't break it," Caron said, inching backward until she bumped into a moose head. "I was wandering around outside this morning, and the sun happened to catch it at just the right angle. I had to crawl under a bush to get it. Otherwise, no one would have found it for years and years."

Ellie reached out to pick it up, but I lunged forward and caught her wrist at the last second. "Don't touch it," I said. "The stain may be blood. The police need to send it to a lab."

"Blood?" gasped Ellie, jerking her hand free and cradling it. "Why would there be blood? Whose blood?"

Maxie struggled to an upright stance. "I think some of us are being overly imaginative, and not for the first time. If the decanter was lying on the ground, then it's only reasonable to assume the brownish material is dirt. I realize that's not nearly as exhilarating as blood, but we mustn't allow ourselves to be swept up in some dramatic concoction. Put down your notebook, Phoebe. Cousin Claire may indulge in her little fantasies, but we have work to do. We need to rewrap the dolls in tissue paper and pack them away where they'll be safe from sunlight and moths, not to mention children who seem to have inherited a propensity for meddling."

"Touch the table and your value will be zero," I said. "I'm going downstairs to call the police. This time, I'll demand an investigation of what happened last night, if I have to call the governor's office. Those two so-called officers will return. They'll send the decanter to the nearest laboratory, where the stain can be analyzed and the surfaces examined for fingerprints."

Ellie sat back and stared up at me. Her expression was as stunned as Pauline's had been when we'd pulled the body from the bayou, and her voice was devoid of any hint of a drawl. "I don't understand what you're saying. Do you think this has something to do with Miss Justicia's death? How could it?"

Despite my history of brilliant deductions and piercing insights into criminal activity, I was totally baffled. "I don't know, Ellie. The decanter was in Miss Justicia's room last night when Pauline prepared her for bed. When the taxi driver showed up at midnight, Pauline looked in on Miss Justicia and mentioned that the decanter was no longer on the night table. This morning, Caron found it outside the window, broken and buried in the leaves."

Maxie gave me the smile she undoubtedly conferred on those who failed to meet the Mayflower Society's rigorous membership requirements. "And you find this puzzling, Cousin Claire? I do not. I think it's evident that Miss Justicia consumed the contents of the decanter, and then threw it out the window. As averse as I am to speaking ill of the dead, I've seen a lot of broken glass and porcelain in Malloy Manor. Whenever Miss Justicia felt the slightest bit vexed, she was apt to vent her frustrations on nearby inanimate objects." Her smile faded, and she paused to wipe away a trace of wetness beneath her eye. "There was in the dining room at one time an exquisite Ming vase, its value astronomical. It was shattered beyond repair when the Brussels sprouts were served without butter."

"Let's stick to the point," I said, unmoved by the account of the tragedy. "Caron said she found the decanter next to the house. It seems more probable that someone dropped it out the window." I held out my hand and opened and closed my thumb and index finger. "Like this."

"Why?" demanded Ellie.

"How should I know?" I curled the same finger at Maxie and Phoebe. "We're all going downstairs together. You may rewrap the dolls after the police have collected the decanter. In the interim, no one will be left up here to tamper with what may be evidence."

Maxie came over to me and leaned forward until I could feel her breath on my face. "You seem oddly determined to wash the family's dirty linen in public, Cousin Claire. Miss Justicia had a drinking problem; that fact is inescapable and may have been a topic of gossip in the parish. However, there is no need to force each and every tawdry incident into the limelight. Miss Justicia finished the brandy and discarded the decanter, no doubt experiencing a twinge of malicious pleasure when she heard it break." She mimicked my gesture. "Like this."

"We must keep in mind that Miss Justicia was a Malloy by marriage," Phoebe said, "although she and her husband were distantly related. Very distantly, that is."

I wasn't sure if that constituted a vindication or a condemnation, but I wasn't interested in finding out which it was. "I am oddly determined, aren't I?" I said to Maxie, although I was frowning to myself alone. "There are some inconsistencies, but I'm not sure exactly what they are."

"What are you doing?" said a voice from behind me.

I spun around. Pauline had stopped partway up the stairs, and only her head was visible. The rest of her body was lost in the darkness, and to put it mildly, this disembodiment was unnerving. I managed a shaky laugh. "Come join us, Pauline. We've discovered something that might have a bearing on Miss Justicia's death."

She floated up the stairs, a handkerchief in her hands and an unnaturally somber expression on her long, pale face. "Why did you come to the attic? You have no business here. This is where the family has hidden its secrets for a hundred years."

"Are we just a little bit too gothic?" Caron murmured, rolling her eyes in case any of us missed the rhetorical overtones of her remark. She then turned her back on us and began to stroke the moose's nose.

"Don't be absurd," Maxie said briskly. "The attic is a treasure trove of memorabilia and insights into the family history. Rather than secrets, there are wonderful photo albums and boxes of letters and documents that must be carefully studied for inclusion in the parish annals."

"And quite a few very good antiques," Phoebe added.

"Why are you here?" Pauline repeated.

Caron glanced over her shoulder. "Why are we *still* here is a better question, Mother. Don't you have a telephone call to make?"

Ellie stood up and brushed the dust off her knees. "I agree. Isn't it about time for dinner?"

I studied the group. Caron was feigning fascination with the moose's marble eyes and flared nostrils. Maxie and Phoebe were hovering above the table, as if protecting the dolls from further outrage upon their appraised value. Pauline was straight out of an early Hitchcock movie—a composition in black and gray.

"Yes, let's go," I announced with the chipper but nevertheless dictatorial authority of a tour guide. I waited by the top stairs until each of them had descended, then looked back at the brandy decanter and the sad assembly around it. The dolls were not toys; their faces were as sour and accusatory as the ancestors decorating the walls below. It was difficult to imagine a pigtailed child cuddling them, whispering to them, even daring to give them frivolous names. No, I thought as I went downstairs, they seemed much more comfortable in their roles as guardians of what might be a murder weapon.

With the exception of Caron, the others had continued downstairs. She was waiting for me in the middle of the hallway, trying to look defiant but not succeeding.

"Did you change the reservations?" she asked.

"We leave at four o'clock Monday afternoon," I said. "I'm sorry if this messes up your plans with Inez, dear. It's not my idea of a good time, either, but you and I have an obligation to your father to represent him at his mother's funeral."

"I know," she said, sighing. "Dad wasn't like these people, was he? He didn't sit around like a vulture, hoping someone would die so he could get money?"

I leaned against the banister. "No, not at all. There were some aspects of his upbringing that he couldn't shake loose. He could never quite relax, or stop feeling as if everyone was judging him and finding him inadequate. It caused him to . . . do things to combat his own sense of worthlessness."

"Like have affairs with his students?"

Her face was obscured by shadows, but I could see unblinking eyes and an unsmiling mouth. I tried to find the right words, but perhaps there weren't any. "The girls in his classes were young and pretty, and they let him know they were eager to idolize him."

"And you didn't."

I considered flinging myself over the banister and allowing gravity to end the conversation. "No, I didn't," I said evenly. "We were adults. Carlton needed a certain amount of nurturing he didn't get from Miss Justicia, but I wanted a relationship between equals—not between parent and child."

"What about Peter? Is he adult enough for you?"

"Possibly, although I have some doubts that our relationship will ever evolve to the point of anything permanent. Are you worried about it?"

"No," she said, opening the bedroom door. "I'm going to be so rich that it won't matter what you and Peter do. I may go to a snooty boarding school in Switzerland. I'll come home during vacations and try not to snicker at Rhonda Maguire's pitiful attempts to speak French."

She disappeared inside the room.

I rubbed my forehead and wondered how I'd failed, when I'd failed, or if I'd failed. Conversations with Caron had the consistency of jellyfish, along with the potential for painful stings. After a few more minutes of futile introspection, I went down to the foyer.

"Here you are!" Stanford said from the parlor doorway. "Rodney and I were beginning to worry about you. I was in the midst of telling him about a real smart colored boy who works in the Pritty Kitty Kollar division, when everybody came tromping down the stairs. Nobody would tell me what was going on, but they sure were acting strange."

I told him what we'd found in the attic, ignored his sputters, and went into the library to call the police. Officers Dewberry and Puccoon were following up on a report of a yellow taxi, I was told, but would come to the house sooner or later. I suspected it would be later.

Dinner was dismal, of course. Everyone straggled in, including Caron and the often-elusive Keith, and said little as we tackled blackened meat of some sort and canned vegetables. Maxie kept an eye on Rodney Spikenard, or at least on his silverware. Stanford's jokes were received without smiles, and his attempts to interest us in his plans for expanding the family business met frosty stares.

Caron put down her napkin. "I've absolutely got to call Inez," she said to me, then left before I could offer any observations about long-distance bills.

Rodney carefully folded his napkin and placed it alongside the silverware, all of which was visible. "I realized the family is in shock over Miss Justicia's untimely demise. I hope my presence has not caused any . . . problem."

"Not at all," Maxie said, gazing over his head. She lit a cigarette and slumped back in her chair. Beside her, Phoebe managed a small smile.

"I hate to see you run," Ellie said, "but you might have a jollier time at the morgue. One little question, if you don't mind. How long do we have to find this olographic will?"

"I must consult Mr. D'Armand about the intricacies of the trust before anything can be done. And the process of probate is lengthy and often delayed."

Ellie shot her father a dark look. "So how much are we talking about, Rodney?"

"Generally, the principal of the trust is the net principal after payment of administration expenses, death taxes, any outstanding debts, and funeral and burial expenses. I've not yet had a current accounting from Mr. D'Armand, so it would be improper for me to speculate at this time."

"But we're talking big bucks, aren't we?" Stanford demanded, utilizing his napkin to wipe his damp face.

"I must repeat what I told you earlier," Spikenard said as he pushed back his chair and rose. "At this time, that question would be more appropriately put to Mr. D'Armand. As probation commences, I will have a complete record of the assets and liabilities of the trust. I'll certainly keep you informed of the situation."

I followed Spikenard down the hallway and caught up with him in the foyer. "I'd like to ask you something," I said.

"I've already said numerous times that I don't have the answers. I can't do anything until I get the records. Even then, it will take time to study them and organize the information."

He picked up his briefcase. "I'm on my way to my office now to call D'Armand."

I went out the door with him, in much the same fashion as a burr on his trouser leg (and as welcome as one). "That's not what I wanted to ask."

"Yes, then?" he said wearily.

"You mentioned Miller Malloy," I said. "He's been dead for thirty years, and, according to his obituary, was survived by only his parents, two brothers, and a few stray cousins. There was no mention of a wife or child."

"No, I don't suppose there would be."

"Then why did you bring up the name? Did Miss Justicia tell you something that led you to believe Miller didn't die in Vietnam?"

He edged away from me but was forced to stop when his back met the railing. "No, on the contrary, she showed me a copy of the official death certificate issued by the U.S. Army and dated December of 1960." His smile glinted in the darkness, and his voice dropped to a husky whisper. "Although she never said she thought he was haunting the manor, maybe she heard rattling chains and creaking footsteps in the basement. Why don't you and the others conduct a séance?"

I felt my face flush with anger. I am not easily provoked, but when I am, I've been told the Surgeon General should issue a warning. "Mr. Spikenard, this is not the time for jokes. Miss Justicia died last night—either accidentally or with someone's assistance. This morning, someone shot at me, and I didn't care for it. These people are beginning to suffocate in their greed, including my daughter, who's packing for Switzerland! I am sick and tired of this whole mess." I advanced on him until I could poke him in the chest. I did so with unnecessary vigor. "However, I am going to sort it out and figure out what happened. Do not underestimate me, Mr. Spikenard."

He did not applaud, but he did have enough sense to get the smile off his face before I did it for him. "My apologies, Mrs. Malloy. What Miss Justicia told me about her eldest son is covered by client-attorney confidentiality, and I would be risking both my license and my self-respect if I repeated it to you. It is possible that Mr. D'Armand might offer enlightenment. The Malloy family files are still at his office, and he might be willing to allow you to look through them for particular documents."

Rodney Spikenard fled to a modest sedan and drove away.

12

I stayed on the porch for a long while, reluctant to go back inside Malloy Manor and face the family. At one point, I went around the corner and studied the shrubs below the library window, but the sound of Caron's insufferably gleeful voice informing Inez of her newly acquired wealth was as much the cause of my indigestion as the food served at dinner.

The discovery of the brandy decanter was a contributor, too. If it had blood on it, and if the blood was Miss Justicia's, then whoever had wielded it then brought it back from the bayou and buried it in the leaves beneath the window. It would seem much easier to toss it in the bayou, where eventually it would sink into the silt . . . if we were not supposed to find it. If we were (this in itself a poser), then why hide it?

The pseudo-driver was the only person downstairs when we'd heard the wheelchair in the yard. Ellie had told me she'd found him asleep on a sofa, and it was possible he'd dozed through the ensuing events. Before he vanished, that is.

My foray into inductive logic was swampier than the bayou, and I reluctantly dismissed it as the ravings of a semistarved gothic heroine. Fully expecting to see a ghostly general on a translucent steed, I sat down on the swing and dejectedly told myself this lapse into lunacy would pass when I had put a reasonable distance between myself and Malloy Manor. Many hundred miles, for instance.

Neither General Richmond Malloy nor Ronald Colman was doing any haunting, but Miller Malloy was stirring up more than his fair share of trouble from the marble vault in the corner of the cemetery. I reminded myself that he was as dead as the General and Mr. Colman. Miss Justicia had shown the death certificate to Rodney Spikenard. I'd seen the brass plaque and read the obituary.

No one inside the house would give me any information. Spikenard had suggested I speak to Bethel D'Armand, who'd choked on his coffee when I mentioned the name. He had not refused to discuss him, though; Ellie had interrupted us and seized the conversation.

I could pace on the porch or I could do something that might alleviate at least a part of my perplexity. I could not, on the other hand, use the telephone to find out if D'Armand were willing to talk to me, unless I waited *a contracoeur* until Caron finished describing, *à haute voix,* her proposed revenge on Rhonda Maguire. *Celui qui veut, peut* (idiomatically: Where there's a will, there's a way).

Glancing over my shoulder every step or so, I went to Ellie's car and ascertained that the key was in the ignition. Surely she wouldn't mind if I was to borrow the car for a brief visit, I told myself without conviction. She and other deposed heirs were busy searching nooks and crannies for granny's will. With a final furtive glance, I got in the car and located necessities like the clutch, shift, headlight control, and brake. I then proceeded to steal the car and sedately drive to LaRue.

The library was closed, as were most of the stores along the main street. Undaunted, I stopped at a convenience store. I found a telephone directory and looked up Bethel D'Armand's office address, purchased sustenance of little nutritional worth to sustain us until our flight, and asked for directions.

A few minutes later, I parked in front of a clapboard house on a side street. The shingle was more of a sign, but it confirmed that Bethel D'Armand, Attorney at Law, conducted business within the premises between the hours of nine and five.

Lights were on in the front room. It was decidely after business hours, but I went up the walk and into an attractive reception room that was devoid of a receptionist, attractive or otherwise. The door to a second room was closed, but light shone from beneath it and I heard a male voice.

A scrupulous visitor would knock and politely announce her presence. I crept to the door and strained to hear more clearly what was being said in D'Armand's private office.

"Just throw a few things in a bag," D'Armand was saying, "and stop worrying. We don't know what the weather will be like, and we can pick up whatever we need when we get there."

I waited for a response, but D'Armand reiterated his suggestion and then fell silent. It was not necessary to let him know I'd been eavesdropping, I decided, especially when I'd heard nothing meritous of the minor breach of etiquette. I returned to the front door, stealthily opened it, and then banged it closed.

"Mr. D'Armand?" I called loudly and ever so politely. "It's Claire Malloy."

In the ensuing lull, I heard a mutter that hinted of his disinclination to receive visitors, but he opened his door and came into the reception room with a smile.

"Why, Mrs. Malloy, what a fascinating surprise to find you here. I was just tying up a few loose ends at a time when I didn't expect to be interrupted." His smile widened, but I was feeling the same arctic breeze I'd felt in the café. "Even though I'm pretty much retired, I still have some clients wanting me to handle minor affairs for them."

I gazed past him at his office door. "I can imagine how irritating it must be to have clients dropping by on a Saturday night."

"What?" he said, looking genuinely puzzled. "No, there's no one else here. I was doing paperwork, and I'd be delighted to take a break. Please, come sit in here and let me offer you coffee or a taste of some fine Kentucky bourbon nearly as old as I am."

His office was befittingly masculine and tastefully decorated with a mahogany desk, leather chairs, bookshelves, and a globe. On the walls hung examples of that which is the epitome of southern macho decor: framed prints of ducks. He waited until I was seated, then took a bottle and glasses from a drawer.

"To what do I owe the honor of your visit?" he said as he handed me a glass and sat down on the far side of the desk.

"To be blunt, Mr. D'Armand, I'm confused," I said with a rueful look meant to elicit avuncular sympathy. "Caron and I arrived at Malloy Manor only yesterday afternoon, and since then, it's been a nightmare." A more skilled actress, such as Ellie, could have produced silver tears; the best I could do was a sniffle. "I hardly had a chance to meet Miss Justicia before she was killed in that tragic accident. Poor Caron is so distraught that she's taken to hiding in the attic."

"Is that so?" D'Armand said dryly, unaffected by the performance. "By the way, I had a call from young Spikenard half an hour ago. He said he'd been out to the house to explain what he could and to have dinner with you all."

"Such a bright young man."

"Oh, yes, a bright young man."

It was evident I lacked even primitive talent in theatrics. "Okay," I said, "he suggested that I ask you about Miller Malloy, and that's why I'm here. My husband never once mentioned an older brother, and the others in the family make odd little noises when they hear the name. But I've been to the cemetery."

"So I heard," he said.

"From Mrs. D'Armand?"

He laughed. "She mentioned it at dinner, but you're underestimating the interest generated by a new face in a small town. The ol' boys in front of the barbershop were still discussing your motives when Ellie and I left the café."

I saw no reason to acknowledge that we both knew I'd lied. "I went to the library, too, and his obituary was published in the newspaper. What's the deal with Miller?"

"The deal with Miller?" He thought for a minute, his eyes drifting beneath the bristly white eyebrows, then said, "I suppose I would have to admit he was a black sheep. Hardly the first in the family, to be sure. Old Richmond was rumored to have had a string of mistresses, despite his less than captivating appearance. There's a legend that his wife went crazy and chopped up one of them in a shack across the bayou. Miss Justicia caused tongues to wag for decades. More recently, there are some titillating stories afoot about Stanford's expensive lady friend in New Orleans."

"Let's talk about Miller. What did he do to have his particular leaf yanked off the family tree?"

"He sowed some wild oats, and then, with encouragement from his parents, joined the army." D'Armand glanced at the antique captain's clock on the bookshelf. "Mrs. Malloy, if you'll excuse me, I need to make one quick call. Afterward, if you're really determined to fret about Miller, I'll tell you in

169

more detail which oats he sowed and where he chose to sow 'em."

"I'd appreciate it," I said.

He picked up a briefcase and went into the reception room. The conversation was inaudible from my chair, and I was making too much progress to risk further eavesdropping. I heard D'Armand replace the receiver, and I was preparing a compliment on the bourbon when a door closed somewhere in the house. Seconds later, a car door slammed. An engine came to life, purred noisily, and then receded.

In that I was loathe to jump to any conclusions, I waited a solid five seconds before I went into the reception room. It and the storage room beyond it were uninhabited, and the gravel parking lot behind the house was empty.

I returned to his office and sat down to contemplate the novelty of the situation. He was gone, but I had no idea if he'd run an errand or run away. The latter seemed more likely, since he'd been alluding to travel arrangements earlier. But he hadn't popped in to say good-bye, which was less than gallant of him, even if he was a lawyer.

I decided to give him fifteen minutes, and took a legal tome from the shelf. It was more entertaining than the fine print on airline tickets, but most of it was cloaked in the convoluted jargon favored by the profession. They did so out of self-preservation; if the law was comprehensible to reasonably literate people, we'd be more likely to take Shakespeare's advice concerning its practitioners.

The *wherewithins* and *wheretofores* eventually lost their appeal. I replaced the book and looked around for less erudite reading matter. Along the wall behind the desk were a dozen cartons, each sealed and neatly marked with the word *Malloy*. Once again, the issue of scrupulosity reared its head. I was a Malloy, but most likely not (or most definitely not) the particular Malloy on the cartons. Then again, my daughter had a legitimate concern in the status of the family financial situation.

It took me another five seconds to resolve this minor moral dilemma. I sat down in D'Armand's chair and opened the nearest carton.

Nearly an hour later, I was lamenting my lack of knowledge of trusts. My eyes were aching, and occasional clouds of dust from antiquated files had kept me sneezing most of the time. The Malloy trust seemed to require numerous ledgers, along with the retainment of every tax document, receipt, inventory, appraisal, invoice, petition, certificate, and yellowed paper with any sort of print/signature.

I reached the penultimate carton before I found a file with Miller's name on it. It was less bulky than the others through which I'd blindly stumbled. I put the ledgers on the floor, pushed stacks of folders aside, and opened the file.

The first paper was a photocopy of his death certificate—the date as expected. A second photocopy was of a letter from Miller's commanding officer, expressing sympathy and praising his valor. It occurred to me I was working through the file in the wrong direction, and flipped to the bottom paper. It was not the record of his birth but, rather, the documentation of his first entanglement with the police.

It did not describe unspeakably vile acts, however. At the tender age of sixteen, Miller had been caught in the possession of a six-pack of beer. He'd been fined twenty-five dollars. I moved on, as he had done. There were several other arrest reports, none for anything more serious than speeding, partying at a bayou, again possessing beer, and a final report of an altercation outside a bar. Misdemeanor charges had been dismissed.

None of it qualified him as a hardened criminal, nor did the next document, his enlistment contract. I was rapidly approaching the photocopies at the end of the file, and all I'd learned was that Miller had required the services of a lawyer a few times and that his father had been billed by the hour.

I was ready to acknowledge defeat and allow Miller to rest in peace when I found the letter. It was written on a piece of notebook paper, and although the handwriting was unexceptional, its content was enough to elicit an abrupt inhalation. The date indicated it was written on June 23, 1960. In the event of Miller's death, D'Armand was to locate Miller's child and see that he or she received the proceeds of a life-insurance policy and any accrued benefits from the army. The final sentence warned D'Armand not to inform anyone of the letter or any actions taken because of it. Miller's signature was a scrawl, but I could identify enough of the letters to confirm it.

I turned it over, hoping for an elaboration. The page was blank, and there was nothing else in the file concerning "he or she." I resisted the urge to fling the whole thing into the air. Miller had fathered a child, gender unknown, mother unnamed. He had written what qualified as an olographic will.

The only person who could enlighten me had departed for a place where the weather was apt to be unlike that of downtown LaRue, or the surrounding parish.

I refolded the letter and put it back where I'd found it, then replaced the file in its carton. I restored everything else as best I could, turned off the light, and went to the reception room. Neither Bethel D'Armand nor his receptionist had returned. I was heading for the door with the telephone rang. To say it startled me would be an understatement; I reacted as if it had fired a bullet at me.

It blithely continued to ring, and I finally went back to the desk, took a deep breath, and picked up the receiver.

"Bethel, it's nearly ten o'clock," said a woman's voice. I recognized it from an earlier encounter. The recognition, regrettably, did not give me any clues how best to respond.

"Did you hear me? Why don't you answer me?" she continued, her pitch rising.

"He's not here," I said. It wasn't inspired, but at least it was true.

"Who is this?"

"It's Claire Malloy, Mrs. D'Armand. I came to your husband's office to ask him a few questions."

"But you said he's not there. Where is he?"

"I don't know. He made a call about an hour ago, and then left without saying anything to me."

"He left an hour ago? Where did he go? Why are you still there?"

They were reasonable questions, I admitted to myself as I desperately tried to fabricate answers that would not implicate me too severely. I finally settled for evasion. "I've been waiting for him to come back. It's getting rather late, however, and I think I'd better return to the house. Shall I leave a note for him to call you?"

"I do not think so, Mrs. Malloy," she said, then hung up.

I left the light on in the front room and went out to Ellie's car. D'Armand had not been discussing luggage with his wife earlier, nor had he informed her of an impromptu business trip. For his sake, I hoped he had a compelling explanation when he returned. If he returned, I amended as I drove back through LaRue.

Once I was on the highway, I chose a moderate speed and let myself consider what I now knew about Miller Malloy. He'd had some minor skirmishes with the law and then enlisted in the military—with encouragement from his parents. The siring of an illegitimate child was probable cause for said encouragement.

The letter was noticeably lacking in details. Miller presumed D'Armand could locate the child; this implied the scandal was local. Ergo, the mother was local. There was no evidence in the file that D'Armand had followed Miller's instructions.

Which meant, I thought as I groped for the lever to turn the headlights on bright, nothing. D'Armand might not have been able to find the mother and child, or he might have followed the instructions impeccably but excluded any telltale papers from the file. Or the child had not survived.

But if the child had survived, he or she would be approximately thirty years old. He or she would be a direct descent of Miss Justicia and entitled to one-third of the estate. He or she would not be popular. Stanford was counting on half of the proceeds. Maxie might have to make an addition to the family tree, with a notation that would not enhance her status in the Mayflower Society. Keith, Ellie, and Phoebe would have a new cousin with whom to contend, as would Caron Malloy.

I hadn't stopped to consider how Caron and I would deal with whatever she received from the estate—particularly if it involved a lot of money. Although our lifestyle would never be the subject of a television show, we survived off the bookstore. There were periods of relative famine, when microwavable entrées were replaced by boxed macaroni and canned soup. We shopped at the discount store, but we also shopped at the mall when I was courageous enough to withstand the sanitized music and the piranhas with their plastic cards. To her eloquently vocalized disgust, she was allowed to augment her allowance by working at the bookstore, and in rare moments of desperation, she did.

But now she was rapidly becoming a greedy green monster. I made a mental note to warn her that probate could take years, especially when several members of the family would contest the intestacy. The legal fees would diminish the estate, radically. Rodney Spikenard might be the only one to realize any profit from the sordid business.

Because, I thought as I dimmed the lights for an oncoming car, he had not written out Miss Justicia's new will. He'd said the reason fell into the realm of client-attorney confidentiality.

Headlights flashed in my rearview mirror, banishing any potential blossoming theories. Annoyed, I slowed down and pulled to the right side of the lane to allow the car to pass me. It was only a gesture, in that the highway ahead of me was devoid of oncoming traffic. "Get on with it," I said irritably.

The headlights continued to blind me. They'd drifted to the right, too, and seemed closer. Feeling as if a dragon were bearing down on me, I decelerated even more and pulled farther to the right until I was partially on the shoulder.

The car behind me did the same. I'd been confused for the last day and a half, and my confusion had deepened in the last several hours. I was not brain-dead, however, and I had a fairly decent idea who was driving the car. Not who, I corrected myself with a grimace. It was the color of the car that was not challenging to surmise, and if it wasn't yellow, then I wasn't hyperventilating while driving down a deserted highway in a stolen Jaguar.

While being chased by a stolen taxi.

A glance in the mirror confirmed my theory. I couldn't think how far away the driveway of the house was. Ellie had made the trip in less time than it takes to plan one's memorial service, but I'd driven to LaRue slowly, and had been returning at the same speed.

And what was he—whoever he was—planning to do? I wasn't going to park at the side of the road, roll down the window, and wait for him to approach the car. If he wanted to follow me to New Orleans, the night was young and he was welcome to try it. It occurred to me it might be prudent to move away from the shoulder. I was assisted by a sudden jolt to the bumper. The steering wheel jerked to one side, but I clenched my hands and steadied it.

"You'd better watch it!" I growled, then clamped my lips together and considered what to do. He wasn't going to wait for me to park, nor was he interested in a marathon chase to the Gulf of Mexico. Instead, it seemed he'd selected the less time-consuming approach of running me off the road.

Shivering, I accelerated as much as I dared. Whenever the headlights closed in, I swerved across the lanes, tapped the brake lights, and in general tried to discourage him. He seemed to interpret my behavior as playfulness. Unless I was willing to continue this unpleasant game, I needed to take some sort of definitive action.

I risked taking a hand off the wheel long enough to tilt the rearview mirror and wipe away an accumulation of sweat. Heroines weren't supposed to sweat in gothic novels, I told myself with a hint of hysteria. Or in traditional mysteries, for that matter. As I drove at a dizzying speed, dodging a maniac in a yellow cab, I tried to think of a fictional ploy that might be useful.

I really couldn't attack him with a knitting needle or a brolly, unless I intended to get within striking range. I couldn't cluck at him and tell him how he reminded me of the vicar's younger brother. I couldn't disarm him with cookies, or even flee across the countryside on a camel.

Clearly, I'd been reading the wrong genre. If I'd forced myself to study the hard-boiled private eyes of both sexes, I'd now have some ideas how to rid myself of the problem.

The problem took it upon himself to remind me of his presence by ramming the bumper. I veered toward the shoulder, veered the opposite way until I crossed the median, and forced myself to drive even faster. I also called him several names more suitable to the latter genre as we sped past the entrance to the driveway that led to Malloy Manor.

In front of me lay a flat black stretch of nothingness. No cars had appeared from either direction since the taxi first loomed on my bumper. The house was behind me, and my distance from it was increasing at more than a mile per minute. At this speed, I told myself with a fierce scowl, we would be out of the parish before too long and on our way into the great unknown.

The headlights tried to engulf me. I bit my lip and put the pedal to the floor. The car leapt forward as if it had been goosed, a reasonably accurate analogy; I clung to the wheel and warned myself not to look at the speedometer.

LaRue was behind us, but I realized the airport was ahead of us. It was not my haven of choice. I could not expect to find a heavily guarded marine base, however, so I started trying to read the signs that materialized and vanished within seconds.

I finally saw the dusty green sign. I adjusted the rearview mirror long enough to determine I had a hundred feet on the taxi, braked abruptly, and squealed into the road that curved toward a low brick building. It wasn't La Guardia, by any means, but the lights were on and a few cars were moving.

I halted at the end of a sidewalk that led to double glass doors, grabbed the key, and sprinted for the interior. Once I was on the side of the door that I preferred, I looked back for the taxi. I didn't know if he'd turned on the airport road, but he hadn't continued to the building.

The decor here was less charming than in D'Armand's office, but I felt a rush of fondness for the harsh white lights, rows of plastic chairs, metal trash containers, and even the bored women behind the car rental counters. Based on their expressions, they were not as thrilled by my presence, nor were the clerks at the airline counters, nor was the custodian pushing a mop across the floor.

The lights above the airline counters went off at the same

time, and the clerks went through doors behind them. One of the car rental agents announced it was eleven o'clock, and before I could realize what was happening, they, too, exited. La Guardia might buzz and hum twenty-four hours a day. Here, the runways were being rolled up for the night. The lovely white lights were going out one by one; the employees were going out the doors in droves.

The custodian, an elderly black man in a khaki jumpsuit, shot me an incurious look as he aimed his mop at a discolored circle in front of a plastic plant. I myself would have been more curious about the entrance of a pale and harried woman, nevertheless becoming, who'd skittered inside the airport as it closed for the night and now seemed resolved to stand by the door on a permanent basis.

"I'm lockin' up in five minutes," he said as he attacked the circle. "Ain't no more planes tonight, comin' or goin'."

This dashed my hopes of hopping on the next plane to Farberville, or to anyplace else. The only car visible was Ellie's, but this did not preclude a yellow taxi parked along the road. I'd drawn the attentions of a psycho or two in the past, but this guy seemed to have dedicated his days and nights to insinuating himself in my affairs in a most unpleasant manner.

"Got to lock the door shortly," the custodian said. The mop was in the bucket, and the floor as pristine as it would ever be. He and I were the last two in the building, and for some inexplicable reason, he acted as though he had other ideas how best to spend what remained of the evening.

"I know this sounds crazy," I said humbly, "but there's someone chasing me, and I'm afraid he's waiting out there for me. Can't we wait inside until he gives up and leaves?"

"You can wait *outside* as long as you want," the custodian muttered. He began to roll the bucket toward a short hallway. "After I put this away, I'm goin' home. I've been here for eight hours, lady, and it ain't that much fun. You got three minutes to pray your crazy man finds someone else to chase."

I scowled at his back. "I thought Southerners were warm and gracious. Here I am, alone and frightened, and . . . a widow! I'm a widow. I'd like to think you might do something to prevent a widow from being murdered in front of the airport."

The bucket squeaked as he went through a doorway.

My oratorical talents were less impressive than my theatrical ones. I looked out the door once again, but all I saw was Ellie's car and an empty parking lot. If the driver was waiting, he'd switched off his headlights.

"Okay," I called loudly, "but don't blame me when you have to mop the blood off the sidewalk in the morning!" I darted into the ladies rest room, gingerly climbed on the commode in the last stall, and pulled the metal door closed. I had a few minutes to read the graffiti, all juvenile and anatomically impossible, before the overhead light went off.

I held my breath as I waited to find out what he'd do if he noticed Ellie's car. Apparently, he was not interested in the whereabouts of the imperiled widow who'd pleaded for help. A lock was secured noisily, followed by footsteps and the sound of a second lock being secured. After several more minutes of self-inflicted oxygen deprivation, I decided I was alone in the airport.

The rest room was as dark as any crypt, thus making my turtlish journey through it an adventure in itself. I eased open the door. The main room of the airport was illuminated by a streetlight near the curb. I stayed in the doorway while I assessed the situation. Even the most moonstruck psychotic might realize the significance of Ellie's car in the drive—and the significance of the departure of the employees.

Who the hell could he be, I asked myself as I dug my fingernails into my palms, and why was he after me? Me, for pity's sake? I peered around the corner and noted that the lock on the glass door was a dead bolt, and, in particular, the kind that requires a key from either side.

I kept a cautious distance from the oblong of light as I explored the small building. The rear exit had a similar dead bolt. The doors behind each counter had more mundane locks, but they were locked, nevertheless.

My pursuer could not get in, which was good. I could not get out, which for the moment was not bad. I had no intention of strolling out to the car and presented myself as a target to be gunned down or run down, depending on his preference of the hour.

I read the board above the nearest counter. The first arrival was at seven o'clock. The other airline was anticipating no action until eight. The airport would open at six or so, I surmised, which meant I had no more than seven hours to amuse myself by memorizing arrivals and departures, and perhaps finding a print-laden ticket to study.

There were vending machines in a corner, but my purse was in the car. There were also pay telephones along the wall, equally inaccessible to those without coins. Wondering if the clerks might keep change in their drawers, I went behind the counter and discovered that I would never know, since the drawers were locked.

My frown faded as I noticed a telephone. I looked at the door to make sure the driver wasn't peering back at me (while drooling on the glass, or preparing to attack it with a hammer), then took the telephone and sat down on the floor behind the counter.

I didn't know the number at Malloy Manor, and I didn't especially want to talk to any of them. Bethel D'Armand would not be at his office, and, for all I knew, had taken the last flight out (the 10:42 to Shreveport). There was one obvious call, but I wasn't yet in the mood to explain how I'd stolen a car and ended up locked in the airport.

I wiggled until I was as comfortable as I could get on unrelenting linoleum, then compounded whatever felonies I'd already committed by dialing Peter's number.

"Yeah?" he answered grumpily.

"So, how was your day?" I asked, charitably ignoring his initial lack of enthusiasm.

"It's after eleven."

"Very good. We must be in the same time zone, although it's more twilight than central daylight down here. Have you made any progress in the thefts in the athletics department?"

"Wait a minute," he said, still grumpy. "Let me turn on a light."

While I waited, I took a quick peek over the counter. I was not exactly the master of my destiny, but I seemed to have the situation in hand, if I overlooked some of the small yet pesky issues that would require resolution at some point.

"Okay," Peter said, "what's going on down there?"

"It's been hectic, and a few things have happened that are causing problems for me. I wanted to let you know that Caron and I are staying for the funeral, and therefore won't be home until Monday evening."

"How hectic has it been?" he asked, missing the opportunity to mention how distressed he was by the delay of my arrival home and into his arms.

"Pretty hectic. Did you fingerprint the coaches?"

"Not yet. What's going on, Claire?"

We yammered back and forth, but I finally gave up and ran through the highlights of the day, including the sniper at the cemetery and his most recent reemergence on my bumper. I lamely concluded with a vague remark about my current incarceration.

He reacted as I'd expected, with snorts and sputters and

tediously repetitive remarks concerning his earlier advice. At one point, I put down the receiver to check the door; when I retrieved it, I doubted I'd missed anything of interest. I let him run down, then said, "Caron and I had an intriguing conversation about her father and about you. You needn't worry, though. She's more—"

"Did you hear what I just said?"

"Most of it, but you were repeating yourself and—"

"Call the local police."

"I will when I get around to it," I said, wrinkling my nose. "They're totally incompetent. I don't know how—"

"Call the local police." He paused, then added, "If you don't promise to stop dithering and call them immediately, I'll hang up on you and call them myself."

"Call them what?" I said lightly. "It would be accurate to call them irresponsible, but to call them irrepressible is—"

Damned if he didn't hang up.

13

"Where were you last night?" demanded Caron.

I opened my eyes long enough to determine she had her fists on her hips and smoke streaming out of her ears, then rolled over, burrowed under the pillow, and muttered, "Go away, dear. We'll discuss it later."

"I said, where were you last night? I searched the entire house, and then went all the way to the bayou to see if you'd drowned or something stupid like that. I stepped on a snake. Well, I thought it was a snake, anyway, and it's an absolute miracle I didn't sprain my ankle when I ran back to the house. Or break it and be permanently crippled."

"Leave me alone."

She jerked away the pillow. "I am not going to leave you alone, Mother! This whole thing is Utterly Crazy, and I've had enough! I'm seriously considering changing my name."

"To Madeline? Then you can live in an old house in Paris, covered with vines . . ."

"I have no idea what you're babbling about, but it's clear that you're just as weird as those other people."

"All right." Yawning, I sat up, then regretted the movement. My neck, back, and upper arms were sore, and my fingers curled involuntarily, as if still clutching a steering wheel. I was relieved to note my knuckles were no longer white.

Caron's nostrils flared more widely than those on the moosehead in the attic. "Well?"

"You want to know where I was last night, so I'll tell you. I went to Bethel D'Armand's office. He disappeared. On my return trip, a demonic yellow dragon chased me to the airport. A policeman named Bo came to rescue me, but he had to go find the custodian's house to get a key. He then asked me several thousand questions, recorded my answers diligently, escorted me to the house, and advised me to seek legal counsel or psychiatric care. He did not imply the two are mutually exclusive. I've decided to make reservations at the Happydale Home. Every afternoon at tea, they serve cucumber sandwiches with the crusts trimmed and little cakes with pink icing."

Caron eyed me coldly. "You're not as weird as those other people. You're ten times as weird. Furthermore, you're not Nearly As Funny as you think you are."

"I suppose not." I went into the bathroom and began to brush my teeth, despite twinges from my fingers. "So what did I miss while I was battling for my life?"

"Nothing. Phoebe made me get off the telephone so she could call her boyfriend. His name is Jules, but when I was leaving, I heard her call him Julie. I thought I'd barf on the carpet."

I finished with my teeth and leaned toward the mirror to examine the puffy bags beneath my eyes. The dark smudges were not of a cosmetic origin but of an organic one. "What about everyone else? Anybody invite you to play Scrabble or conduct a séance?"

"Uncle Stanford stayed in the parlor. Most of the others kind of wandered around, searching for the dumb olographic will." She slumped against the doorsill and sighed. "With my luck, one of them will find it and I won't get any of the money. Then I won't be able to have a big house with a swimming pool, and Rhonda Maguire will keep inviting Louis over to swim until his brain is waterlogged. They'll go steady for the next three years, announce their engagement at the senior prom, get married while they're in college, live in a really cute apartment—"

"Stop, and I mean it," I said as I returned to the bedroom and opened my suitcase. Although it was Sunday morning, church was not on my agenda, so I took out slacks and a shirt. "I assume no one dashed into the parlor, waving the will and shouting 'Eureka!'"

Caron had taken my place in front of the mirror, and was glumly dabbing cream on her chin. "I couldn't say. After I gave up trying to find you, I came up here and read that idiotic book you brought. A butler and a blizzard—give me a break!"

"Did Ellie happen to mention her car?"

"She saw you take it, if that's what you're getting at. All she said was that you'd better not bang it up. When I get the money, I'll find some world-famous dermatologist who's invented zit medicine that actually works, even if you eat chocolate all the time." She put her finger on the tip of her nose, pushed it up slightly, and tilted her head to study the effect. "And maybe a plastic surgeon."

Resisting the urge to make a reference to a Pekingese, I told her I was going downstairs, and was halfway out the door when she said, "The murderer made a really stupid mistake, you know."

I stopped. "What mistake was that, Caron?"

"Hiding the weapon the way he did, of course. Can I wear your blue shirt? Everything I brought is dirty."

I managed to turn myself around, and, with modulated and well-articulated deliberation, said, "What do you mean?"

"Well, on the airplane I spilled a soda on my white shirt, and I brought this plaid thing, but I don't know why because I don't like it very—"

"What do you mean about hiding the weapon?"

She picked up the plaid thing, shook her head, and dropped it on the floor. "Oh, you know, the way Lord Diggs put the knife in the solarium after he strangled his wife and killed the cat. I mean, like the police are so dense that they aren't going to search the—"

"Lord Diggs?"

"In that book you brought," she said, digging through my suitcase and finally emerging with my blue shirt. "Then right at the end, he remembers that his nephew was making love to the parlor maid in the greenhouse and could have seen—"

"Lord Diggs is the murderer? I thought the nephew was guilty. He mentioned that he was allergic to cat hair, and he was sneezing during the investigation."

"And also to pollen, from the flowers in the greenhouse. Didn't you notice when he leaned over the centerpiece to pass the salt to—"

"Of course I did," I said, and left before I further disgraced myself in her steely adolescent eyes.

The house seemed empty, but I doubted I was any luckier than Caron. I went to the dining room and determined I was not. Maxie and Phoebe sat silently, both staring at the tablecloth. Coffee cups, plates, and black crumbs littered the table, indicating others had come and gone.

"Good morning," I said as I headed for the kitchen.

When I returned with a cup of what passed for coffee, I repeated my greeting.

"I'm pleased you find it so," said Maxie. "I myself had a restless night, tortured by thoughts of this house and its contents being lost to future generations. There are so very few examples of plantation architecture left in Louisiana, and it's distressing to see one destroyed"—she snorted—"in the name of progress. It was such a vital era."

"Those unschooled in regional history assume cotton was the major crop," Phoebe inserted, apparently on automatic pilot. "However, indigo was the major crop for export until the market declined at the end of the eighteenth century. After that, sugarcane dominated the area."

"Really," I murmured, wondering how much sugar it might take to counter the bitterness of the coffee, or if there were a handy cane with which to stir it.

"Very interesting, dear." Maxie frowned at me. "The police officers came last night. They were less than impressed with your theory that the decanter has significance, but they agreed to have it tested. I took it upon myself to assure them none of us will be surprised when the mysterious substance is determined to be dirt."

Caron's white shirt was dirty, the brandy decanter was dirty, and so was something else. A pair of something elses, to be precise. I ordered myself to take a swallow of coffee, then put down the cup and said, "Your bedroom slippers are dirty."

"No, they aren't," Phoebe said promptly. "We went over this Friday night, Cousin Claire. You were wiggling your toes at the time. Surely you remember that; heaven knows it's indelibly etched in my mind."

"Not your slippers. Your mother's."

Maxie solidified as if the temperature had plunged. After what Caron would describe as a Distant Lull, she said, "It's possible they're a bit dusty, but the floors are not cleaned on a regular basis, or on any basis whatsoever that I've thus far noticed."

"I'm talking about grass stains," I said.

My comment did not generate any explanations, much less any confessions. The two exchanged quick looks, then stared at me. The temperature had indeed plunged, and we were approaching absolute zero.

"Give me a minute to think," I said, forcing down more coffee. "Let's try this: When we went outside Friday night to search for Miss Justicia, Phoebe returned to change into shoes and told you what was happening. You decided to avail yourself of the fortuitous opportunity to search her room."

"I went to her room in hopes she had returned. I was worried about her."

"If you truly were worried about her, why did you first go outside and peek through the window to make sure she was still in the yard?"

She plucked a cigarette from her case and lit it. "If Miss Justicia had returned, I did not wish to disturb her further by entering her room."

I refused to wince as smoke wafted into my face. "That was very thoughtful of you, Maxie. Did you step on something hard while in the process of being so very thoughtful?"

"I assumed it was a rock. And I didn't find a will, so you can save yourself the necessity of further innuendos."

"But you were outside during the pertinent time, and by yourself. Someone who frolicked in the yard as a child should know the quickest path to the bayou."

"One would think so." She jabbed out the cigarette and rose. "Come along, Phoebe, and bring your tape measure. There is a secretary in the parlor that warrants a second scrutiny. It might have a secret drawer."

I let them reach the doorway before I said, "I discovered Miller's big secret, by the way. Baa, baa, black sheep . . ."

"Who's Miller?" asked Phoebe.

Maxie's hand tightened on the cigarette pack until it crinkled, but her voice remained cool. "He is no one worthy of your attention, Phoebe, or yours, Cousin Claire. Miss Justicia made it clear a long time ago that his name was not to be said aloud in Malloy Manor. Even though she has passed away, we owe her the respect of obeying her wishes in this matter."

"Because he got a girl pregnant?" I said. "Isn't that an overreaction?"

"It was not a topic of debate then, nor is it to become one today." Maxie took Phoebe's arm and led her down the hall.

The coffee wasn't any worse cold, and I sipped it as I inserted Maxie into the night's activities. Like Stanford, Phoebe, and Pauline, she had been alone outside. She was strong enough to shove the wheelchair into the water, and she'd admitted she was in the precise spot where the decanter had been found. But why would she risk killing Miss Justicia until the will—any will—had been perused in private?

I was beginning to regret the decanter had been found. I was regretting quite a bit more than that, such as fishing the invitation out of Caron's waste basket in the first place. Borrowing Ellie's car was high on the list, along with allowing myself to become obsessed with Miller, which was what I'd done and for no reason beyond curiosity.

Also high on the list, and in contention for first place, was taking the yellow taxi from the airport when we arrived. The conversation in the backseat had been lively but had contained nothing to merit the man's continued attacks on me. He'd been agreeable during the drive; now he had an attitude I did not appreciate.

And he'd been following me, I realized. He hadn't shown up at the cemetery by coincidence, and he surely hadn't been cruising the highway at the exact time I was returning from

D'Armand's office. This newest idea turned the coffee in my stomach to burning, churning acid.

The gloom in the dining room deepened. It was probable that a cloud had blocked the sun, but I became uneasily aware of the water-stained ceiling, peeling wallpaper, depictions of raw meat on the walls, and droopy, dusty cobwebs. I could hear no one, not even Maxie and Phoebe in the parlor. The only other person I'd encountered was Caron, and she was likely to be upstairs pondering her chances of getting in the witness-relocation program. I would have welcomed any company, including Stanford, his offspring, or Pauline. I listened, but all I heard were creaks and wheezes, as if the house had developed a malevolent personality.

It seemed we'd moved from gothic to horror, I thought as I pushed aside the coffee, told myself I was losing my few remaining vestiges of sanity, and went down the hall to the parlor.

Maxie and Phoebe were examining the suspicious secretary. "Where is everybody?" I asked.

"Stanford and Ellie are at the funeral home," Maxie said. "The cook doesn't come in until noon. Pauline has not yet appeared for breakfast, which is for the best. I have no idea of Keith's whereabouts, nor do I have any interest in them. Forty-three inches."

"Forty-three inches," Phoebe echoed. She recorded the figure in her notebook, then kneeled and stretched the tape along the base. "If you're that desperate for company, Cousin Claire, try the opium den under the stairs. Forty-eight and one-half inches."

"Forty-eight and one-half inches." This time, Maxie recorded the figure. "There is a discrepancy. This is ever so promising. If you'll be so kind as to excuse us, Cousin Claire, we must concentrate on our calculations. Malloy Manor is at stake."

I returned to the foyer, a now-familiar home base, and frowned at the little doorway. Since I wasn't anywhere near that desperate, I went outside.

Ellie's sports car and Stanford's Mercedes were gone, thus depriving me of both transportation and the means by which to commit additional felonies. Then again, grand theft auto hadn't been all that entertaining, and the mini grand prix to the airport had been downright grim.

The door behind me opened, and Caron came out to the veranda. "I cannot believe we're stuck here an entire extra day," she muttered, her hands in the pockets of her white shorts. They went nicely with my blue shirt.

"Your father was stuck here for eighteen years," I said. I stared at the undergrowth beyond the driveway, but I could see no jarring patch of yellow in the muddy-colored shadows. "Let's take a walk, dear. This house is beginning to get to me, perhaps even more so than its occupants."

"Did one of them murder Miss Justicia?" asked Caron as she and I went down the steps and started along the nearest path.

"I don't know if anyone murdered her. If the lab reports blood on the decanter, we'll have to assume it was used for something more sinister than a nightcap." I hesitated for a minute. "The wheelchair's on the back porch. I wonder if the police checked its back for traces of blood . . . ?"

"You are disgusting, Mother. Once I get my driver's license, I won't mind being an orphan. In the meantime, stop poking your nose in this before you get it—and other things— blown to smithereens."

I headed for the back of the house. "That's what Peter said last night, and not nearly as politely. I really must discourage him from that sort of thing."

"You don't want him to worry about you?"

I faltered, then resumed my pace. "I suppose I do want

him to worry about me, in the sense he's showing concern. I don't like this paternalism, however."

"You just don't want to share the closet space," Caron said under her breath.

"Maybe not," I said under mine.

We came around the corner of the house. The wheelchair was on the porch, folded and propped against the wall. With stern encouragement from me, Caron helped me drag it out to the grass. As Stanford had said, it seemed heavier than a refrigerator and it took us several minutes of struggling to pull the arms apart and open it. The seat was muddy, and bits of slinky green weeds were entwined in the spokes of the wheels.

"Look at this control panel," Caron said, awed.

I chose to look at the back braces. If there had been blood, the water had washed it away. I stepped back and regarded what might have been an instrument of death, rather awed myself by the elaborate controls and sense of massiveness and power. "It must have cost a fortune," I said.

"I hope the water didn't rust the controls," Caron said as she sat down in the seat. "I'll bet this was fun to ride around in. Look, here's the brake, and the joystick to steer it, and the lever to change gears. It goes in reverse, too."

"No headlights?" I said dryly.

"Maybe it still works." Her finger touched a button, and the motor began to drone. "This is neat, Mother. If Rhonda was to step out from behind that bush, I could flatten her. Inez could write it up for the school newspaper, with the headline 'Rhonda Maguire: Miss RoadKill of Farberville High.'"

"And you accused me of being disgusting?" I said, laughing. "Remember, dear, you only have a learner's permit, and it's not valid in this state. We'd better put the wheelchair back on the porch before . . ."

Mother's little darling smiled sweetly. "In a minute."

The drone intensified, and before I could shriek out an

order to the contrary, the wheelchair shot across the grass and disappeared around an azalea. There was no cackle, but I swore I heard a howl of delight.

Feeling a surge of empathy with Pauline, I lowered my head and took off down the path. I soon realized why she'd worn jogging shoes for such occasions. The path was slippery and uneven, and vines and branches grabbed at my ankles. And there were many paths as I went farther from the house, I discovered. Periodically, I could hear the wheelchair, but paths that pretended to go one way took turns that led in the opposite direction.

I finally abandoned the paths and pushed through the bushes to the bayou. I saw nothing, but I heard the wheelchair behind me and well back in the yard. I couldn't blame her too much for wanting to test-drive the chair. On the other hand, I could lecture her at length about ignoring my directives, and I most definitely would.

I headed back into the wasteland, trying to progress in the direction of the sound and feeling a vague kinship with blood-lusting hunters who tracked down animals. I came around a neglected magnolia tree with branches nearly brushing the ground, and caught sight of the barn.

I also caught sight of the runaway, who came speeding out of a path into the cleared area.

"Watch this!" she shrieked as she began to zigzag through the weeds, turning neatly each time.

Images of broken bones invaded my mind. "Stop right this minute!"

She looked back at me and yelled, "Hey, this is Really, Really fun!"

And crashed into the door of the barn.

I ran toward her, alternately cursing and offering sympathy. The chair was on its side, and all I could see were feet and one hand fumbling on the control panel. The motor went dead. Before I could get there to pull the twisted, battered body of my only child from the wreckage, she stood up.

"Wow," she said as I stumbled to a halt. "That was quite a ride. You wouldn't believe how fast this thing will go on a straightaway. I mean, like wow."

"Are you okay?" I gasped.

"I'm fine, but you don't look so good, Mother. Why don't you sit down for a moment?"

"If I sat down, I couldn't wring your neck." I forced myself to take a few breaths. I was calmer but no less angry as I continued. "I have been thrashing through this—this jungle to find you before you killed yourself. Why on earth did you race away like that when I'd just told you we were going to put it back on the porch? You may think joyriding among the trees is perfectly safe, but what would have happened if you—"

"Mother," she said solemnly, "look."

I stopped sputtering and looked where she was pointing. The crash had knocked open the barn door. Less than ten feet from us was the yellow taxi, partially covered by a canvas tarp.

"What's it doing in here?" Caron said, moving toward the door. "It looks like someone tried to hide it. Do you think the driver's here?"

I grabbed her elbow and pulled her back. "Let's hope not. Come on, we've got to get back to the house to call the police."

She gave me a blank look, and I realized she'd missed the updates on the identity of the driver and his recent antics. I explained as curtly as I could.

"That doesn't make any sense," she said, refusing to be dragged any farther. "At least let's see if he's in there. He knows we're out here. I didn't exactly tap on the door, and you were ululating like an coyote."

"Claire!" Ellie called. She came down the path, with Keith slouching behind her. "The lawyer called, and he's coming back to talk to everybody."

"Safety in numbers," Caron said. She freed her arm, went to the door of the barn, and timidly said, "Hello? Is anybody in there?"

"What's the taxi doing in there?" asked Ellie.

"And the wheelchair out here?" added Keith, although with less interest.

I shook my head. "I have no idea about the taxi. Caron was riding in the wheelchair and ran into the door."

"But why would it be in the barn . . . ?" Ellie murmured as she joined Caron in the doorway. "Is he in there? I thought he left the other night . . . ?"

"I don't think he's in here." Caron went into the barn and lifted the tarp. "He's not in the cab, and there's not anyplace else to hide."

"Unless you're a rat," Keith remarked to no one in particular.

Gritting my teeth, I went into the building. Calling it a barn was an exaggeration. It was simply a storehouse with four rough walls and a roof through which sunlight slanted. The walls were substantial enough to muffle the sound of the birds outside; the only thing I heard was heavy breathing, some of it (a good deal of it) my own. There were a few boxes, a shelf holding plastic flowerpots, and a lumpy discarded bag of Pritty Kitty Kibble.

Ellie and Caron pulled off the tarp. The driver wasn't crouched on the backseat, nor was a gun lying on the same. The keys were in the ignition.

"So where is he?" demanded Ellie, her eyes round and her chin quivering. "Why is this here?"

I looked at Keith, who was sitting on a carton, and, from

all appearances, admiring his hangnails. "Was the taxi here yesterday afternoon?"

"No way. Even I would have noticed it."

"Mother," Caron said, wrinkling her nose as she moved around the taxi, "something smells bad. I think it's coming from the trunk."

My mouth turned sour. "We're all going back to the house to call the police. All of us, now."

"Cousin Caron's right," Ellie said as she approached the trunk, making an increasingly carking series of faces. "Something in there smells worse than any meal I've ever had in Malloy Manor. Do you think the driver forgot about his creel?"

"We're going to the house," I said, trying to swallow.

"Don't be a wimp, Auntie Claire. We have to look."

"No, we don't."

Ellie took the keys from the ignition and unlocked the trunk. As it rose, a stench flooded the barn. It was a mixture of sweetness and acridity, strong enough to have color and form and texture, vile enough to be the embodiment of the manor's malevolent personality.

Gagging, Caron stumbled out of the barn. Her hands on her mouth, Ellie backed away from the taxi, tripped over the doorsill, and fell on the ground. She scuttled away from the door, coughing. I managed a quick look in the trunk as I headed for the door, and what I saw was enough to eject the meager contents of my stomach.

The driver lay as if in a coffin, his hands folded across his chest and his eyes wide in a final, frenzied appeal. His mouth was covered with a piece of silver tape. His skin had been pasty; now it had a bluish tint.

Caron grabbed me and put her head on my shoulder, her body shaking violently. I held her tightly. Ellie was kneeling on the grass. Her hair shrouded her face but did nothing to soften her sobs. Keith came out of the barn, the visible areas of his face a pale shade of green, and said, "Nasty, nasty, nasty."

"Nasty?" Ellie cried. "Oh, my God, how can you say that?"

"Well, it is nasty," he said as he braced himself against the side of the building and doubled over as he retched.

I caught Caron's shoulders and steadied her. "Just don't think about it," I said firmly. "Think about something else."

"What?" she said, tears snaking down her cheeks.

"A swimming pool." I gave her an encouraging smile, and then put my arm around her and nudged her into motion. After a minute, Ellie stood up and took Keith's arm. They followed us toward the house.

14

Officers Dewberry and Puccoon came almost immediately. I went outside and explained what we'd found, and agreed to escort them to the scene. As we walked along the path, they asked for details, but this time there were no smirks or derisive remarks. Not until I'd finished, that is.

"Read about you this morning, Miz Malloy," said Dewberry. "Bo turned in this screwy report about you claiming to have been chased across the parish by a taxi. He wasn't real clear about why you ended up being locked in the airport after everybody went home for the night. Something about a commode." Smirk, smirk.

"I indeed was chased by the taxi," I said. "I assumed I knew who was driving it, but I was wrong. The man in the trunk hasn't driven anything in the last few hours."

"You gonna do the preliminary autopsy for us?" asked Puccoon. Smirk, smirk.

"I'm sure you're ghoulish enough to handle it without

me," I said, thus breaking my resolution not to be irritated by them. "I had only a glimpse of the body, but the smell indicated he's been in a hot trunk for some time." I froze as the implications of my remark hit me like a bucket of ice water. "The original owner of the taxi was found dead. The obvious explanation is that this unknown man in the trunk killed him and stole the taxi. He's the one who picked us up at the airport Friday afternoon, and then appeared at midnight, claiming someone had called him. I don't know what that was about, but I do know he didn't commit suicide in a fit of remorse for trying to run me off the road. Someone else was driving last night."

"Maybe your imagination was overheating again," Dewberry said. "Some kids out riding around with a six-pack decide to have some fun with you."

"I saw the hood of the taxi." I stopped at the edge of the grass. "There's the barn, and you should be able to find the taxi all by yourselves. I'm going back to the house to check on my daughter. She was very close to hysteria earlier, and I sent her upstairs to lie down."

"You mean you're not going to supervise us and tell us what all to do?" Puccoon said, giving me a woeful look. "Why, I don't know if Dewey and me can investigate on our own."

"Neither do I." I retraced my steps to the porch. Stanford's Mercedes was back, and from within the parlor, I could hear him hurling questions at Ellie. She seemed to have no answers.

I sat down on the swing and let my head fall back. My thoughts were as tangled and unruly as the yard surrounding Malloy Manor, and although I had as many questions as Stanford, I had no more answers than Ellie. I set the swing into motion. The tiny squeaks and rhythmic motion were soothing, almost hypnotic. My eyes closed, I went back over everything that had been said and done since our arrival, visualizing expressions and replaying conversations.

I was not overwhelmed with crystalline insights, but a few key phrases were beginning to make sense—unless I'd drifted into a stage of semiconsciousness and was merely deluding myself.

The sound of a car door roused me. Rodney Spikenard came up the sidewalk, his briefcase in hand. He wore the gray suit, but his necktie was gone and the top button of his shirt undone.

"Mrs. Malloy," he murmured with a nod. "Please excuse my frayed appearance. I was in a hurry to get here."

Frayed. I tried to hold on the phrase, to attach it to something, but it blinked out. "Good afternoon, Mr. Spikenard," I said.

"The police are here?" he asked delicately.

When I told him the reason for their visit, he dropped his briefcase and sat down on the top step. If his hair had been longer, it would have been mussed beyond repair as he repeatedly ran his fingers through it.

"This is too much for this nice, bright colored boy," he said, shaking his head. "I thought I was being engaged to straighten out some accounts and proffer legal advice. Hold the old lady's hand when she became upset over some imaginary slight, and keep her out of jail. Fend off the relatives when they wanted to borrow against the capital. I didn't know what I was getting into with Malloy dynasty, but I do believe I'll get out as soon as possible."

"Can you?"

"There are plenty of qualified attorneys in the parish, Mrs. Malloy."

"I wasn't suggesting you couldn't extricate yourself from the professional relationship, Mr. Spikenard."

"Oh, really, Mrs. Malloy?"

"There are other relationships less easily dissolved."

"I can't deny that."

All of this was being conducted politely, like fencers warming up for the match. A flick here, an unspoken *touché* there, all in preparation for the first lunge.

I opted for a more diplomatic move. "Miss Justicia made it clear that your arrival for her birthday dinner would have more than a minimal impact on the family."

He leaned back against the end of the rail and crossed his legs. "You may be naive in these matters, but there is a certain amount of racism lingering in Louisiana. Lingering like a bad case of the flu, but nevertheless a factor. You saw their faces, Mrs. Malloy. They weren't shocked at my age or the cut of my suit."

"I won't argue that issue, Mr. Spikenard." I set the swing back into motion. "In that we both know where this conversation's going, there's no need for formality. Why don't you call me Claire and I'll call you Rodney?"

"As you wish, Claire."

"Miss Justicia was bubbling with glee over your upcoming appearance at the party," I said, trying to keep my thoughts in a tidy line. "Part of this may have been caused by her anticipation of the family's reaction to your skin, but I think she had a second bomb waiting to be detonated."

"She implied she was going to read the olographic will."

I pointed my finger at him, although I did not lunge. "She had to write the will because you couldn't. You said the reason for that couldn't be discussed because of client-attorney confidentiality. In that I fit neither category, why don't I discuss it? Miss Justicia let you know that you would be one of the heirs. Therefore, you couldn't prepare the document."

"One of her heirs?" Rodney laughed. "Why would this

ancient Southern matriarch include someone like me in her will? Her eyesight was just fine. I may not be pitch-black, but I'm a long way from being alabaster."

"Because you're her grandson."

"What?" Stanford and Ellie said in unison through the parlor window.

If I myself hadn't been eavesdropping so much lately, I would have commented on their rudeness. Instead, I gazed at the murky faces behind the screen and said, "Rodney is Miller's son. He didn't use his father's name, but I think he used the proceeds of his father's life-insurance policy to finance his education."

"That's preposterous!" Stanford sputtered. "I'm not saying Rodney here isn't a smart boy who did real well for himself by getting through college, but—there ain't no way— no, ma'am, no way at all he's a Malloy. You can see for yourself, plain as day. He's colored."

Rodney smiled. "Keen eyesight must run in the family."

"Why don't we go inside?" I suggested.

"Shouldn't I go around back and use the kitchen door?"

"The front door will do." I opened it and gestured for him to precede me. "Remind me to show you the portrait of General Richmond Malloy. The cook said Miller was the 'spittin' image' of him. She wasn't referring to physical attributes, I suspect, but this inclination to have relationships with black women."

"I've heard stories," Rodney said as we went into the parlor.

"Well, I can't believe the story I just heard," Stanford said. He stood by the cart, attempting to splash whiskey in a glass. His hand, the cart, and the floor were receiving the majority. "Miller got himself in some trouble—that much I knew on account of I heard them talking behind closed doors.

Yelling was more like it, him and my daddy, going at each other like a pair of hounds fighting over a bone. Hell, most of the parish could hear 'em that night." He banged down the glass and gulped from the bottle. "But I'll tell you this—I didn't hear anything about a colored girl."

"Afro-American," Ellie drawled from a sofa. She'd recovered from her earlier shock, and she regarded us with a feline smile. "Poor Daddy is terribly behind the times."

Stanford glared at her. "You watch your mouth, missy. I don't mean anything derogatory when I say *colored*. It's the word I grew up with in this very house, and I'm not going to start with some newfangled term."

"No problem," Rodney said. "I've heard worse."

"And you're not a Malloy."

"I haven't said I was."

I made a face at him. "Well, you are. I explained it to you out on the porch."

"Ah, yes," he said, "but would your explanation stand up in a court of law?"

"Now that's being a sensible fellow," Stanford said to him. He turned to me. "What's this Ellie's been telling me about a body out in the barn? I saw the police car when I drove up, but I thought you'd dragged 'em out here on another of your harebrained ideas."

"Harebrained?" I said. "It wasn't my fault the decanter has blood on it, and I sure as hell didn't kill the taxi driver and hide the taxi in the barn. I only arrived here two days ago. I'm not the one who's been skulking around the house searching for wills, or creeping around the yard at the time of Miss Justicia's death." I fixed myself a drink and stalked to the nearest sofa. "In fact, I'm the only one who *doesn't* have anything to do with all this. Stop gawking at me, all of you!"

"My goodness," Maxie said as she and Phoebe came into

the parlor, "Cousin Claire seems to be frothing at the mouth. Perhaps she might like to lie down with a cool compress."

"Meet your new cousin," I said tartly. "Cousin Maxie, Cousin Rodney. Cousin Phoebe, fetch the notebook; there's an addendum to be made to the family tree."

Maxie's chins bulged one by one, as did her eyes. "I'm afraid you're mistaken, Cousin Claire. Mr. Spikenard is the family attorney—for the moment."

Phoebe straightened her glasses and licked her lips. "It might be wise to retain him on a permanent basis. Yale is one of the best law schools in the country."

"Those aren't the credentials under discussion," Stanford said in a dark voice. "Paternity seems to be the issue. According to Claire, this boy is Miller's son. That makes him my nephew, your cousin, Miss Justicia's grandson."

Maxie and Phoebe sat down on a sofa, each as pale and rigid as the china dolls in the attic. Stanford flopped down beside me, grumbling to himself.

"So welcome to the family," Ellie said, yawning. "Is that why you came out here this afternoon, to tell us the glad tidings of great joy? For unto you is born in the town of LaRue . . ."

"I have tidings," Rodney said, "but they're not glad. Mr. D'Armand told me last night that he would have all the trust information delivered to my office this morning. When no one appeared, I called his house and spoke to Mrs. D'Armand. He failed to come home last night or this morning. She sent Spencer to the office, and he discovered that the lights were on and the doors unlocked." He looked impassively at me. "Mrs. D'Armand claims that the last person to see her husband was Claire."

"What'd you do to good ol' Bethel?" Stanford snarled at me.

I was becoming seriously fed up with the accusations being heaped on me every few minutes. "I didn't do anything to good ol' Bethel."

"Has this been reported to the police?" asked Maxie.

Rodney nodded. "Yes, but he's only been missing since last night. The police won't take any action for forty-eight hours."

"Is that why you stole my car?" said Ellie. "I thought you'd gone to the local tavern for a few beers."

"Stole your car?" Maxie and Phoebe echoed.

"Did you steal it to take Bethel somewhere?" Stanford said, no doubt thinking he was craftier than a church bazaar.

"You people are getting on my nerves," I said.

"This is outrageous," Maxie began, then stopped as the doorbell rang. "Phoebe, answer the door. It's probably a group from the church with food, or someone with flowers. This dreadful conversation will have to wait."

Phoebe rose obediently and left the room. When she returned, the two police officers followed her. Although they held their hats, neither looked respectful.

"Mr. Stanford," Dewberry said, "we came back to the house to use the telephone. Where's our car?"

"Where'd you put it?"

Puccoon looked sharply at me. "Miz Malloy suggested we leave it up here so's not to mess up any tire tracks by the barn. It was in the driveway."

"Jeez, Lester," said Stanford, "don't you realize we got better things to do than baby-sit your car? You boys are officers of the law. Can't you take care of your car yourselves, without intruding on the family in our hour of grief?"

"But, Mr. Stanford," Dewey said, "we—"

"Most of us are here," Maxie said, "and therefore innocent of this latest incident of car theft. I suppose we ought to ascertain the whereabouts of Cousin Keith, Cousin Pauline—and Cousin Caron. One never knows what a negative influence can engender in an adolescent mentality."

"Cousin Pauline hasn't come downstairs all day," Phoebe said. "I knocked on her door earlier and offered to bring her a tray, but she refused to answer."

"So go knock again," Stanford muttered. "Claire, you check on Caron, and Ellie, see if you can dig up that nogoodnick brother of yours."

The three of us brushed past the policemen and went upstairs, although without any sense of jolly camaraderie, and separated in the hallway. I went to our bedroom and found Caron lying on the bed.

"Is everybody dead so we can go home?" she asked.

"Not yet. You didn't steal a police car, did you?"

"Not yet."

"Just checking," I said as I went to the window and pulled back the curtain to look out at the bayou.

"Have you found out who was driving the taxi last night?"

Sighing, I let the curtain fall back. "No, and it's too bad I never had a glimpse of his face. All I saw was the bright yellow of the taxi, and I rashly assumed . . ."

"What?" she said impatiently.

"I rashly assumed that I knew who was driving," I said. My knees began to tremble so violently that I barely made it to my bed. "That's the problem. I saw what I was supposed to see, and it never occurred to me to question it. Nor, obviously, did the others. It's a good thing we weren't a flock of lambs frolicking outside a slaughterhouse. We'd all be accompanied by mint jelly."

"Then who was driving it?"

The plastic bag containing my bedroom slippers had

been kicked into a corner, nearly hidden by a plaid shirt. I picked up the bag. My frayed bedroom slippers only appeared to be frayed. In reality, they were coated with tiny white objects. "Who was driving what?" I said distractedly.

She frowned at me. "The taxi. That's what we were talking about, remember?"

"That's not what I was talking about."

Her frown deepened. "You're beginning to make me nervous, Mother. Did you get a bump on the head last night?"

"I wish I had." I went into the bathroom, applied lipstick, and ran a comb through my hair (one always hopes to look one's best in a classic drawing-room denouement). I picked up the bag with the slippers and beckoned to Caron. "Come along, dear. This is likely to be educational, if not entertaining. Furthermore, you can say a proper hello to your new cousin. His reception thus far has been chilly."

I ignored her spate of questions and went to the hallway. Ellie came out of her bedroom and shrugged at me. "I don't know where Keith is," she said. "Under a rock, I suppose."

I didn't bother to tell her that she was lying. Phoebe joined us at the top of the stairs, saying, "I knocked very loudly on Pauline's door, but she won't answer me. Uncle Stanford will have to break down the door."

"She's not in her bedroom," I said, then went downstairs. I halted only long enough to watch Caron gliding down on the elevator seat, and continued into the parlor.

"Caron's on her way," I announced. "Keith and Pauline are not upstairs."

"Did one of them steal the police car?" Maxie asked, clearly worried about the quality of the lineage.

"No, neither one of them stole the police car." To the officers, I said, "But your car has been stolen. You need to put out an APB immediately. The driver's armed. He's already killed twice, so he'll have no qualms about killing again."

Dewberry gasped. "What's his name?"

"I don't know, but trust me—he's dangerous. He hasn't had time to go too far, so you might want to make the call as soon as possible. The telephone's in the room across the foyer." Once the officers were gone, I went to the cart. "Rodney, shall I fix something for you?"

"Soda water, thank you."

"I don't understand," Stanford said petulantly. "You know who he is, but you don't know his name? Sounds like poppycock to me. I think we ought to stick to familiar faces. It's hard to imagine Cousin Pauline hunkered over the steering wheel, but Keith's missing, too, and it's not hard to imagine him doing anything criminal. Besides, he has a history of car theft."

"Keith did not steal the police car," I said as I dropped ice cubes in a glass.

"You're sure?"

"I'm very sure," I said, nodding.

"Where is Cousin Pauline?" Maxie asked. She looked up as Phoebe, Ellie, and Caron came into the parlor. "Phoebe, what is going on—and where is Pauline?"

Phoebe hung her head. "Her door's locked, but Cousin Claire says she's not inside."

Maxie marched across the room and leaned over the cart. "Then where is she?"

"I don't know her precise whereabouts, but she's not in her bedroom." I gave Rodney his drink and sat down.

He raised his eyebrows as he noticed the plastic bag, but merely said, "Two down, one to go. Do you know where Bethel D'Armand is?"

"No," I said, "but I know why he's missing. And he is definitely missing."

"I think you're missing some brain cells," Caron said as

she sat down near the door. The mumbling that ensued seemed to imply that her opinion was popular in the parlor.

Dewberry and Puccoon came back in the room. "We'll get the sumbitch before he gets out of the parish," said Puccoon. "It might be easier if we knew who he was, but Miz Malloy doesn't seem to want to tell us."

"I'll tell you," I said, "but before I do, let me ask you something. Did you happen to find the remains of a duck beside the bayou where Miss Justicia's body was found?"

"It was an accident," Maxie said. "We have been over this—"

"It was not an accident." I looked at the police officers. "Well, did you?"

"No, ma'am," Dewberry muttered.

I held up the plastic bag. "Then how would you explain the white feathers on my slippers?"

I might as well have asked them how they would explain the subtleties of the Napoleonic Code. Both of them gazed blankly at me, and Dewberry finally said, "Why would we want to?"

"Maybe you're the only one of us to have her ducks in a row," Ellie said. "The only problem is that you've been stepping on the little dears." Her throaty chuckle sounded brittle, however, and she was picking nervously at her nail polish.

"I was thinking the same about you," I said evenly.

She no longer attempted to sound amused. "I don't know what you're getting at, Claire, but let's get one thing straight right now—I didn't hurt Miss Justicia. She was my grandmother, for God's sake."

"I know you didn't, Ellie. But you became an accomplice when you tried to make the murder look like an accident." I flapped the bag with the slippers. "Tiny white feathers."

"What are you saying?" Stanford exploded. "Are you saying that she was in cahoots with a duck that murdered Miss Justicia? I have tried to be tolerant with you, Claire, but—"

"Good grief, Stanford," I said. "ducks don't kill people. People kill people."

"It must be Keith," Phoebe said abruptly. "He's the only one with whom she would be . . . cahooting."

"I realized he was untrustworthy when I saw that hair," Maxie said, nodding smugly. "I tried to warn you, Stanford."

"I didn't cahoot with anybody," Ellie protested.

Caron hopped into the melee. "I Cannot Believe I was going to ask your advice about my complexion."

Dewberry pulled out his gun, then realized he had no culprit within range, and, with a disappointed look, lowered it. "Where's this Keith fellow?"

"Phoebe is mistaken," I said. "Keith did not murder Miss Justicia."

Stanford scratched his head. "Then it was the duck, after all?"

"Forget the duck, okay?" I said, then waited until he gave me a sulky nod. "In a sense, Miss Justicia brought it upon herself by demanding that her would-be heirs be present for her birthday dinner. Caron and I knew nothing of this, but the rest of you realized she would delete names without hesitation. Therefore, it was vital to be here. For some, the trip was inconvenient. For one, it was almost impossible."

"But all of us came," Maxie said.

"Eventually," I conceded. "The problem was Keith's detainment in prison. Ellie was led to believe she and her brother would receive the bulk of the estate—but only if they were in this house for the birthday dinner. The warden was unlikely to sympathize, so she convinced her boyfriend to pose as Keith. The last time she saw Keith, he no doubt was lanky and had long stringy hair and shabby clothes. No one else had seen him for such a long time that she hoped they might get away with it if he avoided everyone and hid behind the sunglasses and headphones."

"Are you sayin we put up with that lout—and he wasn't even Keith?" Stanford said, oblivious to the saliva on his lips, which gave him a rabid look. "I should have tanned his hide when he first walked in the door!"

I ignored him and said to Ellie, "This can all be verified by fingerprints, you know. Keith's are on file with the FBI. Does your boyfriend have a record?"

"Yes, but nothing like the one he'll have when this is over," she said. "You're right about Buzz. I promised him a cut of the money to pretend to be Keith. This problem with Big Eddie's quite a bit more serious than I implied earlier, and Miss Justicia flatly refused to loan me money."

"But why did you suspect this?" Phoebe asked sharply, as if accusing an undergraduate of imprudent logic.

I was on firm ground, for the moment. "Stanford has blue eyes, and he mentioned that the twins' mother had eyes the color of the morning sky or some such twaddle. Blue eyes are a recessive trait; it's impossible for two blue-eyed parents to produce a dark-eyed child."

Ellie lowered hers. "I told Buzz to keep the sunglasses on day and night. We tried tinted contacts, but they caused so much irritation that his eyes were more red than anything else."

I waited until everyone had overtly or covertly determined that her eyes, as well as Stanford's, were blue. "Ellie's scheme worked well through the remainder of the day. After we'd gone upstairs to bed, he crept out of his little closet and into Miss Justicia's room."

"To look for the will," Ellie said. "He was trying to help me."

"The will, or perhaps some cash and jewelry," I said with a shrug. "My guess is that Miss Justicia woke up and confronted him, no doubt in an unpleasant manner. He bashed her on the head with the brandy decanter, then dropped it in the bushes next to the house, where it was likely to remain undiscovered until he had a chance to dispose of it. The next day, however, it was gone."

This provoked gasps and shrieks from all corners of the room, none of them particularly innovative or eloquent. When things quieted down, Ellie looked at me and said, "He came up to our room and swore that she'd clutched her bosom, turned white, and fallen dead from a heart attack. He swore it to me, Claire. He convinced me that we had to make it look like an accident so the police wouldn't investigate too closely and find out he was an impostor. He'd been convicted of burglary a few years ago, and he was afraid they'd get the wrong idea about his presence in her room. It was stupid of me to buy it, but I did. If I'd known he killed her . . ."

"You wouldn't have helped him? In any case, you did. The pseudo-driver's arrival at the door was a fluke, but I'm sure you and Buzz had come up with a plan to rouse the household at the pertinent minute. Once Pauline reported that Miss Justicia was asleep, you—"

"I thought you said she was already dead," Stanford said. Despite my careful pacing, he seemed confused. "I heard Pauline say—"

I wasn't in the mood for replays. "She thought she saw Miss Justicia. What she really saw were pillows under the comforter and white fuzziness, since Keith had already taken the body to the bank of the bayou. What she didn't see was Ellie hiding in the room."

"I myself saw Miss Justicia in the wheelchair," Stanford said, undaunted, "and I myself heard her cackle."

"That's what we assumed, because we'd seen it before and had no reason to be suspicious. Ellie was operating the wheelchair, with a piece of white boa wrapped around her head. She arrived at the bayou, placed Miss Justicia in the wheelchair, and pushed it in the water. She then hurried back to the house, where she had a surprise."

"She did?" one of the officers said.

I did not turn around. "She most certainly did. I may need some assistance here, Ellie, but I'll give it a shot. Pauline knew that so-called Keith was an impostor, so you decided to ply her with whiskey until you could convince her not to talk. You took the teapot and trotted down to the parlor—and discovered the real Keith."

Once again, the room swelled with gasps and mumbles. Ellie was gnawing on her perfect nails, but she forced a smile and said, "I filled the teapot for Pauline and took it to her. Then Buzz and I went back to the parlor to find out what the hell Keith was doing there. It turned out that he and Pauline had been corresponding while he was in prison, and she told him about the birthday gathering. He escaped and made his way here. He admitted he'd killed a taxi driver and left the body in a ditch. He was driving the taxi so he could find out who was coming, and maybe overhear useful conversations." She shrugged. "He said that the tips were good."

"Why didn't Pauline say anything?" asked Maxie, the familial title withheld pending further developments.

"You know," Caron said, "when we drove up in the taxi and she first saw us, she had a really funny look on her face. Maybe she was looking at the driver."

Ellie nodded. "They'd always had some little signal for their midnight raids on the kitchen. Keith appeared on the porch at the appointed hour, but everybody came blundering into the foyer before they could talk."

"I was hardly blundering," I said, seeing no necessity to describe my initial reaction to the ghostly figure in the peignoir. "Well, perhaps I should have wondered how he knew precisely where the parlor was, and why he and Pauline had the same nickname for Miss Justicia."

"That might meet the definition of blundering," Phoebe said thoughtfully. "It's synonymous with making an error, or, colloquially, botching things up."

"Thank you for sharing that with us," I said. "Then, Ellie, you heard people returning to the house?"

"I decided I'd better make an appearance. Buzz told me later that Keith was threatening to expose the charade, but he also told me he'd convinced Keith to split to a motel and wait. That's the last I saw him until today."

"You did seem upset when we found the body," I said, "but I'll be the first to acknowledge your acting skills. Miss Justicia's cackle was perfect, and you fooled me when you claimed to be bewildered by the man asleep in the parlor."

"Buzz is the one who killed them," she said, her eyes welling with tears. "He thought everything was okay until he heard you talking on the telephone about the decanter. He took a few shots at you at the cemetery to frighten you into packing your bags."

"How did he know I was there?"

"The old men in front of the barbershop asked Bethel and me if we knew you were there. I may have mentioned it when I called the house, but I had no idea that he would do anything like that. Last night, he totally lost it when I told him about the decanter's discovery. I tried to stop him, Claire, but he insisted on going into town to look for you."

"And what did you think he was driving? The wheelchair?"

"I didn't ask," she said in a low voice.

"Perhaps you didn't need to," I said. "The cackle was well practiced, and the sound of your humming and singing in the bathroom was taped in advance. You did bring a tape recorder, didn't you? Is it in the closet, along with the pieces of feather boa?"

She bit her lip, then turned to Rodney and gave him a dazzling smile. "Since you're a member of the family . . . ?"

"I'm delighted to be of service," Rodney murmured, "but I bill by the hour in criminal cases, and require a retainer."

"You are such a card, Cousin Rodney," she drawled.

"A veritable ace of spades," he said, glancing at me out of the corner of his eye.

Maxie began to sob, although I suspected she was distressed not by Ellie's involvement in Miss Justicia's death but by Rodney's entrance into the lineage. Phoebe handed her a handkerchief, patted her shoulder, and then looked at me with a cool smile. "Since you've proved how clever you are, Cousin Claire, why don't you impress us more by sharing your theory about the location of the will?"

"She never wrote it," Stanford said as he headed for the cart. "Maybe she was going to, but she was struck dead by that long-haired hippie before she had a chance."

"She spoke as if she had," Phoebe countered.

Maxie wiped her cheeks. "Indeed, she hinted very strongly that the will was ready to be read."

I once again had everyone's attention, including my daughter's. "I think we can assume the house was searched very thoroughly. Miss Justicia knew you all would be sniffing for it every time she turned her back on you. There is one place no one had access to during the day, and limited access at night—unless you were willing to search her room while she was asleep."

"The wheelchair?" Caron said, proving at least some of her genes were from a pool rather than a bayou.

Puccoon cleared his throat. "Excuse me, but when Dewey and me was dragging it back to the house, the armrest fell off." He took a rolled paper from his back pocket. "Is this what you folks are looking for, Mr. Stanford?"

15

After an intolerable amount of spirited debate, it was agreed that Rodney would read the will aloud. Ellie demanded to be allowed to stay, and the police officers seemed in no rush to leave in the midst of the impressively melodramatic scene, even though Officer Bo and the coroner were waiting outside for them.

"It's dated last week," Rodney began, wrinkling his forehead as only a lawyer can do, "and appears to be in order. We'll have to confirm that it is written in her own—"

"If you don't mind," Maxie said, puffing furiously on a cigarette. Ashes littered her bosom, but she was unconcerned, perhaps for the first time in her life, with appearances.

"As you wish. 'I, Justicia Beauville Malloy, being of sounder mind than any of you greedy, slobbering scavengers, am going to do the right thing. Oh, I know you've been kicking each other under the table and stabbing each other in the back, but blood is thicker than swamp water. We've been decaying for generations, and what's left is a sorry lot.'"

"Look who's talking," Puccoon whispered to Dewberry. He realized he'd been heard, and edged behind the door.

"Please restrain yourselves," Rodney said sternly. "There are a few more observations concerning the present individuals, but I'll provide each of you with a copy so that you may read it at your leisure. Shall we cut to the bequeaths?"

An odd ripply noise came from Maxie's flaccid mouth. Stanford harrumphed and downed his drink. Caron's lip shot out as she gazed into a dismal future bereft of wealth and Louis Wilderberry. Ellie softly clapped her hands.

"Good idea," I said, doing nothing at all.

Rodney cleared his throat. "All right, here we go. 'To Maxine Rutherford Malloy-Frazier, an appropriately pretentious name if ever there was one, and her daughter, Phoebe Malloy-Frazier, I leave Malloy Manor and its contents. The house is haunted, but only by termites and dry rot and peeling paint. It's a perfect setting for you."

"Oh, dear"—Maxie panted—"I'm feeling quite woozy. Phoebe, fetch me a glass of sherry. How wonderful of Miss Justicia to ensure that the house will—"

"Get on with it," Stanford said.

"'To my sniveling son, Stanford, I leave all my stock in Pritty Kitty Kibble. I don't know what it's worth now, but if nothing else, it'll make fine toilet paper.'" Rodney paused, but Stanford was slumped over and any comments he was making were inaudible. "To continue, 'To Pauline Hurstmeyer, who dedicated her life to despising me, I leave the proceeds of all my life-insurance policies in hopes that it's not too late to purchase herself a companion.'"

"Where is she, anyway?" Maxie asked, having gained enough self-control to feign curiosity, if not concern.

"Making the last payment on a companion," I said. "Bethel D'Armand, to be precise."

"They . . . ah?" Maxie sought a phrase appropriately genteel to reflect her newly enhanced status. "They have gone away together? Is he the one to whom she referred when she so coarsely mentioned an unrequited love?"

Phoebe blinked at her mother. "She implied it was requited often at the Econolodge. Her exact words were—"

Maxie cut her off. "I remember her remarks. She was in shock at the time and rambling."

"I'm happy for her," Ellie said, "but could we get on with it, Cousin Rodney? These policemen are breathing down my neck and I'd like to hear the rest of the will before I'm dragged away to the dungeon."

He resumed reading. "'Everything else is to be divided among those of my grandchildren who are present at the dining room table of Malloy Manor on the evening of my eightieth birthday. You're the new generation. You might as well enjoy disgracing the family in the future.'"

Ellie's eyes glistened. "Miss Justicia, if you weren't embalmed, I'd kiss you! Let's take roll: Cousin Caron and I were at the table, and so was dear Cousin Rodney. Poor Keith was absent, although it certainly wasn't his fault, since he was dead. We're down to thirds. I could have used all of it, but this is an improvement over nothing. Champagne?"

"Actually," Phoebe said, removing her glasses to clean them on a tissue, "as an accessory to Miss Justicia's murder, you're not entitled to inherit from her estate."

Ellie blanched. "Don't be silly. I still get my share of the money, don't I? I didn't kill Miss Justicia. All of you heard how Buzz did it. I just—helped him make it look like an accident. Big Eddie's getting impatient. I need the money."

"At least room and board will be provided by the state," Maxie said with a malicious smile. "So, Cousin Caron, it seems you and this"—she swallowed what must have been bitter taste—"son of Miller's will divide the money in the trust. Isn't that a lovely surprise? It would be a nice gesture on your part to make a donation in honor of Miss Justicia, to ensure the continued preservation of Malloy Manor."

"Tax-deductible, of course." Phoebe poised her pencil over the notebook to record any offers.

"Yeah," Caron said dazedly, hundreds of miles away in a swimming pool. And not alone.

"I get my share!" Ellie said savagely. Her perfect complexion marred by angry blotches, she stood up and glared challengingly at each of us in turn. "Nobody would get a damn penny if we hadn't hurried along Miss Justicia's death a little bit. You think it's easy to make that sound? You know how much practice it took?" Her hands began to jerk and her voice grew more shrill. "Hours! It took hours! You sorry amateurs never could have done it!"

She threw back her head. The cackle came from her mouth like a ribbon of bile, coiling through the dreary room, stinging our ears, and scalding our skin. The noise hung in the air long after the policemen escorted her out of the house.

Caron rolled her eyes at me.

Rodney's car was the only one in the driveway as he came to the porch. Ellie's had been impounded, and she and Buzz were rumored to be implicating each other more quickly than an gator slipping off a log. Immediately after we'd returned from the funeral (sparsely attended and minus one pallbearer), Stanford had packed his bags and stormed out of the house, muttering about an appointment in New Orleans. Maxie and Phoebe had gone straight to the attic to commence an inventory that would end in the darkest corner of the basement.

Our suitcases were on the porch. I sat in the swing, idly

listening to Caron on the telephone in the library. Rhonda Maguire's future had taken a downward turn.

"Hello," I said to Rodney. "Thanks for offering to give us a ride to the airport. It's going to be a while before I take any taxis. You look exhausted."

"I stayed up all night sorting through the files and ledgers in D'Armand's office," he said as he sat down beside me. "They were jumbled, as if someone had taken everything out and then stuffed it back in without regard to date or content."

"No kidding?"

"No kidding," he said without inflection.

"Did you find the file with Miller's name on it?" I asked. He nodded, watching me closely. "I've been thinking about it. D'Armand kept every last document pertaining to the family—with the singular exception of anything to do with the distribution of Miller's life-insurance policy and army benefits. Supposedly, no one would have access to the files until he retired and turned them over to another attorney, so he had no reason not to include the paperwork. There was no indication he ever attempted to locate the woman and her child."

"And what did this lead you to theorize?"

"Several different things. One is that there was no child," I said. "Bethel D'Armand was the defender of the Malloy family name, and he might have felt an illegitimate child sullied its reputation. The mother, of course, would have to bought off—and kept bought off for the rest of her life."

"Are you hinting that D'Armand convinced the woman to have an illegal abortion, and, in return, she was promised lifelong employment?"

"I could be hinting that," I said, although I was doing more fishing than hinting. "One possibility comes to mind, and she's had countless opportunities for revenge, hasn't she?

I've never been confronted with worse food in my life. Imagine facing thirty years of it!"

"One possibility," he murmured.

I gave the swing a push, and we sat companionably in the sunshine, the squeaks of the swing in harmony with the cries of distant birds and the sound of an airplane taking some lucky souls out of the parish.

"But," Rodney continued, "that would make me an impostor—if I'd ever claimed to be this child. I did not. I was planning to emphasize that yesterday, but I couldn't bring myself to rescue Mrs. Malloy-Frazier from her worst nightmare." He gave me a quirky little smile that melted my frown. "Oh, come on, it was pretty damn funny, wasn't it? For awhile there, she looked as if she'd swallowed her tongue, her teeth, and all of her platinum fillings."

"It was definitely the highlight of the weekend." I stopped to think, then shook my head. "But abortions were hard to come by thirty years ago, even illegal ones. If the woman had moved away, Bethel simply could have pocketed the money and thrown away the paperwork to cover his tracks. She and her now-grown child could be anywhere in the country."

"I suspect we'll never be sure," Rodney said. "In any case, only one qualified heir was at the table Saturday night."

"Which means Caron is the sole beneficiary of the Malloy fortune. She was unbearable as a pauper. I don't know how I'll handle her once she ascends the throne."

"It won't be too high off the ground." Rodney glanced at the open windows and lowered his voice. "You guessed why Bethel fled so abruptly, didn't you?"

I wanted to pretend I had, but the sunshine was an opiate and I'd been malnourished and deprived of sleep for several days. I admitted as much.

"Miss Justicia discovered he was embezzling money," Rodney said. "She wanted to divide the estate fairly—well, somewhat fairly, and she told me to examine everything as soon as possible. He stalled for a week. My call two nights ago sent him over the edge."

"It sent him somewhere," I said dryly. "How bad is it?"

"He'd been stealing money for years, with the aid of Miss Hurstmeyer, who controlled the household accounts and signed Miss Justicia's name to various financial documents. A preponderance of these were withdrawal authorizations. The house has three mortgages. D'Armand was on the board of directors at the local bank, and he persuaded them to make some hefty loans against it, resulting in a considerable negative equity. There's a lien against the contents, too. Mrs. Malloy-Frazier and her daughter are facing some severe challenges, beginning with back property taxes for the last few years."

"Oh dear," I said, clucking softly. "You will let them know before the dealers arrive?"

He nodded. "And you might have a word with Caron before she applies to a Swiss boarding school. There are federal and state death taxes to be paid, along with an accumulation of unpaid debts and claims on the estate. Income taxes are in arrears. The jewelry is missing from the safe-deposit box, but the personal property taxes and insurance must be paid."

"All in all?"

"I'll do my best to cut a deal with the government to allow her to make monthly payments."

The squeaks were loud, but they weren't originating from the chains holding the swing. He caught my hand before I could strangle myself, and said, "Just kidding, Claire. I can jiggle assets and liabilities, and even things out. Neither of you will have to go to debtor's prison."

I stood up. "Rodney, I think I'll let you explain this to the heiress. We have a few minutes before we leave for the airport. I'm going to take a walk." I stopped at the bottom step and frowned at him. "But if you're not Miller's son and a potential heir, then why did Miss Justicia write an olographic will?"

His teeth glinted in the sunlight, and dimples appeared on both sides of his mustache. "Client-attorney confidentiality."

"With a degree from Yale, you must have had tempting offers from prestigious firms all over the country. Yet you chose to open a practice in LaRue, Louisiana, where you knew you'd be faced with a two-hundred-year-old tradition of bigotry and discrimination."

"My mother worked two jobs and took in laundry so that I'd have the opportunity to concentrate on my studies and do well enough to receive scholarships. She was the one who suffered from the bigotry and discrimination, and I promised myself I'd return to the South to carry on the fight. Substantial fees from families like the Malloys enable me to take on clients less able to afford decent representation." His smile of complacency was eerily familiar. "That doesn't mean I'd ever care to make public any entanglement with such a family. I have a reputation to protect, and the last thing I need is to be considered an offshoot of loons."

"But I won't be out of line if I send you Christmas cards?"

"Of course not, Claire. I'll be delighted to keep in touch with you and Caron in the future. I suppose I'd better tell her the bad news."

I went around the house and took a series of paths to the bayou. The silky brown water was placid, although by no means inviting. An egret watched me from the smooth knee of a cypress tree, and a mammal of some sort fled into a hole. Something sent ripples splashing on a mossy log. A few muddy footprints remained in the grass, but the next rain would erase the last vestiges of Miss Justicia's death.

General Malloy might continue to gallop across the yard when the moon was full, but it seemed likely that in the future no one would be watching him from the second-story windows of Malloy Manor. His legend would fade. The moon was waning, and, with each passing night, would less and less be able to diminish the stars surrounding it. As Miss Justicia had diminished those surrounding her.

The only ghosts that would haunt the banks of the bayou were children. Stanford, Maxie, and Carlton, squabbling as they poled a boat in search of gators and gars. Miller, who'd no doubt done the same things for the same innocent reasons.

I tried to picture Carlton as a boy, to put aside the intense professor who'd given me both happiness and pain, who'd never freed himself from the influences of a decaying family. I wanted to see freckles, a gape-toothed smile, eyes bright with mischief or drowsy with idle daydreams. All I could see was Caron's face.

And as I walked back to the house to catch our ride to the airport and flights that would return us to Farberville, to the Book Depot, to Peter Rosen and his many talents, I heard Caron's voice.

"Mother!" she wailed. "This Isn't Funny!"

"Good morrow, Kate, for that is your name, I hear."

I blinked at the young man in the doorway. "Well have you heard, but something hard of hearing. They call me Claire Malloy that do talk of me."

"You lie, in faith, for you are call'd plain Kate, and bonny Kate, and sometimes Kate the curst, but Kate, the prettiest Kate in Farberville. Kate of Kate Hall, my superdainty Kate, for dainties are all Kates, and therefore—"

"Mother," Caron said as she came out of my office, "who is This Person?"

"I have no idea," I admitted.

The peculiar man came into the bookstore and bowed, one arm across his waist and the other artfully posed above his head. He was dressed in a white shirt with billowy sleeves, a fringed leather tunic, purple tights, suede boots with curled toes, and a diamond-patterned conical cap topped with a tiny bell. His brown hair dangled to his shoulders, rare among the traditionally minded Farber College students. "Perchance miladies will allow me to maketh known myself?"

"This milady thinks you ought to maketh known

thyself to the local police," Caron said, edging toward me. "Start with the Sheriff of Nottingham."

He stood up and swept off his cap. "Pester the Jester, or Edward Cobbinwood, if it pleaseth you all the more."

"Not especially," I said. "Would you care to explain further?"

"Okay, I'm a grad student at the college and a member of ARSE. I was assigned to talk to all the merchants at the mall and on Thurber Street about the Renaissance Fair in two weeks. We'd like to put up flyers in the store windows and maybe some banners. Fiona is hoping you'll let us use the portico in front of your bookstore for a stage to publicize the event."

"A Renaissance Fair? I haven't heard anything about this." I noticed Caron's sharp intake of breath and glanced at her. "Have you?"

She nodded. "I was going to tell you about it when you got home this evening. The AP history teacher sent a letter to everybody who's taking her course in the fall. We have to either participate in this fair thing or write a really ghastly midterm paper. I don't think she should be allowed to blackmail us like this. Inez and I are going to get up a petition and have everybody sign it, then take it to the school board. I mean, summer is supposed to be our vacation, not—"

"I get your point," I said.

"Look not so gloomy, my fair and freckled damsel," added Edward Cobbinwood. "It'll be fun. We put on a couple of Ren fairs when I was in undergraduate school. It's like a big costume party, with all kinds of entertainment and food. ARSE will stage battles, and perhaps a gallant knight in shining armor will fight for your honor."

Caron glared at him. "I am perfectly capable of defending my honor without the help of some guy dressed in rusty hubcaps."

"What's ARSE?" I asked.

"The Association for Renaissance Scholarship and Enlightenment. It's not a bunch of academics who meet once a year to read dry papers and argue about royal lineage or the positive side of the feudal system. Anybody can join. The country is divided into kingdoms, counties, and fiefdoms. The local group is Avalon. There are just a few members in town this summer, but when the semester starts in September, Fiona says—"

"Fiona Thackery," Caron said with a sigh, not yet willing to allow me to dismiss her imminent martyrdom. "The AP history teacher. I'm thinking about taking shop instead. I've always wanted to get my hands on a nail gun. Or if I take auto mechanics, I'll learn to change tires and . . . tighten bolts and stuff like that. That way, when your car falls into a gazillion bits, I'll know how to put it back together. That's a lot more useful than memorizing the kings of England or the dates of the Napoleonic Wars."

"You're taking AP history," I said. "If you want to work at a garage on the weekends, that's fine with me."

She gave me a petulant look. "Then you can write the midterm paper. Compare and contrast the concepts of Hellenism and Hebraism in *The Divine Comedy* and *The Canterbury Tales*. Cite examples and footnote all source material. Five thousand word minimum. Any attempt at plagiarism from the Internet or elsewhere will result in a shaved head and six weeks in the stocks."

I cupped my hand to my ear. "Do I hear the lilting melody of 'Greensleeves' in the distance?"

"The only recorder I'm playing," Caron said sourly, "will have a tape in it."

Edward seemed to be enjoying the exchange, but
fluttered his fingers and strolled out of the Book Depot
to bewilder and beguile other merchants along the
street. He must have had a recorder tucked in his
pocket, because we could hear tootling as he headed up
the hill. It may have been "Greensleeves," but it was
hard to be sure. I hoped he wasn't a music major.

"Goodness gracious," said Inez Thornton as she
came into the bookstore. Her eyes were round behind
her thick lenses. "Did you see that weirdo in the purple
tights?"

Inez has always been Caron's best friend through thick
and thin (aka high crimes and misdemeanors). Caron,
red-haired and obstinate, faster than a speeding bullet
except when her alarm clock goes off in the morning,
able to leap over logic in a single bound, is the dominant force. Meek, myopic Inez is but a pale understudy
in Caron's pageant, but equally devious. Encroaching
maturity tempers them at times. There are, of course,
many other times.

"Tell me more about the letter from your history
teacher," I said.

Caron grimaced. "This Renaissance Fair sounds so
juvenile. Everybody has to dress up as something and
go around pretending to be a minstrel or a damsel or a
pirate or something silly like that. There's a meeting
tomorrow afternoon at the high school so we can get
our committee assignments. It's like Miss Thackery
thinks we're already in her class. She shouldn't be allowed to get away with this. It's—it's unconstitu-
tional!"

"That's right," said Inez, nodding emphatically.
"Aren't we guaranteed life, liberty, and the pursuit of
happiness?"

"I'm not sure reading Chaucer and Dante will make you all that happy, but you never know," I said. "You'll find copies on the back shelf. Help yourselves."

Rather than take me up on my generous offer, they left. I would have felt a twinge of maternal sympathy had they not been muttering for more than a month about how bored they were. I'd never been to a Renaissance Fair, but I supposed it was similar to a carnival show, with tents, booths, and entertainment—not to mention men clad in armor made of aluminum foil, bashing each other with padded sticks.

Pester the Jester did not reappear, to my relief. I've always been leery of men in tights, especially purple ones (tights, not men). The few customers who drifted in were dressed in standard summer wear and more interested in paperback thrillers and travel books than in Shakespeare. Business is sluggish in the summer, when most of the college students have gone home and their professors are either wandering through cavernous cathedrals in Europe or sifting sand at archeological digs. The academic community as a whole comprises nearly a quarter of Farberville's population of 25,000 semi-literate souls. Their civilian counterparts tend to do their shopping at the air-conditioned mall at the edge of town when the temperature begins to climb.

At 6:00 P.M. I locked the doors and went across the street to the beer garden to meet Luanne Bradshaw, who owns a vintage clothing shop on Thurber Street. It could have been a hobby, not a livelihood, since she not only comes from a wealthy family on the East Coast but also divorced a successful doctor and left him barefoot in the park—or, at least, penniless in the penthouse. However, she chose to rid herself of most of her ill-gotten gains via trusts and foundations, dumped her offspring on the doorsteps of prestigious prep schools, and headed for the hinterlands. Farberville definitely falls into that category. Despite being in the throes of a midlife crisis that may well continue until she's ninety, she's disarmingly astute.

She was seated at a picnic table beneath a wisteria-entwined lattice that provided shade and a pleasant redolence. Her long, tanned legs were clearly visible in scandalously short shorts, and her black hair was tucked under a baseball cap. As I joined her, she filled a plastic cup with beer from a pitcher and set it down in front of me.

"You didn't mention Peter when you called earlier," she said by way of greeting. "Are you having prenuptial jitters? It's unbecoming in a woman of your age."

"My age is damn close to yours," I said, "and I'm not the one who scrambled all over the Andes with a bunch of virile young Australian men for six weeks."

"I kept claiming I needed to rest just so I could watch their darling butts wiggle as they hiked past me. So what's going on with Peter?"

"The captain sent him to FBI summer camp so he can learn how to protect our fair town if the terrorists attempt to create havoc by jamming the parking meters. It's a real threat, you know. The mayor will have to flee to his four-bedroom bunker out by the lake. The Kiwanis Club won't be able to have its weekly luncheon meetings at the diner behind the court house. The community theater won't be able to stage its endearingly inept production of 'Our Town' for the first time in nineteen years. All hell could break loose."

Luanne failed to look properly terrified. "How long will he be gone?"

"Three weeks at Quantico, and then a week at his mother's."

"Oh," she murmured.

I took a long swallow of beer. "It's not like that. She's resigned to the idea that Peter and I are getting married, or so he keeps telling me."

"But she's not coming to the wedding."

"No, she's not," I said. "She always goes to Aspen in September to avoid the hurricane season."

"Rhode Island is hardly a magnet for hurricanes, but neither is Farberville," Luanne said as she refilled her cup and mine.

"It's a tradition. She goes with a big group of her widowed friends. They take over a very posh condo complex and party all day and night. Besides, it's not as if this is Peter's first marriage—or mine. I'd look pretty silly in a flouncy white dress and veil, with my teenaged daughter as maid of honor. There's no reason why she should disrupt her long-standing plans for a simple little civil ceremony in a backyard."

"She's probably afraid she'll have to eat ribs," said Luanne, "and toast the happy couple with moonshine in a jelly jar. Have you spoken to her on the phone, or received a warm letter on her discreetly monogrammed stationery?"

The topic was not amusing me. "Not yet. Peter thinks we ought to give her some time to get used to the idea, and then go for a visit. Will you loan me a pair of jodpurs?"

"Yes, but they'll make your thighs look fat."

I brooded for a moment, then said, "Did you happen to encounter Pester the Jester this afternoon?"

"Oh my, yes. I couldn't take my eyes off his codpiece."

I told her about the letters Caron and Inez had received from the history teacher. "They're appalled, of course, and were rambling about their constitutional right to spend the summer sulking. I didn't have the heart to remind them that they'd already had their fifteen minutes of fame a month ago, when they were interviewed by the media after that unfortunate business with the disappearing corpse."

"Fame is fleeting," Luanne said.

We pondered this philosophical twaddle while we emptied our cups. The remaining beer in the pitcher was getting warm, and a group of noisy college kids arrived to take possession of a nearby picnic table. I told Luanne I'd call her later in the week, then walked the few blocks to my apartment on the second floor of a duplex across the street from the campus lawn. A note on the kitchen table informed me that Caron and Inez had gone out for pizza with friends. It was just as well, since my culinary interests were limited to boiling water for tea and nuking frozen entrées. In the mood for neither, I settled down on the sofa to read. I hoped Peter would call, but as it grew dark outside I gave up and consoled myself with images of him on the firing range, learning how to take down grannies with radioactive dentures and toddlers with teddy bears packed with explosives. Or librarians and booksellers who refused to turn in their patrons' reading preferences to cloak-and-dagger government agencies.

What I did not want to think about was the wedding, scheduled for early September. Not because I was having second thoughts, mind you. I was confident that I loved Peter and that we would do quite nicely when we rode off into the sunset of domestic bliss, which would include not only more opportunities for adult behavior of a most delectable sort, but also lazy Sunday mornings with coffee, muffins, and *The New York Times*, and occasional squabbles over the relative merits of endive versus romaine. He'd been suggesting matrimonial entanglement for several years, and I'd given it serious consideration. But after my first husband's untimely and very unseemly death, I'd struggled to regain my self-esteem and establish my independence. I hadn't done too well on the material aspects, as Caron pointed out on a regular basis. However, the Book Depot was still in business, and we lived on the agreeable side of genteel poverty.

A distressingly close call with mortality had led me to reassess my situation. The emotional barrier I'd constructed to protect myself collapsed during a convoluted moment when a hitman had impolitely threatened to blow my brains out (not in those exact words, but that was the gist of the message). If commitment meant sharing a closet, then so be it.

The problem lay in my inclinations to meddle in what Lieutenant Peter Rosen felt was official police business. It wasn't simply a compulsion to outsleuth Miss Marple. In all the situations I'd found myself questioning witnesses and snooping around crime scenes, I'd never once done so for my personal satisfaction—or to make fools of the local constabulary. It just happened. Peter, with his molasses brown eyes, curly hair, perfect teeth, and undeniable charm, never quite saw it that way. He'd lectured me, had my car impounded twice, threatened me with a jail cell, and attempted to keep me under house arrest. One had to admire his optimism.